TO SAVE A LOVE

Soldiers & Soulmates
Book 4

Alexa Aston

ARE YOU SIGNED UP FOR DRAGONBLADE'S BLOG?

You'll get the latest news and information on exclusive giveaways, exclusive excerpts, coming releases, sales, free books, cover reveals and more.

Check out our complete list of authors, too!

No spam, no junk. That's a promise!

Sign Up Here

www.dragonbladepublishing.com

Dearest Reader;

Thank you for your support of a small press. At Dragonblade Publishing, we strive to bring you the highest quality Historical Romance from some of the best authors in the business. Without your support, there is no 'us', so we sincerely hope you adore these stories and find some new favorite authors along the way.

Happy Reading!

CEO, Dragonblade Publishing

Additional Dragonblade books by Author Alexa Aston

Second Sons of London Series
Educated By The Earl
Debating With The Duke
Empowered By The Earl
Made for the Marquess
Dubious about the Duke
Valued by the Viscount
Meant for the Marquess

Dukes Done Wrong Series
Discouraging the Duke
Deflecting the Duke
Disrupting the Duke
Delighting the Duke
Destiny with a Duke

Dukes of Distinction Series
Duke of Renown
Duke of Charm
Duke of Disrepute
Duke of Arrogance
Duke of Honor

The St. Clairs Series
Devoted to the Duke
Midnight with the Marquess
Embracing the Earl
Defending the Duke
Suddenly a St. Clair
Starlight Night (Novella)
The Twelve Days of Love (Novella)

Soldiers & Soulmates Series
To Heal an Earl
To Tame a Rogue
To Trust a Duke
To Save a Love
To Win a Widow

Yuletide at Gillingham (Novella)

The Lyon's Den Series
The Lyon's Lady Love

King's Cousins Series
The Pawn
The Heir
The Bastard

Medieval Runaway Wives
Song of the Heart
A Promise of Tomorrow
Destined for Love

Knights of Honor Series
Word of Honor
Marked by Honor
Code of Honor
Journey to Honor
Heart of Honor
Bold in Honor
Love and Honor
Gift of Honor
Path to Honor
Return to Honor

Pirates of Britannia Series
God of the Seas

De Wolfe Pack: The Series
Rise of de Wolfe

The de Wolfes of Esterley Castle
Diana
Derek
Thea

Also from Alexa Aston
The Bridge to Love

CHAPTER ONE

London—May 1798

DESMOND BRETTON BOUNDED out of the coach the moment it came to a halt in front of his father's London townhouse. His legs needing to stretch after the long carriage ride from Eton. School was behind him, at least for a little while. He would take the summer off and then enter university next term. After that, as a second son, he was destined for the army, while his older brother, Ham, would eventually become the Earl of Torrington upon their father's death.

For now he intended to relax. Spend time with his sister, Dalinda—if she could make room on her calendar for him. His twin was in the midst of her come-out and she'd written to him of the busy swirl of social events. For a moment, his thoughts turned to Anna, who would also be making her come-out with Dalinda. Anna Browning lived on the country estate adjoining theirs.

And Dez had been in love with her ever since they were children.

The three of them had been inseparable from childhood. Riding. Walking. Sharing confidences. His favorite times were when they picnicked at the lake that straddled their fathers' estates. It was at that lake that he had finally kissed Anna last summer. Dalinda had taken Jessa, Anna's much younger sister, on a walk, leaving Dez and Anna alone. He couldn't remember what he'd said. Only the feel of Anna's lips beneath his. The taste of strawberries on her tongue. The soft curve of her hips.

They had kissed several times after that. In the gardens of Torville Manor. In the drawing room of Shelton Park, hanging back as others left the room for dinner. In an empty stall before riding. Dez had known it was forbidden but he couldn't resist the irresistible urge that drew him toward the girl he had always loved. When he left for his final year at Eton, they had both known by the time he returned that Anna would be in the midst of her come-out. They spoke briefly about how they knew they had no future and that they would both make the best of what was to come. For Anna, it would be as the wife of some peer. For Dez, he hoped to ascend to the highest ranks of His Majesty's Army.

Billy, his favorite footman who was close to Dez's age, came out to greet him.

"Good afternoon, Mr. Bretton," the servant said cheerily. "Finally done with school, are you?"

"For a bit, Billy. Where is my father?"

"The earl and Viscount Bowling are both at their club, Mr. Bretton," the footman informed him, sending a ripple of relief through Dez, knowing he could avoid both his father and brother for short while.

He had never gotten along with his father. Not that the Earl of Torrington spent any time with Dez. Or Dalinda, for that matter. Torrington had no use for females and had been put out when his countess died giving birth to the twins. As a second son, Dez wasn't lavished with attention as Ham, the heir apparent, was. Ham was five years older and had spent his entire life being cruel to Dez and Dalinda. Their brother blamed the twins for the loss of his mother, so he said. Dez simply thought Ham had a vicious streak that ran deeply through him, one Ham had obviously inherited from their father.

"Is Lady Dalinda home?" he asked.

"That she is, Sir. In the drawing with her friend, Miss Browning. They're having tea."

"Very good. I will join them. See my trunk brought upstairs, Billy."

"Shall I unpack it for you, Mr. Bretton?"

"Yes, thank you."

Dez entered the townhouse and took the stairs two at a time, eager to see Dalinda and yes, even Anna. He knew it would hurt to listen to her talk about her suitors but he loved her enough to know he wanted the best for her. It wasn't destined in the stars for them to be together. He was gentleman enough to wish that she find a good man who would take care of her and treat her well. One who would give her the children she so desperately wanted.

The moment he entered the drawing room, though, he knew something was terribly wrong. He saw Dalinda's arms wrapped around a weeping Anna. His sister sensed her twin's presence and looked up, revealing the tears streaming down her own cheeks. Quickly, he rushed toward them.

"Dez is here," Dalinda said softly and released Anna.

Without even looking at him, Anna turned and blindly latched on to him, her sobs breaking his heart. He held her trembling body close, aching for the pain she now experienced. If it was some rake who had broken her heart, Dez would call him out. Her pain was his and he would do whatever it took to soothe her.

He didn't say a word, just stroked her hair and her back and let her cry. His focus was to bring her comfort and she would tell him whatever was wrong in her own time. Eventually, her sobs ended and she gazed up at him, her clear, sky-blue eyes full of anguish.

"Would you like to sit?" he asked quietly.

Anna nodded and he led her to a settee, sitting beside her, his arm going around her shoulders. She reached for his free hand and pulled it into her lap, both her hands clutching it as if it were a lifeline that could keep her from drowning in sorrow.

Dalinda sat in a chair nearby and she nodded to Anna. "Tell him."

"What good will it do?" Anna asked, her tone laced with bitterness. Then she sighed and Dez heard the resignation in it.

She began to speak, gazing across the room, her voice a monotone.

"Papa called Mama and me into his study an hour ago. I have had several suitors and thought one of them might have spoken to him about asking for my hand in marriage."

His gut tightened as he prepared himself to hear the man's name.

"Papa told us that he knew I was one of the more sought after girls this Season and since so many gentlemen seemed interested in me, it was obvious he didn't need to waste a dowry upon me."

Dez frowned. Custom, which the *ton* clung to, always dictated that a woman bring a dowry into the marriage. It was a huge part of the negotiation of the marriage contracts. If Lord Shelton pulled Anna's dowry, her chances of marriage would evaporate, despite her beauty and charm.

Her hand tightened around his. "He said I had always been a worthless girl and that Mama was incapable of giving him sons and an heir. That I shouldn't have to cost him anything to be taken off his hands. That he should be compensated instead." She swallowed. "He told me he had sold me to the highest bidder. Viscount Needham."

He looked to Dalinda. Anger sparked in her eyes. Without words, they communicated that Dez, not having been a part of the Season, had no idea who this viscount was.

His twin said, "Lord Needham is at least seventy if not older."

"What? He sold you to a dried up prune of a man?"

Anna nodded, still averting her gaze from his. "Papa said Lord Needham was taken by my strawberry blond hair and trim figure. That he needs an heir and will get one off me as soon as possible."

"No," Dez whispered. "No. This cannot be."

Finally, she faced him and Dez saw the misery filling her face. "Though Mama begged him not to do so, he is determined. He said he will announce our betrothal at tomorrow night's ball being held in my honor."

"You cannot allow this, Anna," Dalinda said, determination filling her face.

"What can I do? We are mere pawns, Dalinda. Our fathers have total control over our lives. We wed whom they tell us to wed. Sometimes, it is a gentleman of our own choosing but you know as well as I do that oftentimes it is not."

"It's so blasted unfair," Dalinda declared. She looked to Dez, who felt helpless.

Then he said, "You can marry me."

"What?" both women cried.

He swallowed. "I cannot let you be sold into slavery with this man. You can wed me."

"How?" Anna demanded. "England's marriage laws say we must be twenty-one to wed. We can be younger if our parents give us their permission and the banns are read for three weeks. There is absolutely no way your father or mine would allow a match between us." She shook her head forcefully. "No, it is hopeless, Dez. I will be chained to bony Lord Needham. He will be my jailor and I will live in his prison. There is nothing that can be done."

"Actually, there is," Dalinda said, looking at him, knowing Dez's mind as clearly as her own. "Are you serious about wanting to wed Anna?"

"You know I am." He looked at Anna. "I have loved you for years," he said tenderly. "I would go to the ends of the earth for you."

"It won't require that," Dalinda said, a grim smile on her face. "Only Scotland."

"Scotland?" Anna asked. "I don't understand."

Dez knew where his twin ventured because he had heard of the practice while at Eton. A friend's older brother had eloped, much to the dismay of the family, who disowned the couple. If he wed Anna, he would receive no monetary support from his father. The earl would cut Dez off and they would have to somehow earn their own living with no help from others.

"You will need to travel the Great North Road and cross into Scotland," Dalinda informed her friend. "The first town you come to is called Gretna Green. Scottish marital laws differ from those in England. You can marry there legally without parental consent. I heard about it from some of the girls in the retiring room the other night. You know how I love to eavesdrop."

"What if you misunderstood, Dalinda?" Anna asked.

"She didn't," Dez said. "I know of the practice from school, as well." He paused and took both Anna's hands in his. "It would mean giving up everything you know, Anna. Your father—and mine—will denounce the action. They will cut us off. We . . . we would have to make our way in the world somehow."

For the first time since he had entered the drawing room, he saw hope on her face. She gripped his hands tightly.

"I love you, Desmond Bretton. I always have and always will. Nothing could ever change that. I don't care if we live in a hovel or a castle. As long as we are together, we can meet any challenge."

He brought her hands to his lips and pressed a fervent kiss upon them.

"If you are sure, my love."

Anna's radiant smiled chased away any doubt Dez felt. "I have never been more certain of anything." Then she frowned. "But how will we get there?"

"The mail coach," Dalinda and Dez said at the same time.

"It's uncomfortable, yes," he added, "but it's the cheapest and most efficient way to reach Gretna Green."

"How long will it take?" Anna asked, her eyes filled with worry.

"Probably four or five days," he shared.

"What if they come after us? Try to stop us?"

"They'll have to know where we are headed. No one will," he assured her, thinking quickly. "I will tell Father tonight that I have been invited to a friend's country estate just outside of London. He won't care if I am here or gone. I am no one to him. As for you, do you have an engagement this evening?"

"Yes," she replied. "A rout."

"Halfway through, claim a headache and see if you can be taken home." Dez thought a moment. "Better yet, beg off going in the first place. Say you want to be well-rested for the betrothal announcement at tomorrow night's ball. That you want to sleep until noon. Leave a note for your maid to discover and take to Lord Shelton. Write that you have had a change of heart and don't wish to wed Lord Needham. That you have left for Surrey and home and you don't care about the rest of the Season."

"So, Papa will look for me in the opposite direction," Anna said, a slow smile spreading across her beautiful face. "And your father won't be looking for you at all."

"Exactly," he assured her though nerves now caused him to feel jittery, thinking of crossing both of their fathers and having to earn a living when he had no skills at all. "We need to leave on the earliest mail coach departing London and heading north to give ourselves a fair lead."

"Who will buy the tickets?" Dalinda asked.

A brief knock sounded at the door. Though his arm was no longer around Anna's shoulders, he couldn't bring himself to let go of her hand. She already felt abandoned enough. He couldn't hurt her more.

Thankfully, it was only Billy, who brought a cup and saucer. He crossed the room and then must have recognized something was amiss. "I . . . I brought . . . an extra cup for Mr. Bretton. I . . . thought he needed one for tea."

"Thank you, Billy," Dalinda said graciously, holding out her hand and accepting the extra china from the footman. "We also need you to run an errand for us," she added, her gaze meeting her twin's.

Dez acknowledged it and said to the footman, "I need you to purchase two tickets for the mail coach leaving London tomorrow morning for Scotland. The earliest possible."

Wariness, coupled with understanding, grew in the servant's eyes as he glanced at Dez and Anna's joined hands.

He tugged his hand from Anna's and reached into his coat pocket, removing what coin he had and handing it to Billy.

"Will this be enough?" Dez asked, unsure of how much anything cost. He spent his small allowance freely, where Dalinda always put away whatever pin money she received as a squirrel gathered nuts in preparation for dinner.

The footman thumbed through the bills. "It should be." Still, he looked as if he needed convincing.

Dalinda spoke up. "There will be a crown in it for you if you bring the tickets back promptly."

Billy's eyes went wide. "Yes, my lady. Right away."

"If anyone stops you, Billy, say you are on an errand for me," Dez emphasized.

"And no word to anyone," Dalinda prompted.

"Of course not, my lady," the footman reassured her. "I know how to keep my mouth closed." He rushed from the room, closing the door behind him.

"You have a crown to give him?" he questioned his twin.

"That—and more. I will give you everything I have. You will need to purchase food on your way there. Pay for lodging. Give the blacksmith something for his trouble."

"Blacksmith?" Anna asked, perplexed.

"Yes," his sister said. "I overheard that a couple usually stops at the first place they reach stopping at Gretna Green. Supposedly, it is a blacksmith's shop. They call elopements to Scotland marrying over the anvil and the blacksmith an anvil priest."

"You are certain this is legal?" Anna asked nervously.

Both Dez and Dalinda nodded.

Anna's eyes filled with tears as she gazed up at Dez. "Then I suppose we will be getting married in Gretna Green."

Despite Dalinda's presence, Dez bent and pressed his mouth to Anna's for a long, tender kiss. He finally broke it.

"Pack a small valise," he suggested. "Only your nightclothes and a change of clothing. Slip out of the house. I will be waiting out front at six tomorrow morning. We will make our way to the mail coach office from there."

"Are you certain?" Anna asked. "This will change the course of our lives, Dez. No university or army for you."

His hands framed her face. "Nothing matters except for us being together, Anna. You know it is what we both want." He kissed her again. "Say you will marry me."

She smiled through tears of happiness. "I will marry you, Desmond Bretton. A thousand times over. We will most likely be poor in worldly goods but we will always be rich in love."

He pulled her to her feet and gave her a last hard, swift kiss.

"Go home. Act as natural as possible."

Anna giggled nervously. "All right."

Dez captured her hands in his. "It will be fine. I promise. Go."

She nodded and stepped toward Dalinda. The two locked their arms around one another.

"The next time I see you, you will be Mrs. Desmond Bretton," Dalinda said.

Anna smiled. "Mrs. Bretton. Anna Bretton. I like the sound of that." She embraced Dalinda again. "Oh, however can I thank you? You have been as much a sister to me as Jessa."

Dalinda blinked back tears. "And soon we will be sisters by marriage." She kissed Anna's cheek. "I will see you soon."

"Your father may forbid it," her friend warned.

Dalinda's eyes lit with mischief. "When has that ever stopped me from doing anything?"

The two said their goodbyes and Anna left the drawing room. The moment the door closed, Dez opened his arms and enfolded Dalinda.

"Am I crazy to do this?" he asked his twin.

"Crazy—in love. I always thought the two of you were meant

to be together," she replied. "Let me go to my room and collect what I have. Stay here. I won't be long."

Dez paced the room as he waited, worried about what he was doing. He had always been impulsive, something his father said was Dez's greatest character flaw. He knew it was the right thing, saving Anna from the fate of a horrible marriage to an old codger who would force himself on her night after night until he got her with child. *If* he could get her with child at his age. It didn't lessen his worry, though, with the great unknown ahead of him and Anna. He wondered how he would support her. Where they might live. If Dalinda would be able to sneak away and see them.

His sister returned and handed over the monies she had.

"This is a great deal," he said, startled by what she brought.

"I have something else," she confided and withdrew something from her pocket, taking his hand and placing it in his palm.

Dez looked down and saw a gold band studded with diamonds. He raised his gaze to her, confused.

"What is this?"

"Our mother's wedding band," Dalinda confided. "Don't ask how I came to possess it. But I thought it would be perfect to have Mama there on your wedding day and with you and Anna as you start your marriage."

He wrapped her in a tight hug. "I love you," he whispered.

"I love you."

CHAPTER TWO

ANNA ROSE, NERVES making her entire body tremble. She moved silently, washing and dressing in traveling clothes, which were easier to don versus her everyday gowns meant for the Season. She wound the lone braid she had slept in around and around, pinning it up as best she could. She had never been very good at doing her own hair. From now on, she would be solely responsible for it.

For everything.

Was she doing the right thing, running away with Dez?

Her heart screamed yes—but her mind still had doubts. Not only was she unsuitable to obtain any kind of job but she would be costing Dez his entire future. No university education. No long, worthwhile career in the army. Who knew what Dez was capable of? Did he know how to swing a hammer? Make a cabinet? Haul goods? She had seen him handle tack and groom his horse. Perhaps he could work in a stable. Or at Tattersall's. Dez certainly knew a good deal about horseflesh.

But would the Earl of Torrington allow Tattersall's to hire his rebellious son, where all of Torrington's friends went at one point or another. Most likely, he'd wish Dez banished from London for disobeying him and wedding Anna.

As for her father, she didn't want to imagine his reaction when he found her gone. He had always despised the fact that she and Jessa were females. Especially now, when her father counted upon receiving a goodly amount from Lord Needham in a reverse dowry, it would be unthinkable for him to lose the easy money he thought he could make from selling her into marriage with the viscount. That's why she and Dez needed to escape London as soon as possible, wedding and consummating their union.

Anna smiled. That would be what she lived for. She had always lived for Dez. To see a smile on his handsome face. To make him laugh. To listen to him talk about anything and everything. She had loved Desmond Bretton since before she could even remember. He was a part of her earliest memories. When he had finally kissed her last summer by the lake, it had been as a dream come true. They both knew, however, that their fathers controlled their destinies and had parted with the understanding that they would always care for one another but would need to go off and lead separate lives, wishing the best for one another.

Until yesterday. When Dez offered marriage. And Anna had been too weak to turn him down. She wanted Dez with a passion she could barely conceal. She wanted to kiss him. Hold him. Touch him. Have him touch her. They would be very poor but she hoped they could both find some kind of work. She was excellent at needlepoint. Perhaps she might become a seamstress. Wouldn't it be ironic if she became a modiste and designed and sewed gowns for daughters of Polite Society who made their come-outs?

Bending, she retrieved the small valise she'd packed and slipped under her bed last night, not wanting her maid or anyone else to see it. She tiptoed across the room and out into the carpeted hall, where her steps were silent. Making her way downstairs, she crossed the foyer. A footman sat by the door, sound asleep. She didn't want to wake him and have her plans discovered before she could even leave the house.

Instead, she went to the left and entered her father's study. Pulling the curtain aside, she unlatched the window and pushed it open. She leaned out the window and placed her valise on the ground. Suddenly, Dez was there.

"Front door guarded?" he asked quietly and Anna nodded.

His hands captured her waist and he lifted her over the sill and to the ground before leaning in and pulling the window closed. She hoped it would stay shut. She didn't feel any wind which might blow it open and alert others that something was amiss.

Dez picked up her valise and one of his own. "Come. I have a hansom cab waiting for us around the corner. Don't say anything."

Anna merely nodded, her heart beating so rapidly she thought it might burst through her chest. They approached the cab and the driver nodded. Dez opened the door and placed their luggage inside before lifting her into the cab and then climbing in himself. The horse started up.

Dez threaded his fingers through hers and then gave her a soft kiss. Instead of calming her, it only made her heart race faster.

"The driver is dropping us a few blocks from our destination," he revealed. "We'll walk the rest of the way there."

"Do you have the tickets?" she asked.

He patted his coat pocket. "Right here. Billy came home straightaway and gave them to me. I also have money from Dalinda."

"I have a little, too. Not much but it's better than nothing."

"I love you, Anna," Dez declared. "I have since I was a boy and I will go on loving you the rest of our lives. Now that I know we are lucky enough to spend the rest of our lives together, I cannot wait to see what our time as husband and wife will bring."

Dez kissed her again, a long, deep, and very satisfying kiss. It tasted of his promise and what tomorrow would bring.

The vehicle slowed and came to a halt and he opened the door. Jumping out, he retrieved their valises and then Anna and paid the driver. They walked three blocks, having to dodge people hurrying to and fro. Anna found it hard to believe people were up and about at this time of the morning but the streets already seemed busy. They arrived at the mail coach office and she saw several carriages standing in the yard.

"Wait here with our bags," Dez said, placing them at her feet. "I need to check on which is our coach and what time it leaves."

"All right," Anna said meekly, not wanting to be left in the middle of such hustle and bustle.

She'd never been left alone in the city before. She always had her maid accompanying her and, usually, Dalinda was in tow, as well. Or Mama and Papa went in the carriage with her, escorting her to the various *ton* events. Fear filled her.

"Quit being afraid," she whispered under her breath.

She was on a public street. No one was going to accost her at a little past six in the morning.

Until a man stopped in front of her.

His coat had seen better days. He could certainly have used a haircut and shave. He grinned at her.

"Who have we here?" he asked, a lascivious look in his eyes.

Stiffening her spine, she replied, "I am a lady, sir, and we have not been introduced."

"A lady, you say." His eyes now gleamed and he took her elbow. "Why don't you come along with me?" he suggested, his tone velvet but instilling fear in her.

"Unhand my wife."

Both she and the stranger turned to see Dez standing there, fury on his face.

Immediately, the man released her elbow. "No harm done, my lord." He shuffled off quickly.

Dez stepped to Anna, placing his hands on her shoulders. "Did he hurt you?"

"No," she said unsteadily. "He frightened me, though. But I didn't tell him my name."

"Good girl." He gave her shoulders a squeeze and released them. Lifting the bags, he said, "Our vehicle is this way," using his head to point to his right. "Leaving in ten minutes."

Anna fell into step with him. As they approached, she could already see a good number of people surrounding the coach and whispered, "Where will everyone sit?"

He shrugged. "I suppose a few will ride on top."

"Don't leave me, Dez," she said, gripping his arm.

He smiled. "I won't, Anna. I will never leave you. Even when we argue and you think me a blockhead and wish me gone from your sight, I will linger. I will be with you as we eat our meals. Tend to our children. Climb into our bed at night. You are stuck with me, Anna. For better or for worse."

His assurances brought a calm to her. This man was her world. Without him, she was nothing.

"Thank you, Mr. Bretton."

"You are welcome, Mrs. Bretton," said Dez as he winked at her.

He had told her in the carriage that they were to act as if they were already married, addressing each other as husband and wife. Dez said it would help smooth things along on the road as they traveled to Scotland. She knew what they now did was scandalous and agreed to treat him as her husband and call him thus. In only a few days' time, they would be actual husband and wife.

What were a few days of a white lie to strangers?

GETTING OUT OF the city had taken longer than Dez wanted. It amazed him how much traffic stacked up at such an early hour. Glancing out the window, though, he saw various delivery wagons and knew shops and businesses must be restocking before opening for the day. Once they left London, though, they definitely picked up speed. Anna told him no rain had come for two days, which was a surprise in itself being that it was spring in England. It helped them move faster with the roads dry. A muddy road always slowed a coach and the vehicle could become easily bogged down. A heavy rain would also hamper them, making it almost impossible for a driver to see. He prayed good weather would hold at least for a day or two, putting distance between them and the city.

He had done his part, greeting his father after Torrington arrived from his club, Ham alongside him. His brother barely glanced at him before heading up the stairs to dress for dinner. Dez had accompanied the earl to his study and answered a barrage of questions regarding his final term at Eton and then he had told his father of plans to visit a friend in the country for a week or two. As expected, the older man didn't even appear to be listening and merely nodded in assent. At least he had laid the groundwork so that Torrington wouldn't suspect him to be involved in Anna's escape from London and the very old Viscount Needham.

The mail coach began to slow and Dez figured it was stopping again for a fresh team of horses. They had already stopped once to exchange their exhausted team for a new one. As before, no one was allowed to disembark from the carriage since the hostlers prided themselves on changing out a mail coach team in under three minutes. The coachman had told them as they boarded this morning that the third stop would be long enough to purchase food to eat. They wouldn't have to do so this first time because Dalinda had packed them sandwiches and apples, knowing they needed to save every pound they could. Dez would retrieve the food from his valise the next time the coach stopped.

He looked down at Anna's hand nestled in his and couldn't help but smile. Yes, he knew they had a very rocky road ahead of them. He hadn't the faintest idea what they would do to earn a living but he couldn't help but think their love would get them through difficult times. He realized he had lied to himself, thinking he wanted the best for Anna, having her wed another man. No, he was selfish to his core because he wanted Anna Browning all to himself. He couldn't wait for them to be man and wife, not only in name, but by consummating their marriage. He was wise enough to realize even being married wasn't enough. He had to breach Anna's maidenhead and make love to her in order for all legalities to be settled.

The coach had barely started up again when he heard a thunderous noise. Fear trickled through him. Anna must have sensed it because she gripped his hand. He glanced at her.

"It's all right, love," he reassured.

She wet her lips nervously, nodding. Trusting him.

Dez looked out the window and saw the carriage come up beside theirs. He grew hot and dizzy when he saw it.

It was his family's carriage.

How?

Only Dalinda had known of their plans to make for Gretna Green. Well, his twin and Billy, the footman. He couldn't imagine Billy betraying him—yet the Torrington crest on the carriage that now pulled ahead of them was proof that one of two people had betrayed them. Billy had to be the weak link. Dalinda would have rather been beaten and starved than divulge where he and Anna had gone.

The horses began slowly and Dez met Anna's gaze. She had bitten her lip so hard that he saw the blood.

"He's won," she said dully.

Then she grabbed the lapels of his coat and yanked him toward her for a searing kiss. He tasted her sweetness and the copper of her blood. The kiss went on until the mail coach came to a complete stop. Anna broke the kiss.

"I will always, always love you, Dez. My heart is yours."

"I love you," he echoed. "Until the end of time, Anna. And beyond."

The passengers stirred in the crowded interior, murmuring about why the coach had stopped. The door opened, slamming against the carriage, and Dez saw Ham standing in the opening. His brother spotted him and sneered.

"Get out!" he commanded. "The both of you."

To her credit, Anna rose, her head held high. Dez didn't want Ham's hands touching her and he stepped in front of her, forcing his brother to move aside as he jumped down. Reaching up, he brought Anna to the ground.

Immediately, Ham spun him around and slammed his fist into his face. Dez saw stars as he stumbled back against the carriage. Then Lord Shelton was there, grabbing Anna and dragging her away. Dez watched, his eyes blurring with tears as the viscount forced her inside his carriage and climbed up after her. The coachman took off.

He blinked and saw Ham motioning him. Reluctantly, he followed his brother back to the Torrington carriage, where the door was opened. Both the footman and driver avoided looking at Dez as he mounted the steps and entered the vehicle.

Sitting opposite his father, he clenched his jaw, not wanting to speak. Ham sat next to their father, a smug smile on his face.

Acting more bravely than he felt, Dez turned his gaze upon the earl, who sat stone still, his face brick red in anger. Their gazes locked as the carriage pulled away. Neither spoke. He continued staring steadily at the man he despised, a sick feeling building within him as he worried what would happen to Anna.

After some minutes, his brother said, "You thought you were so clever, telling Father of your visit to a friend. You were foolish to involve a servant in your schemes, Desmond."

So, it was Billy who had revealed where he and Anna headed.

"Murtie told us everything." Ham smiled triumphantly.

Murtie?

Vaguely, he remembered a parlor maid that might go by that name.

Ham continued, "She was sweet on that stupid footman. Told him he better tell Father what he knew else he'd lose his job." His brother chortled. "They both did."

"Enough, Hamilton," their father commanded and Ham fell silent.

The trio rode that way all the way into London. The carriage stopped in front of the mews and they got out. The earl ordered Ham to give them privacy. Dez followed his father into the house, where Torrington ventured to his study. He ushered his younger son inside and closed the door before addressing him.

"This is a debacle," the earl declared. "You have ruined our family's reputation."

"How?" Dez pressed, knowing at this point that he had nothing to lose. "The mail coach continued on the Great North Road, its passengers none the wiser since we never used our names. It is not as if anyone from Polite Society was on it."

Torrington slapped him. It took everything Dez had not to return the slap. He stood stoically, his face stinging.

"Shelton is furious," his father continued. "He claims you are the instigator of this fiasco, along with your sister, whom he called wild."

"Dalinda had no part in this," he protested.

The earl's withering glance silenced Dez. "You would not have gone to such lengths without telling her what you planned. Don't worry. She, too, will pay for her role in this debacle."

Dez winced, sorry he had dragged Dalinda into the scheme. He should have known better. Known that Torrington would find out. That he would pursue him and Anna. Force them to return to London.

The earl glowered at Dez. "As for you, there will be no university. You will go straightaway into the army. I will have the commission purchased by tomorrow morning."

"Go ahead," he challenged. "Do it. I swear I will wed Anna when we are of legal age. She won't care that I am a soldier."

The earl harrumphed. "Shelton will marry off his chit by the end of the week to some doddering old fool that thinks he can get a child off her when he probably can't even find his cock." He paused. "You have shamed this family enough. Accept your fate."

"This family?" he shouted. "We are not—nor have we ever been—family. You and Ham ignore Dalinda and me. There is no lost love on our part for the pair of you. Dalinda is my only family."

The earl glowered. "I have already stated that I will handle your sister. As for you, the army will make you grow up. It will make a man of you. Break you down and build you back up. You are too much of a dreamer, Desmond, and always have been—else you never would have thought this foolish scheme to elope to Gretna Green would have worked."

"I may be a fool for love but at least I know what it is," he challenged. "I found Mama's diary, you know. Three years ago. I read every last entry. She loathed you. She was probably glad she died in childbirth just to escape you."

Torrington slapped him again and then called out. Two burly men rushed in and bound and gagged Dez before he even had a chance to fight back.

"Take him to his bedchamber," the earl ordered and the pair dragged him from the room and up the stairs.

After flinging him on the floor, they left, heartily laughing. Dez couldn't move. His hands were restrained behind his back, the circulation already cut off. His ankles were also tied together.

As the day passed and darkness came, he worried about Anna and what was happening to her. He prayed she would think of a way out of wedding Viscount Needham. Next to Dalinda, Dez knew Anna was the strongest, most resilient woman he knew. She would find a way, he told himself. She would wait for him. They would be together someday.

He had to believe that—or go mad.

CHAPTER THREE

ANNA STARED MOROSELY out the window, her stomach grumbling noisily. She had been locked in her room for two days now, given neither food nor water, and feared her father thought to starve her into submission.

The carriage ride back to Shelton Park had seemed an eternity as her mind whirled, wondering what would become of Dez. She had silently watched the English countryside as the miles passed as she felt her father's intense stare upon her. She refused to acknowledge it or his presence. Finally, as they drove up the lane to Shelton Park, he had asked, "Will you wed Needham?"

"I would rather load my pockets down with stones and walk into the lake," she'd snapped.

He had made no other comments and the carriage had pulled up in front of the house. Their butler, along with two footmen, met them. Usually, Jessa would have been present but Anna supposed her little sister had been forbidden to come and greet the wayward daughter.

"Take her to her rooms and lock her in," the viscount commanded.

Anna had gone of her own free will and stepped inside the room she had thought never to enter again. The sound of the lock turning chilled her soul.

Nothing had happened since then. She had seen no one, not even the gardeners from her window. Heard no footsteps in front of her door. Hunger gnawed at her belly. She'd had no access to water to drink or wash. The chamber pot was almost full, the smell growing stronger by the hour. She had covered it with an old shawl and pushed it under her bed.

For the thousandth time, she wondered what had happened to Dez. How he was being punished. She knew a marriage between them would be impossible now. She also vowed never to wed the elderly Lord Needham. She would rather become a spinster than wife to that dried up, shriveled man.

The sound of the lock being turned drew her attention from the window and she held her breath, waiting to see who might appear at the door. Hope filled her heart as her mother entered, leaning heavily on her cane. Mama rarely left her rooms. She had suffered numerous miscarriages and two stillbirths between Anna and Jessa's births.

"Mama!" she cried and ran toward her, throwing her arms about her.

The door closed and she heard the lock turn again. "Are you supposed to be here?"

Mama smoothed Anna's hair. "Yes, dear. For only a few minutes, though. How are you?"

Through watery eyes, she replied. "Hungry."

"I know. I am so sorry. Your father . . ." Her voice trailed off as she shook her head.

"Do you know anything about Dez?" she asked.

"No. Why would I?"

"I just thought you might have heard something. From the servants. They always seem to know everything."

"No. You must forget about Desmond Bretton," Mama cautioned.

"I know we can never marry," she said glumly. "But I love him."

Mama touched her cheek. "I know, dear girl. I had such high hopes of you marrying a nice young gentlemen." Her mouth trembled. "Not like me."

"Oh, Mama," Anna said, embracing her mother again. "Were you forced to wed Papa?"

"Yes." She shrugged. "It is the way of females, I suppose. We rarely are in control of our destinies." Then her eyes welled with tears. "You will be going away, Anna."

"Where? To wed Lord Needham."

A knock sounded at the door. "It's time, my lady."

"Just two more minutes," Mama shouted harshly.

The lock turned and the door swung open. Their butler appeared in the doorway, two large footmen behind. "No, my lady. Now."

Anna looked to her mother, who said, "Go along with them, Anna."

"Let me get my reticule," she said weakly. "And if I'm to go to Lord Needham, I should at least change my gown."

"That won't be necessary, Anna," her mother reassured her. "Just go along. Everything will be fine."

But Anna saw the haunted look in her mother's eyes. "You're lying," she accused. "No. I am not going anywhere until I know—"

"Bring her," a voice ordered and she saw her father standing in the doorway.

Suddenly, Jessa dashed past him and ran to Anna, throwing her arms about her sister. "Don't go, Anna," she pleaded.

She absorbed Jessa's warmth, drawing a small bit of comfort from it. Then she looked at the murderous look in her father's eyes and pulled Jessa away.

Kneeling, she clasped her sister's shoulders. "It's all right, Jessa. Don't worry."

Then Anna rose and walked from the room. The two footmen latched on to her elbows and began dragging her quickly down the hallway. Suddenly, fear seized her, not knowing where she was being taken, and she began struggling. She fought and kicked the entire way down the stairs and across the corridor, where their stern housekeeper looked at her with pity before hurrying away.

The butler opened the door and she saw the carriage waiting. Anna broke free, dragging her nails against the face of one of the footmen. Blood sprouted on his cheek.

"Bind her," her father said.

A cord appeared and one of the footmen wrapped it tightly about her wrists. She began screaming and saw her father nod. Quickly, a gag was placed over her mouth, silencing her shouts. Her fear now turned to panic as she was taken to the carriage.

Her father said, "This is what happens to disobedient daughters." With that, he turned his back on her and entered the house again.

The footmen forced her into the carriage and slammed the door. The vehicle immediately began moving. She struggled, pulling on her wrists, which only made the cord tighten. Tears streamed down her face.

Where was she being taken?

The carriage rolled on for what she thought must be several hours until it began slowing. Anna's heart beat wildly in her chest as it came to a halt. The door opened and she was removed from the vehicle.

"Had a bit o' trouble with her?" a man asked, cackling.

"Some," one of her father's servants admitted.

"Wouldn't be the first," the man said, looking her up and down, making her flesh crawl. "Hand her over."

She was shoved and then caught by the stranger, who latched on to her elbow and marched her inside a house. It had a small foyer and worn carpet. No paintings adorned the walls.

She tried to speak but the gag only made grunts come out. The man laughed again as he led her up the stairs. He sobered as they began walking down a long corridor. Anna heard screams in the distance and shivered.

Pausing before a door, he said, "Behave yourself with Matron," and then pushed open the door.

A woman dressed in gray looked up from the desk where she worked. She had iron gray hair and a dull complexion. She could have been anywhere from forty to sixty.

"This the new one?" she asked.

"Yes, Matron."

Anna could tell this man was afraid of the woman before her.

"Get the dress off her. Be quick about it but careful," the woman warned. "You know I like to sell them."

She was appalled that a stranger—and a man—would see her without her gown and she began struggling, trying to protest behind the gag.

The woman stepped to her and slapped Anna hard. Stars appeared in her vision. She had never been struck before and was dumbfounded by the pain.

"You're not to speak. Is that understood?"

Anna blinked back tears and nodded.

"Good. You're learning."

The man pulled out a knife and cut the cord restraining her wrists. Immediately, the blood rushed through her, bringing pain. She bit back her gasp, afraid of being struck again, her hands and arms in agony as if hundreds of pins jabbed them.

Without speaking, she stood there as the man stripped her gown from her, handing it over to the woman called Matron. She folded it neatly.

Then he continued removing each of her undergarments. Anna stood there, her face burning in shame as he gave each one to the woman. He removed her shoes and stockings and she now stood bare, trying to cover her private parts as best she could, humiliation seeping through her.

"Leave," Matron commanded.

The man scurried from the room and Matron removed Anna's gag. Her raw mouth hurt from being stretched for so many hours. She tried to lick her lips and had no moisture to do so. Tears streamed down her face.

"You learn quickly," Matron said, approval in her voice. "Most of the rebellious ones don't."

She longed to ask what that meant but held her tongue.

"Do you know where you are?"

Anna shook her head.

"Gollingham Asylum. A madhouse for the insane."

Her jaw fell.

"Careful," Matron warned.

She closed her mouth.

"You did something," the older woman said. "Something that angered a man. Your father. Your husband. Your brother. Whoever was in charge of you. The madhouse used to be for those who were mad. Things changed," Matron said, matter-of-factly. "When a man thinks his female is no longer controllable, that's when we get them."

Fear spread through Anna and she began trembling. Matron went and picked up a gray bundle.

"Put this on."

Quickly, she unfolded the drab fabric and slipped it over her head. It was shapeless, short-sleeved, and hung to just below her knees. At least she didn't feel quite so vulnerable now with something covering her.

"Do you have any questions?"

Afraid to speak, she shook her head vigorously.

"You may ask."

"How long will I stay here?" she managed to get out.

Matron shrugged. "As long as you stay. Some women are retrieved after a few years."

"Years?" she squeaked.

Matron's gaze pierced Anna. "And some never leave."

Panic filled her. Something told her she would never find her way from this place. She turned in circles, wide-eyed, not knowing where to run. She rushed to the door and flung it open. The man who had escorted her inside waited. She slammed the door on him and spun around.

"Do as you're told when you're told," Matron advised. "It makes it go easier."

"What am I to do?" she cried.

"Whatever I say," An evil smile spread across the woman's face. "Sit here." Matron pointed to a chair.

Anna made herself walk toward it and lowered herself into it. Her thoughts swirled, making no sense. She knew she had to escape. The how and when would take time but she knew she would never survive in such a place.

Matron warned, "Don't move," and left the room.

It must be a test. She didn't know if there was a way she could be watched, so Anna at perfectly still.

And waited.

The minutes passed. Then what must have been an hour. Then two. Finally, the door opened and Matron appeared with a slender man wearing fastidious clothes. Matron's eyebrows raised slightly, seeing Anna in the same position, and she nodded in approval.

The man came forward. "Good afternoon, Miss Browning. I am Dr. Cheshire."

Her eyes cut to Matron, who nodded permission to speak.

"Good afternoon, Dr. Cheshire. I must say I am not certain why I am here."

He frowned deeply. "You are here because of your odd behavior, Miss Browning. Your father stated you have been erratic. Unpredictable. Volatile at times. You are here so we can help manage your mercurial moods and inconsistent behavior."

"I have been none of those things," she said. "May I speak candidly, Doctor?"

He nodded.

"My father wished me to wed a man more than four times my age. I was opposed to the idea. Bringing me here is his way of punishing me."

"What of running away?" Cheshire challenged.

Anna took a deep breath. "I was leaving with my fiancé to be married. The man I wished to marry. One I grew up with and have known—and loved—for many years."

The physician shook his head and turned to Matron. "She is

delusional, just as Lord Shelton said." He glanced back at Anna. "There was no fiancé. No other man you loved. And as for your claim that your father was marrying you off to someone? Ridiculous."

She shot to her feet. "No. I am telling you the truth, Dr. Cheshire. I don't know what Father told you, but it was all lies."

He looked back at his companion. She shrugged.

"Please," Anna begged. "I do not belong here."

Cheshire shook his head. "I am afraid, Miss Browning, you are exactly the person who should be contained in an asylum."

"All because I disagreed with my father? Because I didn't want to be chained to a man I didn't know and could never love?"

"See? Even now, your voice rises with hysteria. You are quivering. Your body knows you are lying and is trying to tell you so."

"I never lie!" she shouted. "Never. But my father does all the time."

The doctor turned and opened the door. The man from before entered, accompanied by another one.

"You know what to do," Cheshire said. "Matron."

He hurried from the room as the two men started toward her.

"Don't touch me!" Anna cried. "Don't. I'll scream."

They both looked at one another and then burst out in laughter. Before she could try to move, they took hold of her, forcing her into the chair.

Matron approached, scissors in hand.

"What are you doing?" she demanded.

"Cutting your hair. We don't have time to care for it." She snickered. "It will soon be covered in lice."

As the men held her in place, Matron unpinned Anna's hair. "How very pretty," she remarked. "This will go for a good price, being such a unique color."

She cringed as she heard the scissors and felt the pull against her scalp. In but a few minutes, Matron held long shanks of strawberry blond hair, placing them on a table. Mortification filled Anna, seeing the loss of her hair.

"Take her to the baths," Matron commanded.

The men dragged her from the chair and across the room, down a dark hallway and into a cold room. They tied her to a chair, her wrists to the arms of it and her ankles to the chair's legs. What followed was a nightmare as they doused her with dozens of buckets of freezing water. Her teeth chattered noisily as gooseflesh covered her body. At one point, she thought she might even drown.

Finally, they stopped slamming the water into her and untied her. As they did, they told her she was to have no opinions. She was to comply with every command. She was never to speak unless given permission to do so. As she trembled with cold and hunger, they marched her down the hallway, which was eerily silent, and opened the door to a room. It was bare except for a small bed with a thin mattress. Bars stretched across the lone window.

As they brought her closer, she saw the bed covered with dark specks that moved. She cringed, digging in her heels. They forced her onto the mattress, still dripping wet, and tied her to it, her hands above her head, her legs spread wide apart.

"Why are you doing this?" she cried. "I am not mad."

"That's what they all say," one of the men said. "Now be quiet. If you make noise, you'll suffer the consequences."

They left, closing the door behind them. Her body quaked with cold.

Anna knew she had been left in Hell.

CHAPTER FOUR

A WEEK HAD passed. Anna knew because she counted in her head each morning as she was escorted from her room. She had remained docile and silent yet inside her head she constantly screamed, frantic to find a way out from this horrible place.

She was tired of being meek. Dalinda would have already rebelled if placed in this situation. Anna looked to her courageous friend and decided today would be the day she would begin to fight back. She had to—or she might truly go mad.

An attendant came to her room to bring her to breakfast and she remained obedient as she forced the slop they called food into her mouth. As usual, after the meal she was led to a long hallway lined with benches. The patients were spaced out on these benches and sat for a majority of the day. When Anna was shoved onto a spot, she bounced back to her feet.

Steadily eyeing her attendant, she told him, "I believe I would like to walk the corridor today and take some exercise."

She looked out and loudly said, "Would anyone wish to join me?"

Not one patient looked her way. Heads remained bowed. She could see tension in shoulders and bodies beginning to tremble—but the silence was deafening. She glanced back at the attendant, who shook his head in disbelief, and then he walked away. She glanced around and saw all other attendants had left. She was free to roam as she pleased.

Savoring her small victory, Anna slowly walked the length of the corridor. She spoke to a few of the women but no one returned a word in her direction. Turning, she moved back up the hallway.

At the end of it stood Matron with an attendant by her side, her expression grim.

Anna moved toward the woman with purpose, praying her steps wouldn't falter. She reached Matron and came to a stop before her.

"I have been told you are breaking the rules, Browning. *My* rules," emphasized Matron. She studied Anna a moment and then said, "I suppose I was wrong about you. You caught on quite well your first day here. For a week, you have been submissive and compliant."

"I merely wished to take some exercise," Anna said, her voice quaking.

"Ah, so the queen wishes for exercise," Matron said, her tone mocking. "A turn about the room. So you shall." She glanced at the servant next to her and said, "Bring me a scold's bridle."

As the man hurried away, she heard a few gasps and glanced out. Still, every head remained bowed. Anna returned her gaze to Matron, whose malicious smile caused a trickle of fear to run along Anna's spine. The two women stared at one another until the attendant returned with something in his hands that she couldn't make out.

"Seize her!" Matron cried suddenly.

Two other men had sneaked up behind Anna and latched onto her. As she tried to shrug them off, Matron took the object from the servant's hands and held it up for Anna to view.

"This is a scold's bridle. It gets its name from the nagging, scolding females it is used upon. I place it on troublesome patients, Browning. Such as you."

Matron lifted it over Anna's head and locked the cage around her head, shoving something into her mouth that was attached to this iron muzzle. She had seen—and now her tongue felt—the tiny spikes in it as cold fear filled her.

"I've slipped the curb-plate into your mouth," Matron continued. "It is like a bridle bit for a horse. It will compress your tongue and prevent you from speaking. If you try to say anything, the spikes will pierce your tongue and fill your mouth with blood."

Anna could already taste the tinny blood in her mouth from Matron jamming it in and held herself perfectly still.

"You will suffer mild discomfort," the older woman said nonchalantly. "While you are taking your exercise, of course."

Matron raised her hand, her palm open. The attendant placed what looked like a leash in her hands. The woman attached it to the cage that surrounded Anna's head.

"You are so eager to move about, Browning, that I will be generous and allow you to do so. Notice I said *allow*. I am in charge here. Nothing happens that I am not aware of. Everyone does my bidding." She smiled brightly at Anna. "You will now be walked as a dog. All day. All night. We will revisit the issue twenty-four hours from now and see how you feel about . . . exercise."

With that, Matron handed the leash to the closest attendant. The ones restraining her stepped away.

"Walk!" barked the man.

Anna did as bid, moving to the end of the corridor. She turned and came back toward Matron, who stood with her arms crossed over her chest. Anna turned again, parading endlessly up and down the corridor, humiliation filling her as much as the saliva and blood that flooded her mouth. Matron remained watching for a few hours and then left but the constant walking continued.

For the rest of the day.

Her mouth and jaw ached something fierce. Fatigue set into her limbs. Yet she still was led up and down, over and over, as not one head raised to see her pass. Eventually, evening must have fallen for the patients were removed from the benches. Another attendant replaced the current one and Anna continued walking up and down the corridor throughout the night. Weariness blanketed her yet she knew she couldn't falter. If she did, Matron would win. She drew on a well of bravery she didn't know she had, knowing Dalinda—and Dez—would have been proud of her resolve.

Finally, a new day must have dawned and the patients were brought back to their benches. A few glanced at her in pity before they took their spots and lowered their gazes to their laps.

When Anna made another turn, she caught sight of Matron standing in the middle of the hallway. Though she had been shuffling along, barely able to move, she now picked up her feet and marched to the older woman, halting in front of her.

"Well, Your Majesty, I hope you enjoyed your bit of exercise." Matron barked out a laugh and the attendants nearby joined in nervously.

Anna met the woman's gaze.

"This is what happens to troublesome patients, Browning," Matron said with a sigh. "I do pray that you have decided to be more manageable in the future."

She couldn't speak without puncturing her tongue further so Anna nodded slightly.

"Good. It is always refreshing when a patient learns an important lesson, Browning. I hope you have learned yours and that you will remember that rash actions have consequences." Matron shook her head. "I am not a monster despite what you think. I merely have rules in place so that all patients will comply. It is so much easier if you respect those rules and yield accordingly."

With a flick of her hand, two attendants took Anna by the elbows. A third undid the leash. Matron herself unlocked the cage and removed the curb-plate and lifted the scold's bridle from Anna's head. Relief swept through her even as blood and saliva mixed in her mouth. She swallowed, her tongue painfully swollen and sore.

"Do you require further exercise, Browning?" Matron demanded, glaring at her as if she were an avenging angel yielding a sword of justice.

Anna glanced to the device of torture she had worn for an entire day. Not sure she could even speak, she vigorously shook her head.

"Good," Matron said, satisfaction in her voice. "Place her on the bench."

Two men dragged her down the corridor to a free spot since Anna's legs gave way and she could no longer walk. Sitting on the hard surface, she placed her hands in her lap, her head bent, tears streaming down her cheeks.

A figure appeared next to her but Anna didn't dare look up.

Matron softly said, "I will break you if I have to, Browning. You would be wise to comply with my rules. Submission is expected at all times. I am to be obeyed without question."

She closed her eyes and barely nodded. After a moment, Matron moved away, her swishing skirts the only audible noise.

For the first time since she had arrived at Gollingham, Anna retreated far into herself. They may break her body but they would never touch her mind. She would submit to Matron's terrible rules and pretend to be a shell of her former self.

But inside, Anna would remain true to herself. If she didn't?

She might actually go mad.

CHAPTER FIVE

Twelve years later . . .
Spain—March 1810

MAJOR DESMOND BRETTON took a sip from his goblet and set it down. "At least the wine is good here. That must count for something."

His friend, Colonel Rhys Armistead, chuckled. "I would say it's the only good thing in Spain. I hope when this ends that I never see Spain again." He tilted his glass and finished off the red wine.

"If we weren't at war, I might appreciate the landscape. The scenery. The people," Dez added. "But I am just so bloody tired of all the fighting."

Rhys shrugged. "It's what we signed up for."

He shook his head. "Don't tell me we knew what we were getting into."

The two men had met a dozen years ago. Both were eighteen and wet behind the ears, not yet having filled out their tall frames. Rhys' benefactor had bought a commission for him, while Dez's father had done the same for his second son. Both men got along because they rarely talked about their pasts and they have saved one another's hide on the battlefield more times than they could count.

"Do you think the Little General will ever be defeated?" his friend asked.

"If you would have asked me that years ago, I would have answered without hesitation. I had confidence in the great, mighty, powerful British Empire. Now, after all of these years at war with no end in sight, I couldn't venture a guess."

Dejection filled Dez. Though he knew he was a good officer, he had grown tired of always being at war. Killing the enemy was bad enough but each man he lost took a piece of his soul. He longed for the beauty of the English countryside. To sit back and breathe in air that wasn't heavy with smoke from cannon fire. He wished for a peace that might never come.

It was probably better to be busy at war even with long stretches of inactivity, as now. And though he thought he would be happier in England, he wouldn't be. Every day he lived was a day without Anna in it.

Anna. Who was no more.

He liked to picture her atop her horse, her long braid of strawberry blond hair bobbing up and down as she raced ahead of him, jumping a fence, cutting around shrubbery. Even after all this time, he could recall her laugh. Remember the feel of her lips against his.

Poor Anna hadn't fared as well as Dez. True, he had to forgo his university education but he had learned far better things during in his time in the army. At least he had a few friends, Rhys being chief among them, and leadership duties. He might not be happy but he was useful to his country. On the other hand, Anna had made the decision to leave this earth. Dez supposed she couldn't stomach the thought of a life spent in the ancient Lord Needham's bed. Instead, she had filled her pockets with stones and walked into the lake where they had picnicked at so often.

Dalinda had written to him of Anna's death, which Lord Shelton had said was an accidental drowning. Both twins knew, however, that Anna had taken her own life and the viscount only said what he did to quell the rumors that tainted his family with her death. Dalinda had said there must have been a problem with the local clergyman deeming it a suicide because Anna was buried not in the village churchyard but at Shelton Park. His sister had never visited her friend's grave, having married herself and staying far away from Surrey. Dalinda vowed never to set foot at Torville Manor while their father or Ham was the earl.

"You look contemplative, my friend," Rhys said. "It is unlike you."

Dez lifted his glass. "Pour me more wine."

Rhys obliged and they sat in companionable silence until the flap of their tent moved and a soldier announced, "Mail."

He knew the letter must be for him since Rhys never received mail of any kind. Both his parents were dead, as well as a sister who died when they were quite young. As for himself, he only received letters from his twin. His father had died a year after Dez left England and hadn't written his son once. Now that Ham was the Earl of Torrington, he had continued the practice of silence, which was fine with Dez. The less he heard from or knew about his brother, the better.

Reaching out a hand, he accepted the letter.

"From your sister, I assume," Rhys said.

The one thing Dez did talk about on rare occasions was Dalinda. He had shared a few stories of his childhood with Rhys, usually ones where Dalinda got them into trouble and Dez took the blame. Other than that, neither Rhys nor anyone else in the army knew about Dez's background or life before he became a soldier in His Majesty's Army.

He glanced at the letter he held and frowned. Puzzled at the unfamiliar handwriting, he broke the seal and skimmed to the bottom, seeing that a Mr. Capshaw had signed it.

Rhys rose. "I'll leave you to it." He left the tent.

With trepidation, Dez looked to the top and began to read.

My dear Major Bretton –

I will dispense with all niceties and come to the point of this correspondence. I am the solicitor for your brother, Lord Torrington, and regret to inform you that his lordship and wife drown. They have already been buried since bloating is an issue when death by drowning occurs.

Because of these circumstances and the fact that they had no issue, you now may claim the title as the new Earl of Torrington. All lands and estates, entailed and otherwise, are in your possession.

I suggest you return to England at your earliest convenience in order to see to your affairs. Write to me once you have arrived at Torville Manor and I will come down from London to inform you of your holdings and answer any questions you might have.

Your servant,
J. Capshaw

Dez dropped the letter and it floated to the ground. Stunned, he shook his head, trying to make sense of what he had just read.

He hadn't known Ham had wed. Not that he or Dalinda would have access to that information. All ties had been cut between them many years ago. Still, he couldn't help but feel a moment of pity for the woman who had perished next to her husband. This Capshaw didn't elaborate regarding the circumstances so Dez had no idea where the drowning occurred.

And he was now Torrington.

A name he loathed, thanks to his despicable father and brother. In that moment, Dez vowed to be a better lord—a better man—than his two predecessors to the title.

His first thought was how woefully unprepared he was to take on such a role. His father had ignored him all his life, teaching his heir apparent all about estate business. Knowing Ham as he did, Dez knew his brother hadn't done much managing of the estate once he had assumed the title. Ham had always run with a fast crowd, drinking and gambling with abandon. Tending to estate business would be the last thing Ham might have done well or been interested in. Because of that, Dez couldn't help but wonder what the state of affairs would be upon his return.

He would need to sell his commission immediately. He owed it to his tenants at Torville Manor. And thank the heavens above because this swift turn of events gave him an excuse to leave the ugliness of war. His only regret would be leaving Rhys behind. They had grown closer than any brothers could.

Rising, Dez folded the letter and placed it in his pocket. He left their shared tent and went in search of his friend, finding him watching a card game from a distance. He signaled and Rhys joined him.

"What news does your irascible twin send?" Rhys' lips twitched with amusement. "Have her boys been up to no good again?"

"The letter wasn't from Dalinda. It came from my brother's solicitor." He paused. "Ham is dead."

His friend drew in a sharp breath. "Then you are now Earl of Torrington."

Dez nodded slowly. "I am. And I haven't the faintest idea how to be a titled lord."

Rhys clasped his shoulder. "Dez, you will make for a wonderful earl. You have a keen intelligence. You always seem to have a solution for any problem that arises. Why, I believe you will be the best Torrington the estate has ever seen," he proclaimed. "Better yet, you will soon leave this cesspool behind in order to take up your duties."

He smiled ruefully. "I suppose I must." He studied Rhys a moment. "Will you ever leave the army? I know nothing of your background, other than some patron bestowed your commission upon you."

"It was the Earl of Sheffington," his friend revealed.

"Why?"

"My mother is a distant cousin. The earl's son is not strong. Sheffington hedged his bets. Found me when I was fifteen and saw me tutored for three years before I entered the army. If the viscount dies, I am Sheffington's heir."

The news Rhys revealed startled Dez. "Then you might also one day be an earl."

Rhys shrugged. "I am not counting on it. Raleigh is a year older than I am and he's still alive. Frankly, I don't care one way or the other."

He knew there was much more to the story and hoped one day his friend would share it with him.

"Will you write to me?"

Rhys looked at him as if he'd gone mad. "You really want to hear about . . . this?" He raised his arms and gestured to the hundreds of soldiers around them.

"I want to hear from *you*," he emphasized. "And I will write in return. No one knows me as you do, my friend. I will need a sounding board."

Laughing, Rhys said, "I am probably the last person who should render advice to you."

Dez also laughed. "I am most likely the last person who would take it." He grew serious. "I will miss you. Other than Dalinda, I have never been so close to anyone."

A moment passed between them and then Rhys said, "If this bloody war ever ends, I will come and look you up. That's a promise."

He sighed. "I suppose I should go and speak to someone about selling out."

By morning, Dez had made the necessary arrangements and had officially resigned his commission from His Majesty's Army. He said goodbye to Rhys and caught a ride on a farmer's cart to the nearest town, where he bought a shirt, pants, and a coat. None of them was fashionable but they weren't clothing that reminded him of the army. He was ready to disassociate himself with everything remotely involved with soldiering although he did carry an order that would see him on a ship and safely back to England.

The next day, he boarded the vessel and looked ahead, never once glancing back at Spain.

CHAPTER SIX

Gillingham

DEZ PASSED THROUGH the village of Gillbrook and rode the two miles to Gillingham, home to the Duke and Duchess of Gilford. He had arrived safely back in England and before traveling to Surrey, he had detoured to Kent in order to see his twin, the other half to himself. He would say the other half of his soul but after all these years, that still belonged to Anna, along with his heart. As the new Earl of Torrington, however, it would be his duty to provide an heir. He wondered if it might be better for his older nephew to take the title instead. It would be something he asked the mysterious and yet pragmatic Mr. Capshaw when they met in person. If Dalinda's boy could serve as his heir, Dez would never have any need to marry. He thought that might be for the best because he would make for a terrible husband. He saw no need to put some poor woman through a marriage with him when he still ached for the dead girl he would always love.

He rode directly to the stables, where a groom took his horse, and he was shown toward the house. Dez knocked on the front door and was greeted by the butler.

"I have no calling card," he revealed, "since I have just returned from Spain. I am Lord Torrington, brother to Her Grace."

The butler's brows rose a good inch. "Yes, my lord. Do come

in." The servant opened the door wider and stepped aside so Dez could enter.

Immediately, he saw the grandeur of the foyer and was pleased Dalinda had done well for herself. She had written to him of their father's scheme to wed her off to a much older man and how the Duke of Gilford, a complete stranger, had come to her rescue. Her letters seemed to show she was happy in the match although the duke's health had suffered in recent years.

"Allow me to escort you to the drawing room, my lord," the butler said.

Dez was led to the destination, taking in all the magnificent art and sculptures in the corridor before they even reached the drawing room.

"I will let Her Grace know you are here, my lord. Might you be staying the night—or longer?"

It was already mid-afternoon. Remaining at Gillingham overnight would make sense.

"Yes, I will stay this evening and leave early tomorrow morning."

"Very well, my lord. I will let Mrs. Paul, our housekeeper, know. And I am Bellows. If you need anything, I will tend to it."

"Thank you, Bellows."

The butler left and Dez began idly roaming the room. He caught movement from the corners of his eyes as the door swung open quietly and two shapes scurried in, hiding behind a settee. It had to be his nephews, boys whom he had never met and yet knew so much about, thanks to his twin's letters over the years.

A giggle sounded and one boy shushed the other.

He bit back a smile and said, "I have been in the military since I was eighteen years of age. I know when someone tries to sneak up on me, be they friend or foe."

Two heads popped up and the taller boy, who must be Arthur, punched Harry, his younger brother, in the shoulder.

"I told you to be quiet," he chided.

"Harry didn't give you away," Dez revealed. "I noticed you

come in."

"How?" Arthur demanded.

"I told you. My experience in the military."

"Who are you?" Harry asked. "How do you know my name?"

He smiled. "I know quite about the two of you from your mother."

Harry's face lit in a smile. "You're Uncle Dez."

He nodded and the boy raced from behind the settee, flinging himself at Dez. He caught up his nephew and gave him a sound kiss on the cheek.

Harry frowned and wiped his face with the back of his hand. "I don't want to be kissed," he announced.

Dalinda had written that of the two, Harry was still affectionate with her, while Arthur stretched the boundaries of independence. It seemed the younger boy might be taking his cues from the older one.

Dez released Harry and said, "Come and greet your old uncle, Arthur."

Arthur stepped toward him and bowed. Offering his hand, Dez shook it—and then grabbed him and kissed him as he had Harry. Arthur squirmed and wriggled from his grasp.

"Are you really our uncle Dez?" he demanded.

"The very one."

Arthur turned to Harry. "He's the brother Mama likes. It's the other one who was mean to her."

He wondered at Dalinda's indiscretion, revealing old family secrets to her sons.

Harry nodded. "I remember. Mama told Papa about the mean one that time in the garden." He looked to Dez. "We aren't supposed to listen in when others are talking but sometimes that's the only way Arthur and I learn anything."

Dez couldn't help but laugh. "That is called eavesdropping. It's rude—but something your mama and I did when we were your age. It is a good way to find out the interesting things adults try to keep from children."

"That uncle is dead. Ham, Mama calls him," Arthur said. "Though why anyone would want to be named after meat is ridiculous."

"It was our nickname for him. Which he hated."

The boys giggled.

"His name was Hamilton. My name is Desmond but I have always gone by Dez."

"Do you like us, Uncle Dez?" Harry asked.

"Of course, I do. You are family."

"But why didn't Ham like you and Mama?" the boy pressed.

He took a deep breath. "Sometimes, a person is not very nice."

"Uncle Ham was an earl," Arthur said helpfully.

Dez nodded in agreement. "Even then, not all earls are good. Just because a man holds a title doesn't mean he is good."

"Papa is very good," Harry said. "He's a duke. But Arthur and I won't have titles. Mama says that Reid is the next duke."

"Title or no title, I hope you are the best boys you can be and grow into the best men you can be."

The pair exchanged a guilty glance.

Before Dez could ask what was wrong, Dalinda sailed into the room. "Dez!"

As he went to meet her, he couldn't help but think what a beauty his sister had grown into. She had always been a pretty girl but now she had a maturity and air of authority about her. Being a duchess and giving birth must have added to her bearing. He embraced her, inhaling the scent of roses.

"You look wonderful," he told her as he released her but took her hands in his, happy they had finally reunited after so many years apart.

"You are as handsome as ever but where is your officer's uniform?"

Dez didn't want to reveal in front of his impressionable nephews that he had thrown it in a garbage bin.

"Now that I have left the army, I had to leave my uniform

behind. I bought these clothes."

Dalinda eyed him, frowning, and then he saw she realized the truth. "Well, you must certainly see a tailor soon. No one would guess you are an earl."

The door opened and a servant rushed in, the color high on her cheeks. "Oh, Your Grace, I am so sorry. I lost track of the little lords."

"That's quite all right. My boys have just met their uncle." She looked at her sons. "It is time for your riding lesson."

"Can Uncle Dez come with us?" Harry asked hopefully.

"Not this time," she said. "You have gotten to visit with him. It is my turn now."

"You won't leave without saying goodbye, will you?" Arthur demanded.

"No. I promise to see you after your ride. I will depart for Torville Manor after breakfast tomorrow. Perhaps we could share that meal together."

"In the schoolroom?" Harry asked, his eyes growing wide. "That's where we eat each morning."

"Then I will join you there," he assured them.

"Go along," Dalinda urged.

Harry gave Dez another hug while Arthur merely nodded at him. After they left, Dalinda said, "They are a whirlwind."

"Shouldn't they be in school?" he asked.

"They are . . . between schools at the moment," she said. "We have so much to talk about. And you are staying overnight?"

"Yes, Bellows suggested it."

"Bellows is most efficient," she said. "For now, I would like you to come and meet Gilford."

"Is he up to it? I know you have mentioned he has been in ill health."

Dalinda slipped her arm through his and led him from the room. "He will never be strong again. He has had two heart attacks. The doctor said a third would kill him. Because of that, he spends most of his time in his rooms. That's where I was when you arrived. He is eager to meet you, though."

As they went down the corridor, Dez asked, "Have you been happy with him?"

"Gilford saved me," she said. "Plain and simple. He was a good husband to me in our first years together. He taught me so much, about art and politics and farming. He was a good father to the boys, as well. Those years will always be special to me.

"Now, though, is my time to take care of him as he did me. We live a quiet life at Gillingham. We read together. Sit in our garden. I play the pianoforte for him." She sighed. "I am content, Dez. I live a peaceful life. One of my own choosing."

"Not the man Father would have bound you to."

"Exactly."

"Did you go to Ham's funeral? And when did he wed?"

"No, I didn't go. I received word of his death in a terse note from a Mr. Capshaw."

"He was brief with me, as well. Said Lord and Lady Torrington had drowned but gave no context as to the circumstances."

Dalinda halted. "I know what happened. Do you remember our housekeeper at Torville Manor? Mrs. Abbott and I correspond monthly. I tell her about Arthur and Harry and she writes to me of news regarding the estate. Ham wed his wife last September, at the end of the Season. His bride had just made her come-out. I suppose at thirty-four, he had finally decided he should take a wife. Not that Mrs. Abbott ever said anything, but from what I glean from the gossip columns in the London newspapers that we receive at times, Ham was a terrible rake. Chasing married and unmarried women alike. Drinking. Gambling. Supposedly, his bride brought an enormous dowry with her."

"I wonder if any of it is left," he mused.

"I would think so." She hesitated and then said, "As for their deaths, they drown . . . in the lake between our property and Viscount Shelton's land."

A fresh stab of pain hit him. How ironic to have lost Anna and his brother in the same place.

"Do you know anything about how it occurred? Especially with both of them."

"From what Mrs. Abbott revealed, Lady Torrington was fearful of water. Ham—who was already deep in his cups by early afternoon—insisted he take her rowing on the lake. Apparently, the boat capsized. Though the water isn't terribly deep, Ham would have been too drunk to swim to shore and his wife did not know how to swim at all."

Dez shook his head. "What a tragedy. That poor young woman."

Dalinda pulled him along again. "There is nothing we can do about it. They are gone—and you are now Torrington. Oh, I am so glad you stopped at Gillingham before you traveled home."

"I had to see you. I wanted to meet your boys and the duke. If you don't mind, I would like Arthur and Harry to come spend a couple of weeks with me each summer. I'd like to get to know them better."

He thought especially if Arthur were to be his heir, it would be good for the boy to be familiar with the estate.

"That would be marvelous, Dez."

She paused. "These are Gilford's rooms." Opening the door, she motioned him in and followed. They entered a sitting room and he spied a tall, gaunt man gazing out the window, gripping a chair. He wore a silk banyan and had dark brown hair peppered with gray.

He turned and smiled. Dez could see the kindness in the duke's eyes.

Stepping forward, he bowed and said, "Good afternoon, Your Grace. I am Lord Torrington, Dalinda's brother."

Gilford took his hand and Dez thought the handshake stronger than he would have imagined from one so frail.

"I am delighted to meet you, Torrington," the duke said, his eyes twinkling. "My wife speaks very highly of you. She reads your letters aloud to me."

Dez understood why Dalinda had an immediate kinship with the duke. "She has praised you as well, Your Grace."

"Why don't we sit?" Dalinda suggested and helped ease her husband into the chair.

They spoke several minutes, the duke reminiscing about how he and Dalinda had met, and then she suggested the two men play a game of chess.

"I'll fetch the board," she offered and crossed the room, bringing it back.

He saw the pieces already in place. "I haven't played in a good number of years."

Gilford's eyes lit up. "All the better for me to beat you."

They played for half an hour and seemed evenly matched. Then Dez saw the duke tiring and decided to make an ill-advised move. Gilford pounced upon him and, five minutes later, the duke emerged as the game's victor.

"You are out of practice to make such a novice mistake," Gilford said as Dalinda swept the board away.

Dez realized the duke knew exactly what he had done. "Perhaps I will win the next time we play, Your Grace."

"I'll hold you to a rematch," Gilford said, wincing.

"You are tired," Dalinda proclaimed. "You need to get some rest."

He helped his sister escort the duke into his bedchamber and the two of them got Gilford settled. He was fast asleep before they even left the room.

"Thank you for playing with him—and letting him win," she said gratefully. "I have longed for you to meet one another for many years."

"I see why you like him. He's very sharp. Kind."

"And a bit impulsive," she said, laughing. "After all, he offered for me only minutes after we met."

They enjoyed tea together, their conversation never ceasing. He talked a bit about the army and his relief that the war was behind him. He mentioned Rhys and regretting that he left his dear friend behind.

"I think you would like him, Dalinda."

"If he is your friend, of course I would. It is interesting that he had a benefactor purchase his commission and that he might one day become an earl, the same as you."

"We will have to see what the future holds."

Dalinda went to read with the boys afterward while Dez took a much-needed bath. The twins dined together and talked until midnight before parting for the evening.

The next morning, Dez joined his nephews for breakfast.

"Good morning, boys," he called cheerfully as he entered the breakfast room, finding Dalinda had yet to arrive.

They both murmured a greeting but Harry kept his eyes on his plate, his lips twitching in amusement. Arthur boldly looked Dez in the eyes. Dez could tell from their behavior that something was afoot. His sister had written about the trouble these two could get in to and Dez sensed he was about to be the victim of some boyhood prank. Arthur had to be the mastermind, acting cool and confident, while Harry wriggled in his seat, toying with his food, surreptitiously eyeing Dez.

"Do you like to drink tea or coffee with your breakfast, Uncle Dez?" Arthur asked innocently.

"I generally like both." He paused. "Perhaps I should drink a cup of milk this morning as you boys are doing."

Harry's head popped up, his jaw falling open. Arthur took his uncle's words in stride, however, and was obviously the instigator of what was to come.

"You don't have to do that, Uncle Dez," Arthur said. "Why, I cannot wait to be old enough to be allowed to drink coffee."

"Then coffee it is," Dez proclaimed. "For both of us," he told the footman, who approached with a coffeepot. "Bring a cup and saucer for my older nephew," he instructed the footman, who poured the hot brew into Dez's cup. "It's about time he tried some."

"Really?" Arthur asked, intrigued by the thought of drinking coffee. "Mama wouldn't approve. She's says a man shouldn't drink coffee until he is old enough to shave."

"Then you better finish it before she arrives," Dez advised sagely.

A cup was placed before Arthur and he sat up straighter. The footman poured coffee into it, the rich smell inviting. Coffee, real coffee, was something Dez had missed during his time at war.

"Coffee is better with a bit of sugar and cream in it," he advised.

Harry's hand went to his mouth, trying to hide a smile, letting Dez know that something had been placed in the sugar or cream—or both.

"Oh, I can drink it this way," Arthur said.

Dez doubted it but said, "Go ahead and try."

Bravely, Arthur brought the cup to his lips and took a sip. He scrunched up his face.

"Bleech!"

"See, I told you. Coffee smells delightful but needs something to take the edge off it." He poured milk into his cup and then spooned some sugar into it. Pushing both toward Arthur, he said, "Try some of both. It will make it quite tasty. I guarantee it," wondering how Arthur would get out of the situation.

"No, really, Uncle, I think I prefer it black," his nephew said shakily.

Harry stifled a giggle and scooped some eggs on his fork, stuffing them into his mouth as he watched them.

Dez stirred his coffee, knowing for the prank to succeed he needed to take at least one sip. He brought the cup to his lips, both Arthur's and Harry's eyes wide now, watching him anxiously. Dez tilted the cup toward him but kept his lips together. The boys wouldn't be able to see that he didn't drink anything and he would save himself from whatever had been placed in his cup.

He quickly lowered the cup, screwing up his face, pushing his tongue out several times as if he tried to rid himself of a foul taste.

"Oh, that's horrible!" he exclaimed.

Harry started giggling. Arthur waited a moment and then burst out laughing.

Playing along, Dez asked, "Good lord, whatever did you put in it?"

"We didn't put anything in your coffee," Arthur said innocently.

"Semantics, Arthur," he chided. "Nothing was in the coffee itself but something was in the sugar or cream."

Arthur smiled triumphantly. "You were the one who added those in, Uncle Dez. Not us."

"So I was," he said thoughtfully and then began laughing.

"You aren't mad?" asked Harry carefully.

"No. Just surprised. You got me good," he said, smiling at his nephews. "And what will happen when your poor mama comes and tries to put cream and sugar into her tea?"

Arthur smiled knowingly. "Mama takes chocolate at breakfast. She doesn't use cream or sugar."

Dez nodded admiringly. "You are very clever. The both of you."

"You really aren't angry?" Arthur asked. "I'm sure salt in your coffee tasted terrible." He wrinkled his nose. "Actually, coffee tastes terrible. I don't know if I'll ever want to drink it again."

"No, of course I'm not mad. Your mama and I did far worse things at your age," he confided.

"You and Mama played pranks on others?" Arthur asked, amazed.

"All the time," Dez said. "Trouble seemed to follow us wherever we went."

"You won't tell on us?" Harry asked.

"Why would I?" he replied.

"Good," the pair said in unison.

After that, both talked nonstop and he found them to be endearing boys. He would enjoy having them visit him once he settled into his routine at Torville Manor. Dalinda joined them, none the wiser, as Dez winked at them and conversed normally with his sister.

After breakfast, Dalinda walked him down to the stables and clung to him for a moment.

"I hate to let you go," she said. "We never got to say goodbye that last time and look how many years have passed. I am afraid the same will happen again."

He smoothed her hair. "There is no one to keep us apart now. No Father. No Ham. Let me settle into my responsibilities and see that things are being run well and I will be back for a visit. I do want the boys to come see me. I would suggest you do, as well, but I know you don't want to leave Gilford."

"No, I belong here with him." Dalinda kissed his cheek. "Take care, Dez. Write to me of all that is going on."

"I will."

A groom brought his horse and Dez swung into the saddle. With a wave, he rode out from the yard.

And toward the estate that now was his.

CHAPTER SEVEN

Torville Manor—May

DEZ FINISHED LOOKING over the papers Paul Lexington, his estate manager, had given him. It looked as if the May harvest would be quite productive. He set aside the last page and turned to his correspondence, answering letters to both Rhys and young Harry.

It was the first letter he had received from the battlefront from his friend since they had parted. As always with the army, everything was hurry up—then wait. Rhys said he might well die from boredom before a bullet did him in. Now that Dez was away from the military conflict, he could only hope Bonaparte would soon be squashed like a bug or that Rhys might be fortunate enough to return to England and take his place as a fellow peer.

As for Harry, his penmanship was atrocious. Dez struggled to read the writing and finally figured out what his nephew wrote about. He was touched that Harry thought to write him. It was the second letter that the boy had sent. None had come from Arthur, however. He was a cool one, most likely feigning indifference toward Dez and then pumping his brother for news of what their uncle had written about. He made a note to write Dalinda next to see when the boys might want to come for an extended stay at Torville Manor.

Dez had been in his former home for almost six weeks now. It had taken him a bit to become accustomed to his rooms, ones he remembered his father occupying and which later must have seen Ham using them. Mrs. Abbott had given him a tour upon his arrival and pointed out the items that needed to be addressed. He'd taken up her list with Lexington, going over the books of the estate in order to see where matters stood.

The very unique Mr. Capshaw had also paid a visit shortly after Dez's return. He brought with him paperwork and ledgers and frankly made Dez's head ache. In the end, though, he received a clear idea of his financial situation, which had been aided by the huge dowry brought by his brother's wife. Mr. Capshaw said that in some instances, when a marriage lasted less than a year, the bride's family might request the dowry be returned. That had not been the case this time. Dez had offered to contact her family and ask if they wished it returned but Capshaw nearly exploded at the idea, telling him he would be foolish to throw away found money. The solicitor convinced him that, as the new earl, the money was his by rights. Though he still felt guilty, he knew very little about financial affairs and decided to take the solicitor's advice on the matter.

He stood and stretched his arms high above his head, tired of sitting behind his desk. He decided to go for a walk on the estate. He had ridden it several times and stopped at every cottage on Torrington property, meeting tenants and their wives and children. When he saw someone now, a name usually popped into his head and he delighted when he recognized the tenant and could put the right name to his face.

Instead of leaving through the main entrance, Dez merely walked through the French doors of his study and into the warm sunshine of the spring day. Though he told himself he had no destination in mind, he found his feet led him to the lake where so many happy memories had taken place. He had only come down here once since his return, with his valet, Coral. Coral knew everything that happened at Torville Manor and far beyond its boundaries. He was friendly with many people in Draymott, the nearest village and spent time in the Draymott pub every week.

Dez had come to depend upon Coral's fount of knowledge, which was why he discussed Ham's accidental drowning with the valet. Coral had been one of the servants who had gone to the lake when the earl and countess did not return from their boating excursion. The valet had been the one to wade into the water and retrieve Lord and Lady Torrington's lifeless bodies and stayed with them while others brought a cart to convey her and Ham home. Coral didn't mince words since the former earl was dead in his grave and had told Dez exactly what he thought of his lordship—none of it flattering. Fortunately, Coral believed Dez a grand step up as the new earl and they got along well.

He arrived at the lake and sat on a fallen log near the shore. He remembered bringing picnic hampers filled with food that Cook had supplied to him and Dalinda. Anna would meet them, bringing Jessa along once she got old enough to accompany her big sister. They, too, would have treats from their kitchen. In cooler weather, he would build a fire and they would gather around it, drawing from its warmth while they told ghost stories and sang. Those were good times and he found himself thinking of them with fondness now. His memories honored Anna and were the best part of his life. He had decided to push away the sadness of her death and concentrate on those happy moments. The only thing he regretted was that Anna had not been buried in Draymott, preventing him from visiting her grave.

Finally, he rose and before returning to the house, he went to the small cottage nearby where he and Dalinda had played as children. He didn't remember which tenant had moved out from it, only that it had stood empty for as long as he could recall. Gradually, he and Dalinda had brought various items to the tiny abode. A few chairs they'd found in the attic. A table with a broken leg that they had propped up with books. An old shelf where they placed more books and a few toys. They had invited

Anna to come to the cottage once it was fixed up.

Dez opened the door and glanced around. He had asked Lexington if any tenant had been assigned to it. No one had. Once he knew no one lived here, he had instructed his housekeeper to send maids down to clean and air out the place. The broken down furniture had been removed. The floors had been washed. Dez had gone through Torville Manor and chosen a piece here and there and had footmen bring the furniture under the butler's watchful eye. The cottage was now cozy. It had a table and two chairs for someone to eat a meal. A settee and another chair. A desk which sat next to the window, where a glimpse of the lake could be seen. In the small bedchamber, he'd placed a bed and wardrobe and had the maids bring linens. He doubted it would ever be used but it captured a time for him that he missed. He might even come here and work every now and then at the desk, enjoying being closer to nature.

Closing the door, he returned to the house, slipping back into his study. It surprised him to find Meadows, his butler, waiting for him, an anxious look upon his normally placid face.

"There you are, your lordship. We had no idea where you had gone."

Dez smiled. "I am sorry if I worried you, Meadows. I will keep you better informed of my whereabouts in the future."

"That would be most appreciated, my lord." The butler cleared his throat. "In the meantime, you have callers."

"Who?" he asked, puzzled since he had issued no invitations. He knew, sooner or later, he would need to start becoming acquainted with his neighbors but he had been so busy up to this point.

"Lord and Lady Shelton and Miss Browning."

He froze at the words then forced his limbs to relax. Lord Shelton, Anna's father, had died recently, according to the ever-knowing Coral. The valet said that the viscount had passed away a month before Ham had. Dez supposed this was the heir and his wife. The Miss Browning would be Jessa. Dez thought a moment, calculating how old she would be and determined she would likely be seventeen or eighteen.

"Where are they?" he asked, recovering his composure.

"I placed them in the drawing room and asked Cook to serve them tea."

"Good thinking, Meadows. I will go to them now."

As he ascended the stairs, he hoped that the new Lord Shelton would be nothing like his predecessor, especially since they were to be neighbors. Dez entered the drawing room as a maid left. She bobbed a curtsey to him and told him tea had just been served and that she'd brought a cup for him in case he returned in time to join his guests. He thanked her and crossed the room.

Immediately, Jessa sprang to her feet. "Dez!" she cried and came toward him.

"Hello, Jessa. It is so good to see you." He embraced her and pulled away to study her. "My, you have certainly grown since I last saw you. And grown tall."

Where Anna had been petite, just a few inches over five feet, Jessa was much taller. She had a willowy frame and the same sky-blue eyes her sister did, though Jessa's hair was blond. He seemed to recall Lady Shelton having blond hair.

"I am just turned eighteen," Jessa said. "Which makes you thirty."

He winced. "Don't remind me." He glanced to the couple who smiled at him and moved toward them. "Desmond Bretton, Earl of Torrington. You must be Lord and Lady Shelton."

The two men shook hands and his neighbor said, "We are. It is certainly good to meet you, my lord."

He turned and greeted the viscountess, a pretty, plump girl with brown hair and brown eyes. "It is a pleasure to make your acquaintance, Lady Shelton."

"I would say the same, my lord."

"Please sit. Tea is here. Would you pour out, Lady Shelton?"

She agreed and soon they all had teacups and saucers in hand.

"You have not been Viscount Shelton long, I hear," he commented.

"No. Only a few months. Jessa's father passed away mid-February. Since he only had daughters, I inherited the title. I was his nephew though he and my father were estranged for many years." The new viscount paused. "I hope that you and I will have a cordial relationship, Lord Torrington. My uncle was a vindictive, spiteful man. I want to be a far different viscount than he was."

Already, Dez liked the new Shelton. "I am in a similar situation. I inherited from my brother, who was not well liked and didn't care much for the running of Torville Manor and our land. I am sorry not to have called upon you earlier but I have been trying to sort out the mess he left me."

Lord Browning held up a teacup. "To good neighbors—and hopefully, good friends."

"I will drink to that," Dez said, laughing.

They talked a little about the neighborhood and their estates and he believed being neighbors with Lord and Lady Shelton would prove most pleasant. Then he noticed Jessa had begun to grow anxious and wondered what troubled her. She caught her cousin's eyes and something passed between them with no words being spoken.

Immediately, the viscount said, "We have come to you on a curious matter, my lord. I need to speak to you about an invoice I received in yesterday's post."

"Why me?" Dez asked, puzzled. "What information might I have that could aid you regarding some bill for merchandise or a service?"

Looking uncomfortable now, Shelton said, "I have discovered through our servants that you loved my cousin, Anna. That the two of you ran away together to Gretna Green in order to wed."

Even all these years later, hearing the words aloud hurt him to no end. "Yes," he said brusquely, hoping to bury the flood of emotion that hearing Anna's name brought. "Our fathers were not in favor of the match and prevented us from reaching our destination. I was shipped off to the army immediately. Anna drowned." Frustrated, he added, "I don't understand what this has to do with some bill."

"That's the thing," Shelton said. "I don't think Anna drowned."

Dez grew still, afraid to move. Finally, he said, "What of her grave? Dalinda, my sister, wrote to me when Anna died. She said Lord Shelton didn't bury her in the village churchyard but rather chose to lay Anna to rest at Shelton Park."

"There is no grave," Jessa said firmly. "There never was."

"What?"

Tears welled in Jessa's eyes. "I was so young. It is hard for me to remember clearly but I do know that Anna was taken somewhere. She was locked in her room for a time, I suppose after Father brought her back from your elopement. Then the door was unlocked and I recall Mama being with her. And the servants taking her out. I hugged her and begged her not to go but they took her away."

"Took her away," he echoed, his throat tightening.

"Yes. She began struggling. Screaming. I ran and watched from a window." Tears began cascading down Jessa's cheeks. "They tied her wrists."

"What?" Dez roared.

"They shoved her into a carriage. Father watched them do it. He must have told them to. Then I remember being with Mama and her crying for a long time. A few days later, Father came to us. I was reading with Mama. He told us both that Anna had walked into the lake on purpose, her pockets full of stones. That she'd drowned. That we would never see her again."

Jessa stood and began pacing. "He said we were never to mention her name again. He had all traces of her removed. The servants were also warned never to bring up Anna's name or they would lose their positions. Father said she was dead and would stay dead."

She stopped in front of Dez. "Even as a small child, I found that turn of phrase odd. That she would *stay* dead." Jessa looked to her cousin. "Tell him, Tom."

The viscount removed a letter from his pocket. "I think this may be where Anna is."

Though stunned, hope filled Dez. For the first time in years, he felt a burden lifting from him. Lord Shelton handed the letter to Jessa and she passed it to Dez. With trepidation, he opened it.

It contained two pages. The first was a document that resembled any he had seen for the cost of goods sold or services performed. It referred to the yearly renewal of the set contract for *AB* and listed an amount. The second page was a brief, handwritten note signed by a Dr. Cheshire of Gollingham Asylum. A cold lump formed in Dez's belly.

In the note, the doctor said that no progress had been made and that he could offer Lord Shelton no encouragement. The situation regarding *AB* seemed hopeless and the best that could be done was to continue treatment as requested by the viscount.

Dez had heard vague rumors regarding what occurred in an asylum. One of his acquaintances at Eton had an aunt who had been carted off to one. It was said the aunt had become difficult and was judged by a physician to be mad. His friend had actually visited the aunt once and said he never would again, claiming the experience too horrific to recount.

Was Anna imprisoned in one of these madhouses?

"She is alive," Jessa said with determination. "I know she is. You must help her, Dez. You and Cousin Tom."

Dez stood. "We will do more than help Anna," he promised. "If she is truly alive, we will move heaven and earth to bring her home."

CHAPTER EIGHT

D EZ SAID, "THE first thing we need to do is find out where this Gollingham Asylum is." He looked to Shelton.

The viscount shook his head. "I haven't a clue, Torrington. The correspondence I received from Dr. Cheshire this morning is the first I had heard of the place. I tore apart my uncle's study, trying to find any kind of documents related to having Anna committed and found nothing."

"What of servants?" he asked Jessa. "Surely, one of them would know something."

She looked at him helplessly. "I don't know, Dez. It happened so long ago. A parlor maid or footman wouldn't necessarily know anything. I asked Beauchamp, our butler, about it years ago, when I was eleven or twelve. He was retiring, being pensioned off. Beauchamp warned me sternly never to mention my sister's name and that she was gone and dead."

"Do you know where he is, Jessa?"

"In Draymott last I heard. His brother runs the local inn and tavern."

Finally, a place to start.

"I will go into the village now and see if Beauchamp is still there and learn what he knows."

"I will go with you," Shelton said. "After all, Anna is my cousin."

Jessa huffed. "You aren't leaving me behind."

"We shall all go," proclaimed Lady Shelton, who had re-mained quiet throughout the discussion. "Two hotheaded men might not learn nearly as much as two ladies who practice politeness."

Dez had to agree with the viscountess. At this point, he want-ed to bash heads and murder someone if Anna had been taken to such a place.

"Very well. We will leave now."

"Our carriage is already ready," Shelton said. "We should take it."

The four quit the drawing room and went to the viscount's carriage for the short journey into Draymott. They seemed the longest three miles in Dez's life. He wanted to hope beyond hope that Anna was alive but knew to temper his emotions. Jessa had been very young and might have misconstrued the events she saw. Still, the butler's warning and the viscount himself announc-ing Anna's death—with no grave—gave Dez pause for concern.

They reached the inn and went inside. He skimmed the room. It was early evening and several tables were occupied with people eating or drinking.

"That's him. Beauchamp. In the corner."

He looked to where Jessa indicated and saw a man in his early to mid-seventies, his hair white as he hunched over a bowl, shoveling food into his mouth.

She started toward the former butler but he caught her arm.

"We don't wish to air anything in public. We must speak to him in private."

"There is a room in the back," she told him. "A private one for traveling parties coming through. We could use that."

Dez looked to the viscount. "Talk to the innkeeper and see if we can use it. Grease his palm if necessary. And bring back a tankard of ale."

Shelton nodded and moved to where the innkeeper stood behind the bar. He wiped his hands on a towel and, after a moment, nodded. Shelton handed over some coin and the owner poured a tankard and handed it to the nobleman.

Returning to them, he asked, "What is the tankard for?"

Dez took it. "Go to the back room. Beauchamp and I will join you shortly."

The trio crossed the taproom without questioning him. He watched Beauchamp and saw the man look up—and the moment he recognized Jessa. He ducked his head and grew still, trying not to draw attention to himself as they passed by.

Once they were out of sight, Dez moved toward his quarry, who now visibly relaxed.

"Good evening, Beauchamp." He placed the tankard on the table. "I have brought you some ale."

Wariness sprang into the old man's eyes. "Who are you?" he asked, his tone belligerent.

"Desmond Bretton. The Earl of Torrington."

Beauchamp's eyes widened. Whether in recognition of Dez himself or the title, he couldn't say.

"I would like to speak with you privately. Stand. Pick up your drink. Accompany me."

"Why should I?" the man asked defensively.

"Because if you don't, I will break your jaw—and force you to speak to me anyway."

Acceptance caused the former butler's shoulders to sag. He stood and gripped the tankard, walking slowly to the back room. Dez followed, closing the door behind them once they arrived. He saw a large table with ten seats around it. Lord and Lady Shelton and Jessa were already seated. Beauchamp went and stood at the head of the table, where he tipped the tankard and downed its entire contents before setting it down and taking a seat.

Dez sat on the man's right, across from the other three. Beauchamp's gaze rested on the table.

"Tell us everything you know about Anna Browning," he said, his tone brokering no nonsense. "What happened the day she was taken from Shelton Park. Where she is now."

Beauchamp sighed. "I knew it would somehow come to this." His eyes remained downcast as he continued. "His lordship returned with his daughter after she tried to elope. With you. She was locked in her room and Lord Shelton left for a day. When he returned, he had me summon two of our largest footmen to take Miss Browning to the carriage. I did as asked."

"Did you know where she was being taken?"

The old man cleared his voice. "I had an idea, my lord. It was confirmed after the carriage left. Lord Shelton told me that disobedient, rebellious daughters needed to learn their place and that his daughter would learn her lesson at Gollingham."

Dez gripped the table in order to keep from striking the man. "You knew she wasn't mad. And yet you did nothing to stop things?"

Beauchamp met his gaze and defiantly asked, "What was I to do, my lord? I was a mere servant and Lord Shelton a powerful viscount. He exercised the rights he held over his own child. If I would have protested, I would have been tossed from the house without a reference. As it was, both footmen and the coachman who accompanied Miss Browning that day were let go within a month. I knew which side my bread was buttered on." He shrugged. "Besides, she must have been mad to cross her father the way she did. Everyone knew what he was like. No one dared test Lord Shelton. If they did, they would suffer the consequences."

Frustration filled him, knowing the man spoke the truth. No servant would ever stand up to his master, especially one as vindictive as the dead Shelton.

"Do you know where Gollingham is located?" he asked, his jaw tightening.

"Somewhere in Hampshire. Near Alton." Beauchamp shook his head. "You know everything I do."

Dez rose. His companions followed suit. They left the inn and waited to speak after the carriage started up.

"We must go now," he declared. "I cannot let her stay another night in such a place."

"No," the viscount said. "We only have a vague idea at this point. It will be dark soon. Even if by some miracle we could find our way there, Torrington, they wouldn't receive us in the middle of the night. It would be better to wait until daylight and leave. We will ask to speak to the physician in charge of the facility. As head of the Browning family, I am legally responsible for Cousin Anna. I am the one who can free her. If she is there."

"She is," insisted Jessa. "I feel it in my bones."

"Very well," Dez agreed. "We leave at first light. I will ride to Shelton Park and we can take your carriage."

"I am going with you," Jessa said stubbornly.

"No. You aren't," Lady Shelton said. She took Jessa's hand. "It will be difficult enough for the two men to see Anna in these circumstances. You will wait with me. We will be strong for Anna once she returns."

Tears welled in Jessa's eyes. "I want to go—but I know you are right."

"I am," the viscountess assured. She looked to her husband. "Even if they claim Anna is not there, you must find her. Tear down the place if necessary, Tom."

"They won't want her once they learn I am no longer willing to pay for her to be there," her husband said. "I will take Cheshire's letter and invoice. That is proof enough she is there."

"Is it?" Dez asked, despair filling him. "Anna could be dead and this doctor might have continued sending his bills. I doubt Shelton went even once to visit his daughter."

"We won't know until we arrive," the viscount said. "If she is there, we will bring her home."

"Agreed," he said, a silent prayer echoing in his mind that they would find Anna alive.

DEZ SAT ACROSS from Shelton, both their expressions grim. They had left Shelton Park as the sun broke the horizon, traveling west to Hampshire. In Alton, they stopped and discovered that Gollingham Asylum was a few miles southwest of their current location, just outside a small town called Grantham.

The carriage now slowed and he glanced out the window. They had reached Grantham. The driver knew to stop in the village so they could ascertain the asylum's exact location and brought the carriage to the door of the local tavern. Dez sprang from the vehicle, Lord Shelton right behind him.

"We are close," the viscount said. "We will find it. I am certain."

They entered the tavern. It was deserted at this hour of the morning. A large man with a bald pate and dark eyes greeted them.

"My lords, what can I do for you? Have you worked up a bit of thirst on the road this morning? Perhaps I can bring you some ale and a bite to eat. Perhaps some bread and cheese?"

"No," Dez said succinctly. "We seek information."

He removed a guinea from his pocket and tossed it to the man, who caught it and stared at it in surprise.

"Yes, my lord?" he asked anxiously.

"We are looking for Gollingham Asylum and know it lies nearby."

The man nodded sagely. "Have a lady need putting away, I assume."

"Why would you say that?" he demanded.

The man shrugged. "That's them who goes there. Ever since the Madhouses Act."

"The what?"

"Parliament passed it. Must be a good thirty years or so now. They began regulating madhouses in London. It kept new ones from being established. That's why the trade in lunacy sprang up. Private madhouses dot all of England now, my lord. Gollingham Asylum is but one of those which came into existence. Being outside of London, it can get around the law—if you know what I mean."

Dez was afraid he did know. How that might affect Anna.

"Can you give us directions to it?"

"Of course." The man grinned. "Anything for a guinea."

The innkeeper told them and they had him repeat it once to make sure they wouldn't get lost. Shelton passed along the instructions to his driver and they started up again. Nervous energy rippled through Dez.

He worried what they would find when they arrived at the asylum. That Anna had been there and was gone. Or worse—dead. If she were truly alive, he had to prepare himself. She would not be the Anna he knew. The girl he had known and loved years ago would have changed after being locked away from the world for a good dozen years. She would be angry at having been abandoned. Most likely hurt and withdrawn. He would need to go slowly.

Because if he did find her, he planned never to leave her again. She would become his countess. They would have the marriage they had sought so many years ago. They would raise the family they had talked about.

And they would find her father's grave and spit on it.

"I think we're close. Look." Shelton pointed out the window.

Dez saw a large house. He swallowed, his mouth dry as if it had been stuffed with cotton. His heart began pounding. He urged himself to remain calm. Not to knock out the teeth of this Dr. Cheshire who had written, asking for his yearly sum to keep treating Anna.

His gaze met Shelton's and both men nodded at one another, an unspoken agreement between them to save the woman they hoped would be found inside.

The carriage slowed and then stopped. He threw open the door and hurried toward the house, Shelton on his heels. Knocking on the door, Dez took a calming breath.

He was about to knock again when the door swung open. A

servant wearing a surly expression glanced at them.

"No one's expected."

"We are here to see Dr. Cheshire," Shelton said.

The man screwed up his face. "He might be in. I'll see."

Before he could close the door, Dez placed his foot over the threshold and said, "We will wait inside."

The servant shrugged. "Suit yourself."

He turned and walked away. Dez and Shelton stepped into a small foyer. The man disappeared and they stood there, an eerie silence blanketing them. His gut told him there was something very wrong with this place.

Then from a distance, a piercing scream erupted, sounding like a wounded animal whose leg had been caught within a trap in the forest. It chilled Dez to his soul. Abruptly, it ended and the silence grew.

Finally, the servant reappeared. "The doctor can see you now before he goes on his rounds. You got somebody you need put away?" he asked, sounding cheery.

"No," Dez said flatly, tamping down his anger.

The servant walked away again and they followed him. He indicated a door and they entered without knocking.

The man he assumed to be Dr. Cheshire sat behind the desk. He was thin. Brown hair and brown eyes. Nondescript in every way. His lips twitched as they came to stand before him.

"Their names?" he asked in a tired tone, glancing at the servant.

"Uh, I forgot that part, Doctor."

"Very well. You are dismissed. Go see if you can help upstairs."

"Yes, Doctor."

Dez waited for the servant to leave and then said, "I am the Earl of Torrington. My companion is the Viscount of Shelton."

That got the little man's attention. He sprang to his feet. "Shelton. I see. I suppose the viscount recently passed?"

"In February," the new viscount said. "I received your statement regarding payment for my cousin. We are here to collect her."

The physician began shaking his head furiously. "No, no, no, that wouldn't be a good idea at all, my lord. Not at all."

"Why not?" Dez challenged.

Cheshire glanced from him and back to Shelton. "The patient is very ill. You would not be able to control her in a home environment."

"*Control* her?" he spat out, drawing the doctor's attention again.

"Yes, my lord. Control in a precise word. The patient—"

"She has a name," he said. "Miss Browning. Use it. I insist."

"Oh, dear," the doctor said and sighed. "This is very unorthodox. Patients just don't . . . leave Gollingham. They are mad, you see. They may seem to have moments of lucidity but they are quite insane. Their behavior can deceive you. One minute they are completely mild-mannered. The next they are wild. You cannot let them fool you."

"We aren't talking about all of your patients. Just Miss Browning," he emphasized. "I know for a fact she is not mad and has never been. Her father placed her here because she defied him."

"Yes, yes, yes. I understand. Defiance is definitely a part of madness, especially in women. We see it frequently here."

"I don't care what you think you see. We are here to claim Miss Browning and take her to her home."

The doctor crossed his arms. "I am afraid that is impossible. She is feral. Savage in her behavior. She goes for long spells where she is docile and then she erupts in violence. She cannot be controlled, certainly not by those who are not professionals."

"You are telling me that man who just left us is a professional?" Shelton asked. "*He* looks after patients?"

Cheshire shifted nervously from foot to foot. "He doesn't have to know the purpose behind the treatments of my patients. Only that he follows my orders. Quite frankly, most of the attendants are a bit dull and slow. Otherwise, I am sure they would be negatively affected by being around the mad all day."

"Enough talk," Dez said. "Whether your agree or not—whether your professional opinion sways you one way or another—we are here for Miss Browning and won't leave without her. I demand you take us to her now."

"Very well. But I highly recommend that you hire professional help to watch over her. Frankly, I don't know if you will make it half a league before she jumps from the carriage and dashes into the nearby forest. She is highly volatile. Full of rage."

"There are two of us," Shelton said. "And we both care for Miss Browning a great deal. We will be able to handle things."

A knowing look came into the physician's eyes as he looked upon Dez. "Ah. You are the man she tried to elope with."

"You know of that?"

"Of course," the doctor said. "It was the chief reason she was brought here. Defiance and rebelliousness are the main signs of insanity in females. A sane woman knows her place—and knows the men in her life know what is best for her. The very act of elopement goes against the obedience owed by a daughter to her father. Lord Shelton had every right to place his daughter under my care."

"For over a decade?" he asked, his tone anguished. "What have you done in all of the years to cure her madness, Doctor? Her supposed madness. What?"

"We have our methods," the man said. "The public wouldn't begin to understand them."

"Anna was a sweet, loving young woman. You tell me she is now violent and abusive. What have you done to her to turn her into someone such as that?"

"It was in her nature all along, Lord Torrington," Cheshire insisted. "She is only showing her true nature."

"I want her released. Now!"

"I second that," the viscount said. "As the head of my family, Anna is my responsibility. I will not put another farthing in your pockets, Doctor. Take us to my cousin."

"Very well," Cheshire said. "But you won't like what she's become," he said ominously. "My guess is you will leave her care to us once you see her."

CHAPTER NINE

WITH TREPIDATION, DEZ followed Dr. Cheshire from the room. He glanced to Lord Shelton, who didn't bother to hide his worry. They moved along a corridor and up a flight of stairs, the sounds of silence heavy.

They reached the first landing and he heard a keening, once again in the distance, and wondered if the noise was made by Anna. At least they knew she was alive. He doubted the picture Dr. Cheshire painted of her being some wild, uncontrollable woman. Dez thought the man did so merely to keep Anna as his patient and keep the money flowing into his coffers.

The stench hit him as they moved higher. He saw rats scurrying about brazenly. The doctor ignored them.

When they made it to the first floor, he gazed down the long hallway, startled to see long benches on both sides. Various women sat upon these benches, wearing drab garments that resembled gunny sacks. No one spoke. No one looked at them as they passed. Dez found his feet faltering as he longed for just one woman to meet his eyes.

Then one did.

He halted and stared at her. Dirt smudged her face. She wore the same thing all the others did and, up close, he could see the coarse, rough fabric. The shapeless garment struck her mid-calf. Her feet were bare and filthy, probably because of the waste covering the floors.

"Please," she whispered. "Help me."

He stood before her, speechless, seeing the agony in her eyes. She couldn't have been more than twenty years of age.

"Who is this woman?" he demanded.

Dr. Cheshire stopped and retraced his steps. He glared at the woman. "You know you are not to speak," he chided.

Fear flashed in the woman's eyes. Quickly, she bowed her head, remaining perfectly still.

"Who is she?" Dez asked again. "Why is she here?"

"She has been diagnosed as mad," the physician said smugly.

Dez knelt and placed a hand over the woman's. Her nails were jagged and broken, dirt ground deeply into her skin, as if she were some laborer.

"Who are you? Who placed you here?" he asked softly.

"Jergens," she said, so softly that he barely heard the word.

"You are Lady Jergens?"

She nodded.

"Come along," Cheshire urged. "The patient is already breaking rules left and right."

"What rules?" he asked. "They are not allowed to speak?"

"No. They aren't," Cheshire informed him. "It is part of disciplining them. Sitting on these benches is also part of their program."

Dez recalled the lilt of Anna's voice. How he enjoyed hearing her sing. To think she had been silenced for years was criminal.

Gazing back at the woman before him, he said, "Did your husband send you here?"

She nodded again, her mouth trembling. "He only wanted my dowry. Once he got it, I was brought here. We never even consummated our marriage." A single tear cascaded down her cheek. "I want my papa."

"You are to cease this at once," Cheshire proclaimed. He motioned to an attendant. "Take her."

The man roughly grabbed Lady Jergens and hauled her from the bench. He struck her face with his fist. Blood spurted from her nose. He struck her again and she fell to the ground. Dez stood there in shock, not believing what was unfolding in front of him. The attendant then kicked the downed woman viciously in the belly, glee on his face, before hauling Lady Jergens to her feet. She began wheezing and sobbing as he led her down the hallway and then began to struggle. Another attendant latched on to her and they dragged her away.

"Where are you taking her?" Dez shouted, the shock wearing off as he glared at the man in charge of the asylum.

"It is none of your concern, my lord," Cheshire said coolly. "The baths will calm her."

"Your people struck a *lady!*" he exclaimed. "They beat her. I have never seen such brutal, savage behavior."

"There are no ladies present at a madhouse," the doctor said blandly. "Only patients who need to be kept in line. Discipline is important to maintain."

Dez glared at the physician. "You are as malicious as your attendants," he spat out. "Evil and cruel. You aren't trying to help these women. You are torturing them. This place is vile and inhumane."

He quickly hurried down the corridor. The men had turned and he tried to guess which room they had entered, trying the knobs on several doors.

Then he came to an open room and saw Lady Jergens had already been restrained, her wrists and ankles tied to a chair. Both attendants retrieved a bucket of water and as they tossed it at her, he raced to block them. He was too late and the woman took the brunt of the water. What spilled from her onto him was frigid.

"This is freezing. Why are you doing this?" he asked as Lady Jergens' teeth began chattering.

"It's the treatment," one man said. "They disobey and they get the water."

The other picked up a full bucket and dashed it against Lady Jergens again.

"Stop!" Dez demanded.

"Come here at once, Lord Torrington."

He turned and saw Cheshire standing in the doorway, a shocked Lord Shelton beside him.

He rushed toward the man. "This is inhumane. Why do you do this?"

"The water actually soothes them," the physician said, arrogance pouring from him. "You know nothing about medicine."

"Neither do you if you subject innocent women to this barbaric—"

"You may think the method is barbaric but it has proven most effective."

"Have you done this to Anna?" he demanded.

Cheshire remained silent. "Come along."

Dez raced back to Lady Jergens. "I will get you out of her, my lady. I promise." Then he rejoined the other men and they left the room.

"You shouldn't have told her that," Cheshire admonished. "It will give her false hope. Her husband is the only one who can legally remove her from Gollingham."

"Then I will find him and convince him to do so."

The doctor smirked. "Be my guest."

"Take us to my cousin," Lord Shelton said, his voice quivering. "And if you think I would leave her in this place after what we just witnessed, you are sadly mistaken."

Cheshire shrugged and continued down the hall. They passed another dozen women, sitting mute, and Dez tried to put them from his mind. He needed to focus on Anna's welfare now.

They stopped before a door and an attendant rushed up, key in hand.

"It's been a bad day, Doctor."

Cheshire turned and gave them a knowing smile. "You will see that she is demented. That her case is hopeless. Open it," he said to the attendant.

The key went into the lock and Dez tried to brace himself for what he would see as the door swung open.

The first thing to hit him was the horrendous smell, much worse in here than in the hallway, which had been awful enough. Bars covered the lone window, which was closed. The air felt heavy. His eyes swept across the room and found the single bed near the corner. A shape lay on it. He rushed toward it and faltered, gasping.

He could barely tell it was a woman, much less Anna. Her beautiful, strawberry blond hair had been shorn short and was so filthy he couldn't tell what color it should be. She lay motionless on the bed, her eyes closed, a rope wrapped around her several times and underneath what was a cot, effectively tying her to it. What puzzled him was something that bound her, her arms crossed in front of her.

"What is this contraption?"

"It is called a straitjacket," Cheshire replied. "Quite effective, I must say. Restraints are often needed to control behaviors such as tearing clothes and demonstrating lewd behavior."

Dez shuddered.

The doctor continued. "We find restraints helpful in stopping patients from harming themselves or others. It also keeps them from attempting suicide at night when no one is watching them."

He couldn't believe what he was hearing and looked at Lord Shelton in disbelief.

"*You* are insane, Cheshire, if you believe this helps individuals committed here, the vast majority which I assume are not mad. You are shutting innocent women away from the world."

The physician shrugged. "They are deemed mad by their families, my lord. I am merely providing a service. We don't promise a cure. We do confine them so they and their loved ones are safe."

"Get this . . . thing off her at once," he barked at the attendant.

The man looked to Cheshire, who nodded grimly.

The attendant first loosened the ropes that bound her to the cot. When he flipped Anna over, Dez could see all the many ties up the back.

Then Anna began jerking and making wheezing, guttural noises.

⸨

ANNA HAD GONE to her special place. She only went there when she was placed in her room. Not when she sat on the hard wooden benches for twelve hours a day. Others were around her and even though they never spoke, she liked to keep her world private.

She imagined being at the lake again, the one that sat in the middle where Shelton Park ended and Torrington lands began. So many happy days had been spent at this lake. Skimming stones. Swimming. Picnicking. Walking along the shore. She pictured the blue of the water sparkling in the sun. A clear sky. Birds chirping in the trees behind her as the woods started.

Her legs were straight out in front of her as she sat on a blanket. Her hands were propped behind her, her arms straight, as she lifted her face to the sun and tried to feel its warmth penetrating her. She sensed Dez sitting beside her and imagined the smell of his favored sandalwood soap wafting toward her.

Near the water, Jessa was hopping on one foot. Then a butterfly caught her eyes and she began chasing after it. Dalinda followed Jessa as she scampered away and they moved into the trees. She sighed. Now came the best part.

One which she had relived a thousand times. No, a thousand times a thousand. Maybe more.

Slowly, she turned her head toward Dez. His handsome face smiled down upon her, his brown eyes rimmed with amber. A breeze caught a lock of his dark, wavy hair and he pushed it from his brow. Then he leaned toward her. Every time she knew it was coming and yet she cherished it as if it were the first time. His hand cupped her cheek. His lips met hers.

And she relived her first kiss.

The kiss was sweet. Lingering. It told of his love for her and promised good things to come. Anna reveled in it, enjoying it anew, yearning for the time when a simple kiss had been her whole world.

Dez broke the kiss and gazed upon her. She froze that image in her mind and let it stay. This was her favorite moment of her life. When she had been young. Pretty. Carefree. Her whole future ahead of her. She would take out this memory and examine it. Replay it. Relish it.

It was unlike the white times. Those were for when Fiend punished her with the abominable treatments. Anna had learned during one of those to go to her quiet place. It was all white. Pure. No color. No sound. No motion. A vast expanse of nothingness where she could hide from the mean people who did bad things to her.

She went back to Dez. Thoughts of him calmed her. She hadn't been calm earlier. It had been one of her rebellious days, one where she couldn't sit for twelve hours without moving or talking. She had screamed and shouted until her throat ached and she grew hoarse. Even the ice-water treatment hadn't made her cease. Eventually, her throat became scratchy. Her pitch fell. Then she lost all ability to speak and retreated to the white place. She didn't remember anything done to her after that, only that she was now here, in her room, the awful straitjacket pinning her arms across the front of her body, tied so tightly that it was worse than a corset.

But it was still blissful because she was alone. Left with her cherished memories.

From afar, she heard voices. Men's voices. They frightened her. Perhaps the attendants had told Fiend of her abominable behavior and he had sent them to beat her again. The beatings left her battered and bruised. They crushed her spirits. It took her a long time to heal from them.

She wouldn't think about it. She would go to the white place.

Where it was serene. Where nothing invaded. Devoid of anything or anyone.

Then she was roughly turned and she knew an attendant was untying the restraints. She couldn't help it. She began thrashing about, trying to scream, wheezing grunts coming from her. She had endured too much today. She couldn't take anymore. Tears streamed down her face as she wished everyone would go away. Leave her. Let her finally die.

Suddenly, the straitjacket was ripped away from her. Her arms ached as the blood began rushing back. What was amazing, though, was she felt an embrace. Someone stroked her hair and murmured to her. Anna caught a whiff of sandalwood and relaxed. Warmth enveloped her.

What was happening?

She had never been able to conjure anything so complex. Yes, she could imagine things in clarity with brilliant, bold colors. Yet she had never been able to create smells. Sounds. Touch. Keeping her eyes closed, she smiled. The heavenly warmth continued. The sandalwood scent became stronger. Anna inhaled deeply, drawing it into her lungs. My God, she had imagined Dez here. With her. This was an entirely new level she soared to. Anna had no idea how she had done it, only that it was the most wonderful thing that had happened to her since she had come to Gollingham.

Then she was being lifted. Carried somewhere. Oh, how marvelous. Her cheek rested against a beating heart in a hard, muscled chest. Dez moved so fast that she felt as if a breeze gently touched her. Then she bounced a bit, moving down stairs.

Fear struck her.

No. She couldn't do this. She couldn't carry her fantasies so far. She had never imagined trying to leave the asylum, at least not after those first few gut-wrenching weeks. She'd thought of nothing but escape then. Ways to flee. And had been shown just how foolish those notions were. She had been hurt so badly as to never wish to think about leaving on her own again. Even her fantasies of Dez coming to rescue her had been shoved away, placed so deeply within her that she dare not let them out.

Suddenly, bright light slammed against her, as if she had been taken outside in the blinding sunshine after the darkness of the asylum. She squeezed her eyes tightly shut and whimpered. This was going too far. She heard the sweet song of a bird. Felt the breeze. Smelled the fresh air of a spring day. She began weeping copiously because she knew her greatest fear had final come and swallowed her whole.

After all this time, Anna finally had gone mad.

CHAPTER TEN

D EZ'S HEART ACHED with each step he carried Anna. They exited the darkness of Gollingham Asylum and he headed toward their waiting carriage. The wide-eyed footman placed the stairs down and opened the door and Dez entered the carriage, a sobbing Anna held close. He took a seat on the bench and kept her in his lap, reluctant to release her. She had yet to open her eyes. He didn't know if she spent so much of her life terrified that she kept them closed to keep out the world or if the bright light hurt them. To think a creature of light such as Anna had been locked away for a dozen years in filth and darkness caused his heart to ache.

Shelton climbed in and took the opposite seat, his emotions worn on his sleeve.

"The poor girl," he said as the carriage started up. "Do you think she knows what is happening?"

"I doubt it. She hasn't looked around. It's as if she's deliberately gone deep inside herself."

The viscount shook his head. "Can you blame her? She's been in that hellhole for well over a decade." He paused. "Do you think . . . that she truly has gone mad after so long a time away from society?"

He shrugged. "I cannot say. All I know is she has been liberated and I will do everything in my power to see her restored to good health, both physically and mentally."

Dez had seen her limbs covered in old bruises, faded to the ugly shades of yellow and green. He wondered how often Anna had been beaten. If any bones had ever been broken. If her spirit had been broken.

He understood why she couldn't speak. She had ruptured her vocal cords from screaming or shouting too long. It had happened more often than not on the battlefield. He himself had even experienced it. Officers, in particular, were prone to the ruptures as they shouted orders, trying to be heard over the sound of cannon fire exploding and the many guns discharging. The strain created the rupture. The first time he had witnessed it, an army doctor explained to him that, within the throat, the vocal cords were layers of mucus membranes. These membranes vibrate, which allows speech. If the layers are ruptured, vibrations cease, causing the loss of a person's voice. It hadn't been painful. He'd had no difficulties breathing. He'd merely been hoarse and his throat scratchy. After two days, he'd regained his voice.

This must have happened to Anna over and over again through the years. Who knew what damage had truly occurred? At least Dez had an idea how to help her. The doctors had had him keep his throat moist, which relaxed the vocal cords and hastened the healing process. He also was told to avoid extremes of hot and cold food or beverages. He had gargled with warm water dosed with salt and drank honey mixed in warm water.

The most important thing had been resting his voice. The same would be true for Anna. She would need to keep silent for as long as possible before starting to try to produce a stray word or two. Eventually, she could build up to phrases and then, finally, full sentences. From what he had seen during his short time at Gollingham Asylum, she had been trained to be silent for long periods of time. Dez shuddered, still not comprehending the number of women present at the place. And only women.

How many were there because they truly were insane versus how many had been put away by the men in their families, as had been done to Anna and Lady Jergens? He ached hearing the brief story Lady Jergens had shared. It struck him that she had said her marriage had not been consummated. If that was the case, he wondered if she were legally wed. It would be worth pursuing. Contacting her father, whom she had wanted so desperately, and seeing if he could claim legal rights over his daughter and annul her marriage to Lord Jergens.

"Do you know Lord Jergens?" Dez asked Shelton.

Distaste crossed his neighbor's face. "I know of him. I have never spoken to him. His gaming debts are enormous. I had heard he wed Lady Alice." He shuddered. "To think that was her . . ."

"I know. We must contact her father and see if he can help."

"I agree," Shelton said. He looked at Anna. "How are we to help her?" he asked.

An idea had been taking shape and Dez decided to share it.

"I think Anna will have a great fear of people after her experience. I am afraid to say this—but you and Lady Shelton are strangers to her."

"I thought the same thing," the viscount admitted. "I have not seen Anna since we were children. And even Jessa will be a stranger to her because she was so young when Anna was spirited away. She wouldn't recognize the grown woman Jessa has become."

"Because of that, I feel that I am the only one she will know. I want to help her, Shelton. Bring her back as far as I can to the girl she once was."

Doubt flickered in Shelton's eyes. "Is that even possible, Torrington? I am afraid with Anna having been at that madhouse for so long, she may never be normal again." He paused. "Do you still love her?"

"I always have. I always will. No matter what she is like. Would I wish for her to be whole again and make her my countess? Of course. Is that even a possibility?" Dez glanced down at Anna, who still wept softly. "I have no idea. But I want to do whatever I can to bring her back."

He took a deep breath. "I want to be in sole charge of her."

Shelton's brow creased. "What do you mean?"

"There is a small cottage where the three of us—Anna, Dalinda, and I—would play as children. It had been abandoned and never had a tenant move in. Over time, we brought odd bits of furniture to it. Toys. Books. Games. Since my return, I found it still unoccupied and have had it filled as though occupied. I even placed a desk in it so that I might work from there at times. I thought I might find great comfort in doing so, recalling the good times the three of us had spent there.

"It would be perfect for Anna."

The viscount shook his head. "I am not sure I understand. Do you mean for Anna to live there?"

"Yes. For a time."

"No, Torrington. She cannot look after herself."

"I will stay there with her."

"What? That's impossible. She is unwed."

Dez's gaze bore into the other man. "Are you telling me you would pander to the strict rules of the *ton* when Anna's very life and sanity are at stake?" He shook his head. "I will care for her. I will talk to her. I am the one, familiar face she will know. If anyone can bring Anna back to reality, it will be me."

"It sounds preposterous."

"Do you have a better idea? You cannot keep her as a caged animal at Shelton Park. What if she does grow violent and neither you nor your servants can contain her? Please, Shelton. Let me try. I won't frighten her. She knows me. She loved me once. I can help her, I know I can. Just give me the chance."

"For how long?"

Dez looked at the man helplessly. "I haven't a clue. For as long as it takes, I suppose."

"Jessa won't like it. She'll want her sister at Shelton Park."

"Tell Jessa what you saw at Gollingham," he urged. "Tell her of the deplorable conditions. How Anna needs the quiet and solitude. Give me at least a week. No, better two. Then you and

Jessa may come visit," he added, hoping that would be enough time for visible improvement to occur.

"I will want daily reports," demanded Shelton.

He thought a moment. "Coral, my valet, will be our go-between. In fact, when you take Anna and me to the cottage, call at Torville Manor and ask for him. Tell him to bring a basket of food and ink and parchment to the cottage. I will have him look in on us daily and he can ride and speak to you in person regarding Anna's behavior and progress."

Dez smoothed her hair. She had quietened and he thought her now asleep.

"A doctor should see her."

"I agree but I pray that we wait on that. I don't want any strangers approaching her. She already cannot speak."

He explained about her damaged vocal cords and how he knew what to do since he had suffered from a similar affliction during his military service.

"We have both been to war, Shelton. To Hell and back. If anyone understands Anna's suffering, it is I."

The viscount was silent for some minutes and finally he said, "I agree. I know how much you care for her and would never abuse her. I will ask for my footman and driver not to reveal what they have witnessed. No one at Shelton Park will know of Anna's return. The same should be true beyond your valet. If Anna can be restored to anything close to what she was before, I would not see her reputation ruined by her having been alone with you."

"I do love her," Dez said. "I would die for her. My fondest wish would be for us to see our dream of marriage come true. If it can't, I will remain devoted to her the rest of my life."

"You would choose not to marry?" Shelton asked.

"There is no one for me but Anna," he said softly. "I have two nephews. The elder will be my heir."

"Very well."

Shelton rapped on the roof and the carriage began to slow. When it stopped, he exited the vehicle and spoke to the driver and then returned.

"My coachman knows where to take you. How far is it to this cottage?"

"Probably a quarter-mile."

"You will carry her all that way?"

Dez glanced down, love for Anna overwhelming him. "I would carry her to the ends of the earth if needed. Besides, look how thin she is. She will be no burden, I assure you."

He stroked her hair again, hating once more how it had been chopped off. It fell a couple of inches below her ears and was matted and dirty. From the conditions he removed her from, he assumed she had head lice. He had seen both in the army and knew of ways to rid her of it. Dez began composing a list in his head for all he would need Coral to bring to the cottage.

The men fell silent after that. It surprised him that Shelton had relented so easily to such an outrageous plan. A bachelor harboring an innocent, unmarried woman. Living together for God only knew how long. There were things Dez would have to do—intimate things—that Shelton probably had not thought of or was reluctant to bring up. It didn't matter. What was important was healing Anna's mind, body, and spirit. Frankly, he didn't know if it were even possible. He would remain optimistic but prepare himself for the worst.

His gaze fell to the sleeping woman in his arms. How many times had he longed to do this very thing? Hold Anna in his arms as she slept. He vowed he would move heaven and earth to help her grow into the independent, spirited girl he had known.

They reached their destination and Shelton promised he would see that Coral came to the cottage as quickly as possible. The viscount descended the stairs the footman had placed beside the carriage's door and he helped guide Dez down them.

He turned and said, "I would offer my hand to you, Shelton, but I am rather tied up."

The viscount grinned. "After all of this, I feel we are meant to be good friends. Call me Tom." He placed his hand on Dez's shoulder and squeezed it then cupped Anna's cheek and said, "Get well, Cousin."

"I am Dez," he told the viscount. "Short for Desmond—but no one I like ever calls me that."

Tom smiled. "Then Dez it is. Take care, my friend."

He nodded, his throat tight with emotion. Tom reentered the carriage and gave a wave. Dez began walking and, in a few minutes, caught sight of the blue waters of the lake. He went to the cottage and opened the door.

"We are here, Anna," he told the sleeping woman. "I pray I can help you find yourself again."

Going inside, he went to the settee and sat. Anna continued sleeping. It made him feel good that she had enough trust in him—whether she knew it was him or not—to fall asleep and stay that way.

Sometime later, Coral arrived. Dez saw the valet standing in the open doorway, a wicker basket in his hand.

"Come here, Coral," he said. "Take a seat."

Over the next half-hour, he told his servant the entire story, holding nothing back. How he and Anna had grown up and tried to elope. How they both had been sent away. And how he and Lord Shelton had discovered Anna was alive and retrieved her from the inhumane conditions they found at Gollingham Asylum.

"Thank you for your trust in me, Lord Torrington," the valet said solemnly, his gaze on Anna. "I hope Miss Browning will be restored to full health."

"I am counting on your discretion, Coral. There's to be no gossip about this unusual situation. In fact, I don't even want anyone to know she is here. I will depend upon you daily for many things."

Dez explained the kind of supplies he would need. The daily trek to Shelton Park. How Coral was to tell everyone from Meadows to Mrs. Abbott to Paul Lexington that Lord Torrington was working on a very important project and had retreated to a private space. He was to be left alone until he returned to Torville

Manor proper.

"You can count on me, my lord," the valet promised.

He had Coral build a fire and put water on to heat. Coral removed some of the food from the basket and placed it on the small table in front of the settee.

"Go and get the things I need most now. The soap and towels. The vinegar and cheese whey. The kerosene and comb."

"What of clothes for you and Miss Browning, my lord?"

"I can wait for those until tomorrow's trip. Check in my sister's former bedchamber and see if any gowns were left behind."

He knew Dalinda had wed Gilford in London during the Season and she had never once returned to Torville Manor. His hope was that his twin had left some gowns more suited to the country in her wardrobe and that his father and Ham had been too self-centered to even think of them being there, much less removing them.

"Yes, my lord. I will return within an hour." The valet hesitated. "Might I say something, my lord?"

"Speak freely, Coral."

"It is a shame what happened to Miss Browning. I admire you for trying to help her. Not many men would."

Tears stung his eyes. "Thank you, Coral. I only hope I *can* help her."

Coral's head bobbed up and down several times and he took his leave. Dez sat holding Anna, not fighting the tears that began to stream down his face.

And then she opened her eyes.

CHAPTER ELEVEN

ANNA HAD HEARD talking again, like bees buzzing in the background. She had stopped listening to others a long time ago. When she'd first gone to Gollingham, she had strained to hear every word spoken. In the end, she had learned it led to nothing and only gave her false hope. So she had not bothered to listen. To the attendants, who had gossiped like magpies and played cruel jokes on the patients in their care. To Fiend, who pestered her with questions and no matter how she answered, told her she was wrong and stupid and mad. To Matron, who was cruel and abusive and taunted Anna.

Not hearing what went on around her allowed her to be in her own world. The one of her own making. It was a far more pleasant place to spend her time, especially during the long hours of sitting on the benches that lined the hallway. During those hours, she tuned out anything that occurred around her. If someone spoke to her, she never answered because she never heard their voice. If a patient was carted off for treatment, she never realized it occurred.

In her world, Anna created beautiful things. She lived in a wonderful house. Not as large as Shelton Park but still roomy and airy. Only she and Jessa lived there. No adults were allowed. Thoughts of Mama hurt too much for her to dwell upon. Mama had been in ill health and something told Anna that Mama was dead. As far as Papa went, she refused to think of him at all. He was the one who had put her in the bad place with Fiend. She had spent hours when she first arrived at Gollingham thinking of ways to kill him. Stab him. Shoot him. Push him off a cliff or the roof of their London townhouse. Cut him with a thousand slices until his blood flowed freely and the life drained from his eyes.

She had pushed those kind of thoughts aside. In her world, everything was perfect and so she had stopped thinking of Papa at all. Her world had beautiful colors. The house had furniture that she designed in her mind and she often moved it around, finding new ways to please her. Every room had freshly-cut flowers in crystal vases, flowers of every color of the rainbow and beyond. She and Jessa took their tea on beautiful china plates, where each time they sat, Anna varied the pattern and colors.

Her bedchamber received the most light and had the largest bed she had ever seen. The adjoining room was filled with nothing but exquisite gowns. She spent hours trying them on, sometimes with Jessa watching her, nodding her approval and clapping her hands when one especially delighted her. Anna had worn every type of fashion under the sun. She had even imagined times when she donned the clothes of a man. She had done so once when she was about twelve, taking a pair of trousers that Dez had brought her, and slipping out of the house to ride in them. It was ever so nice to be able to move and walk and ride in something so comfortable.

The stables were perhaps her favorite part of the world she created. More than anything, she had loved to ride and felt more comfortable in the saddle than anywhere else. Her stables had horses of every color and size. Her favorites were a tall black of seventeen hands who was a handful, spirited and energetic, and a chestnut mare with white socks who had the gentlest nature and enjoyed the apples Anna brought to her.

A good portion of her time was spent riding. She rode the perimeter of Shelton Park and cut through the woods in order to take the shortcut to Torville Manor. When she went there, Dez and Dalinda were always waiting for her. They would mount their horses and the three of them would ride out. They explored places she remembered and new ones she invented on the spot. They rode into the small village and would stop at the baker's for a treat. Sometimes a cinnamon bun. Sometimes fresh scones.

She rode back now, the sun shining because it was always a sunny, rain-free day in her world. She led her horse into the stables and returned to the house. Magically, she stepped inside wearing a sapphire blue gown and went to the drawing room, where Jessa should be waiting for her and they would have tea.

Her sister wasn't there, though. Dez waited for her instead. And she kept hearing the buzzing. Then it stopped and she relaxed, content to pour out the tea and tell Dez about the carrot cake she had made that he was about to eat.

Then she heard crying. No, she didn't hear it. She sensed it. The tears flowed. She instinctively knew this—but no sobs came.

Who might be crying?

No one cried in her world. No one was ever sad or unhappy or jealous or angry. Everyone was happy and satisfied and enjoyed every minute.

Slowly, she opened her eyes.

Glancing around, she didn't know where she was though it seemed incredibly familiar. She felt warm and smelled sandalwood again.

Dez...

Anna decided she had taken her world to a new level but realized she no longer had control of the creation of it. She was somewhere she didn't know. She smelled someone she would never see again.

For some reason, she had avoided looking at the person who held her but she couldn't avoid doing so any longer. Her gaze turned to whoever held her. Her breath caught.

It was Dez. A much older Dez than the boy or young man she remembered. This Dez was very much a man. His face was tanned as if he spent a good portion of his day outside in the elements. His thick hair, always with that slight wave, was a rich brown. She steeled herself and looked into his eyes. Oh, they were exactly the same, a deep brown with amber circling them.

And Dez was the one crying.

His eyes glittered bright with unshed tears, while others ran along his cheeks. Without thinking, Anna reached out and cupped his face. His eyes grew wide but he didn't speak.

How had she done this? Made Dez into a man? He looked older. Harder. Full of anguish. She had to do better. She had to make him happy. Her fingers grazed his cheek and touched the corner of his mouth. She tugged on it, trying to make it move up. When it didn't, she took her other hand and brought it to the other side. Using her thumbs, she pulled the corners of his mouth up into a smile and let go.

Her Dez now smiled on his own. His tears flowed freely, which she didn't like, but she supposed they might be tears associated with happiness. She had once cried those, just as she had cried tears of misery. She had learned that tears did nothing. They only made a person appear weak and then someone might take advantage of you. She still cried sometimes but only when no one else was around and she was in her room, lying on her cot.

"Anna."

His voice was deep. Deeper than she remembered. She liked it, though. She liked him. It would be fun to visit with this new Dez. Perhaps she could think and make herself appear older. Wouldn't it be fun if they could dance in her world? She played the pianoforte there and sang because Jessa enjoyed music so much but she had never thought to dance. She had learned to dance just before they eloped because she was going to be making her come-out with Dalinda and it was important to know the steps of all of the different types of music which would be played at balls.

She frowned. She had not wanted to make her come-out. She had not wanted to be parted from Dez. They had talked about it and both had understood that they could not be together. Until her father told her about arranging for her to marry some ancient lord with a name she refused to remember and Dez had said they should run away and they did and then everything horrible happened.

"Anna," he said again.

Hmm. She didn't know how to make up conversation for a mature Dez. She knew what he should say when they climbed trees and swam and went out on the lake in the rowboat. But not what a grown-up Dez would talk about.

"You are free."

Her belly tightened. She didn't like that word. It brought up foolish ideas that she had abandoned long, long ago.

She shook her head furiously because she couldn't speak.

"You are," he insisted quietly. "Your father is dead. Your cousin, Tom, has become the new Shelton. And I came home from the war. Tom and I found you. We have—"

Anna pushed hard against him, her hands covering his mouth. She didn't like this kind of talk. It made her head hurt. She scrambled away, breathing hard, daring him to rise.

"I will sit here," he told her.

Good. He understood. She had at least made that clear to him. She needed him to go away, though. She blinked several times but he remained. She closed her eyes and counted to twenty. One hundred. One thousand. Counting had been a different way to pass the time and she did it often. When she finally opened her eyes, he was still there.

She tried to say a curse word but only strained air emerged. She remembered she had screamed so much that her voice was gone. It would be for several days. Would she have to put up with this adult Dez because she couldn't shout at him and make him disappear? That wouldn't do at all.

Turning, she began taking in her surroundings. The familiarity tugged hard on her memory. She had been here before. But where was this here?

Anna walked around, touching items. The floor was smooth

and clean beneath her feet. She glanced down and saw her usual dirty, bare feet, her legs covered in bruises as they stuck out from the drab garment she wore every day. Matron gave her a new one every now and then. She said it was for Christmas but Matron kept giving them to her. She knew that many Christmases couldn't have come and gone. Else she would be old. So old. Like this Dez. Even if he did appear handsome.

The open door drew her attention and she went to it. The closer she came, the more her legs began shaking. She reached it and stood in the doorway, grasping it in her hands.

The lake . . .

She had dreamed of this lake. Imagined it over and over.

A choking sound came from her. She dropped to her knees. She slammed her hands against the ground, over and over.

Then Dez was beside her. He took her wrists and stilled her hands. His legs came around and stretched out so very long, with her in-between them. His arms wrapped around her waist and nudged her until her back pressed against his chest. His arms remained lightly about her. Anna leaned against him. He felt so good.

"Untuck your legs," he said gently.

Somehow, she managed to get them from under her and stretched them out like his were. She pushed her legs against his, feeling how solid they were. For the first time in a long time, she realized she was utterly content. A grown-up Dez had come to comfort her. He hadn't forgotten about her. This was his way of rescuing her. The real Dez would never find her hidden away at Gollingham but the Dez she had created had found her. He would take care of her.

They sat together and she listened to her surroundings for the first time. Two birds warbled, answering one another. The wind made the leaves in the trees ripple. And she could hear—and feel—Dez's steady heartbeat against her back.

Anna liked this new world. It had taken her by surprise. She hadn't known she could create something as wonderful as this.

She might just stay in this world forever.

Then she heard something. A horse's hooves. A creak. Suddenly, a cart appeared in the clearing in front of the cottage, driven by a man with a shiny bald head. He slowed the horse and jumped down. She could see he was short but stout.

Fear rippled through her. She had let her guard down. Something terrible had entered her perfect world. He would be a new attendant. He would take her and do awful things to her. Anna began struggling, trying to make sounds to force him to go away.

"Leave, Coral," Dez said from behind her. "She is afraid of you."

"But the horse, my lord," the man protested.

"You can come back for it. Go."

As the man hurried away, Dez's arms felt secure around her. Anna quit her struggles.

"He's gone, my love. He only brought us some supplies. Something to help clean you and for you to wear. He also brought food earlier. Are you hungry? Would you like to eat?"

My love . . .

Had Dez ever called her that? She couldn't recall. This new Dez was like the old, familiar one but he was still different. She liked being called his love. Her heart told her she would always love Dez.

He stood and brought her to her feet when he did. He was very strong, she decided. Dez turned her until she faced him. His hands lightly held her waist. He gazed down at her with such tenderness that Anna's chest hurt, a tightness that spoke of long ago and promises forced to be broken. She couldn't think about it.

"Come and eat, Anna," he said.

She didn't like to eat but she couldn't tell him with no voice. She hated the daily bowl of gruel broth. The bread that was mostly dried dough. The occasional beef which was spoiled and made her belly ache and her bowels run loose.

He took her hand. His large one swallowed hers. Once again,

the nearness brought her comfort. Slowly, they moved toward a table, where she saw food—real food—sitting out.

"That was Coral who drove the wagon," Dez said as he helped her into a seat, as if she were some fine lady and he a gentleman at a fancy dinner party. "Coral also brought this food."

He took the chair next to her. "What would you like?" he asked.

His question overwhelmed her. This much food overwhelmed her. Her mouth trembled.

"It's all right, Anna," he said, taking her hand. "I will fix something for you."

She watched as he took a plate and placed items on it. Things she had forgotten about. Large, plump strawberries. Cold chicken legs. Fresh bread, which he buttered. Her mouth salivated at the thought of creamy butter.

He placed the plate in front of her and then reached for something in a jar. A memory tugged at her and then she smiled.

"Ah, you remember when Cook would send lemonade for us."

Cook . . .

If he mentioned his cook and she had been the one to send this to them, Anna feared she had stumbled into Dez's world. This one wasn't made by her, after all. It was his.

But how had she gotten into his?

She lifted her eyes and met his. A single tear rolled down her cheek. It was all pretend. It had been fine when she was the one who pretended and dreamed because she had controlled what she imagined. Now, though, she had lost the thread of reality and things spiraled out of control. She had thought it and had rejected the idea but she couldn't any longer.

She had become the demented lunatic Fiend and Matron had told her she was. Her slender hold on reality had finally broken. Everything Dez said—even the fact that he was here—wasn't the world of her making. Madness had set in and Anna knew she had descended into a place from which she would never emerge.

CHAPTER TWELVE

D EZ SENSED THE shift within Anna. He thought he had been making progress with her. She hadn't tried to run away or strike him. She had gingerly explored her surroundings. She had allowed him to hold her. It had shattered when Coral arrived, frightening her, but Dez had once again calmed her and Anna seemed to accept things.

He could tell she had been overcome by the display of food on the table. What he considered simple fare must have seemed like a feast to someone in her position. He wondered at the rot they must have fed her at Gollingham, seeing how thin she now was. Yet he still thought it was going well until he mentioned Cook and the lemonade. His words had triggered something inside Anna. She had begun to withdraw. The look on her face changed, tremendous sadness spreading across it. Why would the idea of lemonade bring unhappiness?

Unless it reminded her of earlier, happier times and what had been lost to her.

With that in mind, he decided to continue speaking to her gently as if everything were perfectly normal. That two old friends were merely sharing a meal. He wouldn't hide what had been done to her. He would address it and continue to do so, all the while letting her know the asylum was behind her and she had nothing to fear again.

"Lemonade will be good for your throat," he said matter-of-factly. "You have strained it. That is why you've lost your voice. It has happened to me before."

Dez took the lemonade and poured it into a cup, placing it before her. He did the same for himself and took a sip.

"Ah, nice and tart. Try some," he encouraged.

Anna looked at the cup and back at him. Then her gaze returned to the cup longingly.

"It is very good." He took another sip. "When I strained my throat, the doctor told me that I should avoid very cold or very hot beverages. I had thought a spot of hot tea would do the trick but he had me gargle with warm salt water. You can do that, too. Coral brought us some supplies."

Pausing, he added, "I think I will bring them in from the cart. Go ahead and start eating. I'll join you shortly."

He rose and left the cottage, going to the wagon. It contained several boxes filled with the items he had requested. He also saw three valises and hoped they contained things for Anna to wear. Once she had some food in her, he needed to bathe her and get fresh clothes on her. Lifting two of the valises, he carried them into the cottage, not looking at Anna as he went to the bedchamber. He opened them and saw women's clothing, even recognizing a dress he recalled seeing Dalinda in.

Returning outside, he brought in the remaining valise and, after several trips, all of the boxes, as well. He had watched Anna surreptitiously and saw she was eating, totally focused on the food, as if he weren't present at all. Dez wondered how much she understood of what occurred around her. He didn't think her mad in the least, especially if after all this time she was still shouting loud and long enough, protesting her presence at the asylum. He believed she must retreat far into herself for great periods of time. That was what had saved her sanity, not driven her into madness.

The key would be to bringing her back to a safe present—and keeping her here.

He rejoined her. "Everything is inside now," he said, keeping his tone conversational. He wanted Anna to see that he treated her normally and didn't look at her with any uncertainty. "There are new things for you to wear, things Dalinda wore."

She stilled at the mention of his twin's name. Then she turned the strawberry she held over and over, studying it. Finally, she bit into it.

"You must wonder why I lost my voice. It was when I was a soldier."

He busied himself spreading butter on a slice of bread but felt Anna's eyes upon him.

"My father sent me to be in the army when I left Torville Manor. I had to grow up quickly. England is currently at war with France. Bonaparte has thought to conquer all of Europe. The war rages on, even now."

Dez covered Anna's dirty hand with his. Gazing into her eyes, he said, "The war was terrible. Men died in droves. As an officer, it was my responsibility to lead them into battle. I would shout orders. Encouragement. It was hard to make myself heard with all the gun and cannon fire. I lost many men, Anna. And it hurt."

Tears brimmed in her eyes. He thought her lips formed the words *I'm sorry* so he said, "I know you are sorry. I am also sorry for what happened to you."

She flinched. Jerked her hand out from under his. Crossed her arms protectively over her breasts.

"I hated the war, Anna. I saw monstrous things. Things I will never be able to forget. You, too, were subjected to horrible things. Though you won't ever forget them, you can believe me when I say you are safe now. You will never see Gollingham Asylum again."

Tears streamed down her cheeks. She looked up and shook her head violently. Dez leaned over and clasped her shoulders gently.

"I will never let anything happen to you like that, Anna."
Doubt flickered in her eyes.
"Your father is dead. He died a few months ago."

Dez let that information settle in. He could almost see the wheels turning in her head as Anna absorbed it.

"Your cousin, Tom, is now Viscount Shelton. He is the head of your family. He came with me to claim you. To remove you from Gollingham."

Her gaze fell. She shrugged his hands off and reached for the bread, smearing an enormous amount of butter atop it and then greedily shoving it into her mouth. He sat back, telling himself it would take infinitesimal steps to bring Anna back. At least she had the knowledge that her bastard of a father was dead and had no control over her. Tom Browning seemed like a good man and Dez believed the viscount would also do everything in his power to help his cousin.

Anna finally pushed her plate away, crossing her arms again, a sullen look upon her face. He couldn't help but ache, seeing the bruises covering her arms. The jagged nails on her dirty hands.

"Would you like to have a bath?"

She shot to her feet, terror in her eyes as she ran to the door and threw it open. As she rushed outside, Dez cursed the mistake he had made. To Anna, the idea of a bath would mean the frigid buckets of water dumped upon her head and tossed against her body. What a fool he had been.

He leaped to his feet and followed her outside. She turned in circles, as if she were an animal trapped by hunters. A faint noise came from her and she slumped to the earth, slamming her palms against the ground in frustration.

Approaching her, he held his open palms to his side, trying to show he was no threat. Dez knelt a few feet from her.

"Anna, I am sorry. I know what my thoughtless words meant to you. You are no longer at the asylum, though. I only thought that you might wish to be clean and wear one of the gowns Coral brought. Remember? Something of Dalinda's. You'd like that, wouldn't you?"

He prayed he had gotten through to her.

She stopped beating the ground and looked at him, her suspicion obvious.

"I had Coral put water on to heat. He also fetched clean, cool water from the lake to mix in with the hot. There is a small tub in the corner of the kitchen. I will mix the water together. It will be warm. I promise that it will feel good. Can I do that for you?"

She nodded abruptly.

"I will also need to check your hair for lice."

Anna shuddered.

"I know. They were rampant in the army. If you have any, they need to be gotten rid of. Can you understand that?"

Again, she nodded her head.

"It would be best to do it outside." Dez looked up. "It looks like we have another hour of daylight. That's good. We'll use it." He rose. "Stay here."

Minutes later, he returned with a box he'd filled with what he would use, along with a chair that sat on the cottage's porch. He had also removed his coat, waistcoat, and cravat and rolled his shirt's sleeves to his elbows, knowing he would get wet in the process.

"Sit here." He reached out his hand and she took it. He thought it important to continue to touch her. Any touch she was used to had been threatening and hurtful. He wanted to emphasize over and over to her that she was safe with him.

Anna took the chair, hunched over. He eased her shoulders back.

"I will tell you everything I plan to do. Nothing will be a surprise," he promised.

She jerked her head up and down and he supposed she was agreeing with him.

He retrieved a bowl and set it in her lap. "Hold this, please. It's cheese whey."

She frowned and he said, "It is the liquid that remains after milk has been curdled and strained."

Dez fetched the vinegar and poured it into the bowl before taking a wooden spoon and placing it into the bowl.

"Here, you stir this together. Mix it well."

A small smile appeared briefly and he supposed it was the first time she had been allowed to do anything other than sit. She stirred slowly at first and then gleefully.

He brought back a small can. "This is lamp oil," he said. "It will smell something terrible but it is effective at killing the lice. May I have the bowl?"

She looked puzzled.

"Once I apply the lamp oil to your hair and scalp, I will rinse it with the cheese whey and vinegar." He smiled. "I learned about this in army. Trust me."

Her guileless, sky-blue eyes searched his face and then she nodded. Dez wanted to dance with glee, feeling he'd cleared a major hurdle with her.

She offered him the bowl with the mixture and he set it aside on the ground.

"Tilt your head back. It will burn, so be prepared."

Anna did as asked, squeezing her eyes shut. He slowly poured the oil over her head, saturating it, then massaging his fingers along her scalp. Her face screwed up at first, the pungent smell overwhelming, but his fingers appeared to calm her. He continued longer than he needed to merely to keep touching her. Then he picked up the comb he'd set down and ran it through her hair. It took a good while because the short tresses were so tangled.

Once he finished it, he moved to the bowl and brought it back, pouring small bits of it into her hair and using his fingers to work it into her scalp. Then he combed through her tresses again, the lice falling away.

"One last thing," he told her. "Honey."

He picked up the jar of honey and emptied it into her hair, again massaging it into her scalp.

"I might have to repeat this process again in a few days. We'll see how successful we were at ridding you of the lice."

Anna nodded, her face turned up to him as she kept her head

tilted back. Her features were now relaxed and he could see bits of the girl she had been.

"Stay here. I need water to rinse out all of what I have placed in your hair."

She shivered.

"I will mix cool with hot."

She nodded.

Dez brought back two buckets and slowly rinsed her hair, pausing several times to run a new comb through it. When he finished, she raised her head.

And smiled.

It was a smile the Anna of old would have given him. Sweet. Playful. It tugged at his heartstrings.

"I think we did a good job," he praised, wanting her to think of them as a team.

She nodded, her enthusiasm obvious.

"Now, we need to repeat some of this and let you bathe."

Dez explained that he would need to remove what she wore. She didn't seem to react to this and he thought she might be desensitized to nakedness.

"Can I bring the tub out here? No one is around. It would make things easier."

Anna nodded eagerly, like a child wanting to please a parent.

He went into the cottage and dragged the wooden tub back into the small clearing and then made several trips, filling it with water of different temperatures and stirring it with his hand to mix it. She watched him with curiosity.

"I am going to get soap and towels now. Wait here."

When he returned, Anna had stood and left the chair to peer into the tub. She dipped her hand into the water and swirled it around, her face in awe. Once more, his heart seemed to tear in two, seeing her marvel at water that wasn't used as a weapon.

Without being asked, Anna reached for the hem of the sack she wore and yanked it off, tossing it aside and climbing into the tub. He saw the welts on her back and more bruises before she sat and fought the tears that misted his eyes.

"I am going to scrub you, Anna. It will hurt some. Not like at the asylum, but I need to penetrate the dirt ground into your skin. We will bathe you every day until it is gone and then you'll want to take a bath because it will be a pleasant experience."

She nodded sagely, taking in his words. Then she held out her hands.

"Do you want the cake of soap and the brush?" Dez handed both to her. "I think that's an excellent idea for you to take charge of this. When you have finished, I will wash your hair for you." He paused. "I am going to the lake to retrieve more water and put more on to heat."

She shrugged and took up the brush and soap. He left her to her ministrations and hauled water back and forth, working up a sweat. He would need a bath himself by the time this was all over. With no valet to give the order to the kitchens to do so and bring water to him, baths were a difficult undertaking. Still, Dez felt he had committed to the right path to help Anna heal.

By the time the water warmed enough to be brought to her, Anna had scrubbed herself thoroughly. Her skin looked rubbed raw in many places but he knew she washed away not only the dirt but the stain of the asylum's soul upon her. He proceeded to wash her hair, working up a lather and rinsing numerous times to rid her hair of the various items he'd used to kill the lice.

Holding a bath sheet open, he said, "Let's dry you off. It's a good thing because the sun is setting."

She stood, the water sluicing from her thin frame. He refrained from looking at her in a sexual way but as a doctor would, in a professional manner. The realization that he might never kiss Anna again was a strong possibility. Her time in the asylum might have left her so untrusting that she would never wish to give control of her body to another.

Even to the man who had loved her since childhood.

He wrapped her snuggly and then placed a smaller towel around her hair.

"Come inside," he suggested. "Let's see what all Coral brought for you to wear."

Anna sat on the bed as Dez unpacked the valises. He talked about each gown he removed and then thanked Coral silently for also including a few chemises and two night rails.

"Let me help you put this on," he said, taking one of them and bringing it to her.

Anna let the towel fall from her, once more seeming to be untroubled by him seeing her bare form as she slipped into the night rail. Then he handed her the dressing gown and helped her shrug into it, belting it for her.

"It's time again to comb your hair."

She huffed.

"I know. It seems like a lot but I don't want you to sleep with it tangled else we might never unsnarl it." He smoothed her hair. "It has been a very long day, Anna, but I promise that you can sleep soon."

Dez had her return to the other room and sit in a chair so he could stand behind her. With her hair clean now, he could see some of the color though it was still wet. He couldn't wait to see it in the sunlight tomorrow. Anna's hair had been one of his favorite things in the world, her strawberry blond locks distinguishing her from anyone else of his acquaintance.

By the time he finished undoing the snarls, she was yawning repeatedly. She tried to stand and seemed too tired to do so. Dez swept her off her feet and carried her into the bedchamber. He placed her on the bed and saw she already was asleep. He took a quilt at the foot of the bed and covered her and then sat on the bed, stroking her hair. Her face looked younger now, resembling more the girl he had once known.

This day had been the most eventful in his life. He had found the woman he loved and brought her out of the darkness she had lived in for too many years. Now she lay here and he swore he would make sure no one would ever hurt her again.

"I love you, Anna," Dez said softly and kissed her brow.

CHAPTER THIRTEEN

ANNA AWOKE TO light. Confusion filled her. Gollingham remained in darkness. Few candles or lanterns were ever lit. The windows had iron bars across them, which hampered light from streaming inside. She opened her eyes and saw a strange room. No, she had seen it before. Last night.

When Dez had brought her here.

She looked down and saw her arms and legs free. No restraints restricted her movements. She couldn't remember the last time she had gone to sleep without being tied down or laced inside the straitjacket. No wonder she felt so refreshed from sleep. She glanced around and saw Dez in a chair brought close to the bed. Her gaze focused on his forearms, corded with muscle. A tingle swept through her, something she recalled from long ago but couldn't think of what it was associated with.

He was asleep. His chest rose and fell, his breathing even. She studied him, wanting to touch his face but refraining from doing so. He looked older, much older than the last time she had seen him. When they had made for Gretna Green. A wave of sadness swept through her. They had been barely more than children. She was in the first few weeks of her come-out and Dez had just finished at Eton. Though he was remarkably handsome, his face matured and his frame filled out, instinctively she knew he had experienced pain.

She remembered him talking of the war. Lord Torrington

must have shipped him off to the army once he and her father had caught up to them. At least, that is what her imagination was telling her. She knew what she was seeing and hearing and feeling wasn't real. That she had finally been broken by the Fiend and Matron and retreated into a world of madness. Funny how she had fought from doing so for such a long time. Now, here in the grips of madness, she found it so very peaceful. She was with Dez. They were far from Gollingham. She had been able to create an entire world based upon one she once knew. Anna knew this cottage, though not the furnishings. She remembered the clearing and could see the lake. Why, she had even been able to recall gowns which Dalinda had worn, the ones the man called Coral had brought.

That was the only thing she didn't like. Anna didn't know where Coral came from. He didn't look like any of the attendants at the asylum and he wasn't a servant she had ever seen. Dez didn't seem to think Coral was a threat to her even though his appearance had frightened her. She would let things play out. If this Coral bothered her, she would make him disappear.

With her arms free, she stretched lazily as a cat might. Oh, how she had missed cats and all the other wounded animals and birds she used to rescue. She had always loved nature and had helped plant flowers with the Shelton Park gardeners while growing up. She, along with Dez and Dalinda, had explored the woods on both estates. Sometimes, they found animals that had been hurt or a bird with a broken wing. She had insisted on bringing each one home and nursing it back to health. Only then would she try to find a home for it or release it back into the wild.

Anna hadn't thought of any animals besides horses in a long time. Perhaps in this new world that was slowly unwrapping around her, there would be animals, ones that she could take care of. She could fill the cottage with them and tend to them, Dez helping her. She would wait for that, though. She didn't want to push things too far or too fast and have this new world crumble into dust. If it did, who knew how long it might take her to recreate it again?

She scooted up, pushing the pillows back so that they rested at her back. She rotated her wrists and then saw how clean her hands looked. The nails were still broken and jagged but her hands were free of dirt. Her arms, painfully thin, still were marred by old bruises. She supposed she couldn't wish everything away. In time, though, she might learn how.

Smoothing the night rail she wore, she reveled in how white and pristine it was compared to the faded, gray garment given to her by Matron. She wore it until it began to disintegrate and then finally she received a new one. New was a relative word. It was new to her but it always looked old and already soiled every time Matron handed it to her.

Dez stirred in the chair and she hoped she could wake him soon. She liked this Dez. She had always liked Dez. As children, he had always protected her and Dalinda, though they were all the same age. Dalinda had been the mischief-maker. Anna had been the follower, going along with whatever her friend wished to do. And Dez had made sure they were always safe.

She watched him for several minutes until he yawned and opened his eyes. She liked his eyes. They were unique. A deep, rich brown like his hair but outlined in amber.

He smiled. "Good morning, Anna. I see you are awake."

She nodded.

"I hope you enjoyed awakening in a bed with clean sheets. Wearing something different than before."

Anna smiled, wishing she could say something. She couldn't, though. Her imagination only went so far. It must take a great deal of thinking to make Dez and this wonderful cottage to exist in her mind. She would hope in time that she could make her voice return, as well. She would like to talk to him.

He pulled a chamber pot from beneath the bed and told her he would go to the lake to bring fresh water.

"I'll also put on water for tea though you'll still need to drink yours lukewarm because of your throat. We'll stir honey into your cup, which the army doctors also suggested. And I want you to gargle with warm salt water. We never did that yesterday and can start today."

She nodded eagerly, wanting to show him she appreciated his thoughtfulness. As he stood, she caught his hand and brought it to her lips. Pressing a kiss upon it, she hoped he understood how grateful she was that she was now in his world, away from the vile asylum and horrible attendants and ghastly treatments.

Dez gazed at her with tenderness, causing a lump to grow in her throat. He pulled his hand, bringing hers with it, and repeated her gesture, kissing her fingers.

"Thank you, Anna," he said softly.

After he left, she used the chamber pot and then went to the window. She unlatched and raised it, thrilled with the view and the slight breeze that ruffled her night rail. That made her remember the pretty gowns and she went and sorted through until she found a pale blue one. She placed it on the bed and also set a chemise beside it then sat in the chair, waiting for Dez.

He returned and brought two pails in, pouring water into a small basin that rested on the table.

"Wash with this. I will be putting on the tea and getting us something to eat."

Once he left, she used the water and splashed it on her face. It felt cool and clean. He had mentioned another bath today and she looked forward to that. Bathing at the asylum had been seldom and when it did occur, the bathwater was rarely changed from patient to patient, only growing more filthy. The attendants never cleaned the tubs, which stayed stained and dirty. The patients were made to share bath towels, as well, and she hated touching the sheets against her skin, especially when she saw skin inflammation and open sores on others.

She lifted the night rail from her and set it aside, picking up the pretty chemise. It was soft from wear but it felt good against her bare skin. She took the blue dress and held it against her, reveling in the fact that she had thought of something so pretty to wear. This had been one of her favorite dresses that Dalinda possessed. The two girls had sometimes traded dresses since they were almost the same height, Dalinda being maybe an inch taller. Mama hadn't minded them doing so and Dalinda's mother had died after giving birth to her and Dez so no one at Torville Manor said she couldn't switch gowns every now and then.

Sadly, the dress was quite loose on Anna. She didn't have the power to wish away being so thin. She would work on that. She wanted to look good for herself and for Dez. He had once looked at her with longing. With desire. He had kissed her and made her feel like a princess.

The thought of kissing him brought conflicted emotions. When Dez had kissed her long ago, she had felt possessed by him. She would have done anything he said and had proven it when he suggested they run away to Scotland together. Now, though, the thought of someone having such power over her bothered her. She would rebel against that ever happening, even if it was only in her make-believe world.

Yet the Dez she had brought to life was very much a man. An incredibly handsome, patient, kind man. Part of her did want to kiss him. Desperately. She would have to think on this. Examine her feelings. See if she could learn to kiss him and still somehow hold him at bay. Oh, this world was very hard! But it was infinitely better than living in the one she had for however long she had. Time had meant nothing at Gollingham. One day blended into the next until it was a series of endless hours.

She laughed—or at least tried to, as much as her damaged vocal cords would allow. She had hated wearing a corset and it struck her that the delightful Coral had brought none. Even when she wasn't trying, she was already creating a better world for herself. She couldn't fasten the back of the gown, however. Dez would need to do that. She left the bedchamber and heard him whistling. She had forgotten he did that and was proud that, somewhere deep inside her, she was resurrecting new things. She still had no control over what was happening. That would come in time. For now, Anna would simply move through her imagination and enjoy what unfolded.

Dez heard her and turned. "Ah, don't you look lovely, Anna? I think so." He grinned. "And it must be liberating to wear no stockings or slippers. At least the weather is warm and you won't catch a cold. Come and let me help fasten the gown for you."

She went to him and presented her back. She could feel his fingers along her spine as he moved, once again sending a little thrill through her. She determined to kiss him at some point and see how much of her feelings she was able to control.

"Coral has come and gone," Dez told her. "He came for the horse and cart last night but he's brought new supplies for us today. More food, as well. Before you sit at the table and eat, let's have you gargle."

Anna had never been good at gargling as a child, always laughing because of the sound it made, which allowed some of the salt water to go down her throat, defeating the entire purpose and souring her stomach. She determined she would succeed this time.

Dez poured some water into a mug and doused it with salt, stirring it with a spoon. He offered her the mug and she accepted it, taking it outside. If she could, she would spend every waking moment outdoors. She moved away from the cottage and then brought the mug to her mouth, taking in a bit of the salted water and then tilting her head back. She gargled, making sure not to giggle, and then spit it out, repeating her actions several times.

Once she finished, she returned to Dez and gave him the mug.

"Very good, Anna. I hope it will promote healing. Come to the table. I have breakfast waiting for you. Coral brought things for us. He will do so every day, several times a day, whatever we need."

She thought that very convenient to have a servant at their beck and call but still not a part of her fantasy. Coral was becoming quite indispensable. She determined not to act frightened the next time he appeared. After all, he was of her making. What had she to fear from a servant she herself had manufactured?

They had bread, which Dez smeared with peach jam, and slices of ham. Fresh fruit and a few slices of a sharp cheese. She had always loved cheese and was glad this Dez had remembered so. She even helped him with washing the few dishes and then dried them with a small towel.

"I will be back," he told her. "Coral packed one of the valises with things for me. I would like to wash and put something fresh on."

He left her and went into the bedchamber, closing the door behind him. Restless, Anna walked about the cottage. It bothered her that he had shut her out. Doors were forever being closed and locked at Gollingham. She didn't want her new world to resemble it in any manner.

So she went and opened the door.

Her jaw dropped. Dez was bare to the waist, wearing only his trousers and Hessians. His shoulders seemed so very broad. His chest was muscular, covered in a fine matting of dark hair which ran down his flat belly and into his breeches. She couldn't help but look at his beauty. Her feet carried her forward and her palms flattened against that magnificent chest.

He sucked in a harsh breath and gently took her wrists, moving them away.

"Anna, when a door is closed, that means privacy is requested. It is different here than at Gollingham. It is not proper for you to see me half-clothed."

She frowned, unhappy at his words. This was what she wanted. To touch him. She placed her fingers against his chest again.

"No," he said firmly, removing them again. "I know at Gollingham you had no say over who touched you. Who hurt you. You aren't there, Anna. You are back where you should be but you must respect the rules of Polite Society. You cannot see me this way. I did not ask for you to touch me. I have the right to tell you no because this is my body. *You* also have that right and no one will touch you unless you want it."

But she did want it. She grabbed his wrists and jerked them toward her, placing them on her breasts. Dez froze. Anna wore no corset, only the dress and a thin chemise beneath it. He could feel the swell of her breasts beneath his fingers, soft pillows he longed to suck and lick. She wanted his touch. He could see it in her eyes as she stared defiantly at him. More than anything, he longed to tug the clothing from her and bury his face between her breasts. Knead them. Let his tongue follow their gentle curves. He yearned to tweak her nipples. Tease them with his tongue and teeth. Make love to her as he had wanted to all those years ago.

It wasn't the right time, however. Anna didn't know what she truly wanted. He had to be strong. For both of them. Hopefully, the right time would come when they could be together. Not yet. It was much too soon. Regretfully, Dez withdrew his hands, forcing them to his sides. Anna stomped her foot, letting him know it was what she wanted.

"No. I won't touch you that way. Not now. Not until you have a voice and can tell me what you want." He smiled sadly. "Even then, it is something that should wait until you are stronger. Feeling better. Do you understand?"

No. She didn't understand at all. Once more, the world she created was spinning out of control, leaving her helpless. It was Dez's world. He was making the rules. She didn't like this at all. She stormed from the room and out of the cottage, her breathing rapid. She spun in a circle, unsure of where to go. A bit afraid, actually, that if she went anywhere she would lose the thread of Dez, who had linked her to this world.

What if she became lost—and couldn't find her way back?

She slumped to the ground, tears of frustration falling onto her gown. She had never thought she would want to go back to the dark world of the asylum but it was familiar to her. Of course, she had no idea how to get back there. Even if she could, she understood she now danced between madness and sanity. She had slipped into madness. But wasn't it possible to have periods of lucidity? She had seen it with others at Gollingham, women who truly were mad—or had been driven mad by years spent at the horror chamber.

Anna closed her eyes, bringing her hands over them to block out the light of the morning sun. If she thought hard enough, maybe she could get back for a few minutes. See Fiend as he walked past in his superior manner. Have Matron slap her or an attendant trip her. Something to help her get a grip on her wild emotions.

Then she felt Dez near. She could smell the faint scent of sandalwood. Feel the warmth of his body behind her.

He slipped his arms around her, drawing her up and carrying her to the porch, where he sat in a chair. He murmured words to her but she didn't think on their meaning. His tone was soothing, which was all that mattered. She had felt rejected and angry and unwanted but that had changed. She was with Dez again.

And that was enough.

CHAPTER FOURTEEN

DEZ HELD ANNA, hoping he reassured her as he sensed the tension melting from her. He had wanted to give her control of the situation and her body, firming up her belief in herself.

He decided she suffered from what he'd seen in other soldiers who had been affected by the war. Some called it being hipped or blue-deviled. The few men he had been in contact with behaved recklessly and had trouble sleeping. They had wild mood swings and would endanger themselves—and sometimes others—on the battlefield. They usually drank too much and no longer acted morally.

He supposed Anna had been affected in a similar way. It would explain her sudden mood swings and the weeping. The distance she placed between herself and him, as if she were in another world at times. She seemed to have no regard for propriety and boundaries between men and women. He would have to take care and make a special effort when her behavior changed radically. Not scold her but continue to speak calmly and patiently, trying to help her come back to the world she'd left, with all its rules, both spoken and unspoken. He feared that would be the greatest hurdle to climb. Anna might never function well in Polite Society again.

It didn't matter. She could live in the country at Shelton Park. Or he hoped with him, as his wife, at Torville Manor. They would have no need of London and its gaiety during the Season. He only hoped that could be a possibility. If not, he would have to respect her need for solace and merely be a visitor. A friend to her. No matter how much it pained him.

"Would you like to go for a walk?" he asked. "We could go through the woods. Down to the lake."

She pushed against him and clambered to her feet then grabbed his forearm and pulled him to his. Anticipation lit her face.

"Where first?" he asked. "Why don't you lead me where you wish to go?"

He wanted to give her choice and control as much as possible. Eagerly, she took his hand and he threaded his fingers through hers.

"Slow down," he said, laughing, as she began pulling him quickly. "You have always loved nature. Let's enjoy the day and take our time."

He watched her consider his advice and then she began moving, more slowly this time. Anna led him to the water. They stood looking across the lake for some minutes, no words necessary. If anything, the outdoors would help to restore her to the Anna of old, or at least as much as she could be after all that had happened to her. Dez still wanted to string up Dr. Cheshire for taking a beautiful, spirited girl and almost crushing the life from her. Dez could still see sparks within her, though, of the Anna she had been. Being away from Gollingham and its inhumane practices was the first step in her recovery.

She pulled away from him and began searching along the shore, collecting rocks. He knew what she was doing and he did the same. Soon, they skimmed rocks along the water.

After flinging another stone, she huffed and slammed the rocks she held to the ground. Dez caught her by the shoulders.

"You are merely out of practice, Anna. Be patient. Keep trying. Remember, it is all in the wrist action. Will you try again?"

She looked contrite and knew the flash of temper was merely

frustration on her part. She bent and retrieved the stones she'd dropped and began again. After several minutes, she had regained her old form and her tosses bounced three, four, five, even six times. Gleefully, she clapped her hands and then hugged him.

"See? I knew you could do it. Don't forget that there are many things you haven't done in a good while. Try to be patient and take your time and I am sure they will come back to you."

She sighed and her head bobbed up and down in agreement.

After she grew tired of tossing stones, she hiked her dress to her knees and ventured into the water. She gasped, her eyes going wide.

"Yes, it is cold. It's only May now. Remember that we used to wait until June or later before we went swimming."

He sat on the ground, his hands stretched out behind him, and watched as she skipped through the water. She kicked it. Twirled. Grinned. Her happiness spilled over to him and he laughed easily at her antics.

Then she pointed to the woods.

"You wish to walk?"

Anna nodded and grabbed his hand, urging him to his feet.

"We will need to tread carefully," he told her. "You have no shoes. I will see if Coral can bring some. I know you and Dalinda switched gowns sometimes but I can't recall you doing the same with shoes."

She shook her head furiously and he gathered that their feet were not of a similar size.

Tucking her hand through the crook of his arm, he said, "Come then. Let us explore."

They went into the woods, daylight coming and going based upon the thickness of the trees. Anna seemed happy and Dez decided they should spend as much time as possible outside the cottage.

Then she froze, tilting her head slightly. Her brow creased in concern. Then she took off, running like a wood nymph. He followed, calling after her to slow down, and finally caught up to her when he saw her kneeling.

As he came closer, he heard the noise she must have heard before. A fox keened eerily, its paw caught in a trap. Anna looked at it, desperation in her eyes, begging Dez to do something. He recalled how she had always found hurt animals and birds in the woods and brought them back, keeping them in the Shelton stables and nursing them back to health.

"You want me to free it?" he asked.

She pointed at the fox and then jabbed her thumb into her chest several times.

"You want to care for it?"

Anna rewarded him with a radiant smile.

A hundred things could go wrong. The fox could bite either of them. Attack them. It might be rabid. He didn't want to take such a risk but looking at Anna let him know he had no choice. Dez unknotted his cravat and, taking the ailing fox unaware, quickly slipped it around the animal's jaws and tied it.

"This is so it won't bite us," he said.

Understanding dawned in her eyes. She went to her hands and knees and then lay next to the frightened animal, softly stroking its fur. The fox calmed and Anna placed her hands on its body, bringing her head to rest gently between the fox's ears. Dez took hold of the trap and pulled with all his might. The fox hissed as he freed it. Anna tightened her grip, her body draped on the injured animal, keeping it in place.

He whipped a handkerchief from his pocket and bound the bleeding paw. Somehow, the fox must sense they were trying to help it and the creature stopped struggling. Anna lifted her head and kissed the fox between its ears over and over, petting it with both hands. Then she scooped it up.

Fear filled him, the thought of a hurt, wild animal slashing her. But Anna had always had a way with animals and the fox seemed to know the person who held it had a heart for the hurt.

It struck him that Anna herself was a wounded animal.

She walked slowly back to the cottage, nuzzling the fox. They arrived and went inside. She motioned what he thought was towel and he retrieved one, wrapping the animal in it with her help, only its paw sticking out. His cravat had held the animal's snout, keeping the fox from biting them.

"We need to clean the paw," he said.

She nodded and he began gathering items to do so. Pouring water in a basin. Finding ointment that Coral had brought for Anna's wrists and bruising, which Dez had forgotten to use after her bath.

"Hold her head, Anna."

She looked at him questioningly.

"The fox is a vixen," he shared. "I saw her teats as we secured her in the towel."

Anna looked dismayed.

"Yes, she must have a litter of kits. We'll need to tend to her and then release her so she can go back to them."

Nodding, she stroked the fox's head, pressing more kisses upon it. Dez unwrapped the handkerchief and cleaned the paw of the squirming vixen and then doused it with ointment. He fetched one of the spare cravats Coral had packed and wrapped it around the injured paw.

"Let's carry her back to the woods," he suggested. "That way, she doesn't have to walk so far on her injured paw."

Anna nodded and lifted the fox in her arms, holding the animal close to her. They went back to where they had found the fox. Anna turned in a circle, her head cocked as she listened. Without warning, she strode off and he followed.

She slowed and searched the woods around them. The fox began making a sound beneath the cravat and Dez heard some noise. A mewling. He took Anna's arm and guided her in that direction.

They discovered the litter, four kits in all. He knew they were born blind, deaf, and toothless. These little ones looked as if they were on the verge of their eyes opening, so they must be about two weeks old.

"Place the mama close to her kits," he said softly. "Hold her while I untie the cravat and let go quickly. We have helped her but she is a beast of the wild and still may attack."

Anna dropped to her knees and rested the vixen on the ground. The kits began making their way to her. Dez undid the cravat and pulled it away, grabbing Anna's elbow and swiftly moving them several feet back, his heart beating wildly in his chest.

The kits swarmed their mother and she began licking one of them. Suddenly, another fox appeared next to the litter, studying the human invaders warily. Dez remembered foxes usually traveled in pairs.

"We only wished to help your wife," he said quietly. "She is back now with your babies. Take care of your family."

With that, Dez led Anna away.

When they reached the clearing before the cottage, she threw her arms around him in gratitude, pressing her body against his. Memories flooded him of holding her. Kissing her. Longing to make love to her. As she snuggled closer, he thought how they seemed like two halves, coming together as a whole after years of separation.

With a recklessness that he couldn't resist, Dez lowered his mouth to Anna's. He brushed his lips against hers softly, just wanting to be near her. To convey how much he loved her. Cared for her. How he would do anything to see her made whole once again.

She grew still. He knew he had acted too quickly. Had probably destroyed every bit of trust he'd gained with her. With sadness tinged with reluctance, he lifted his mouth from hers.

Meeting her gaze, something flickered in her eyes. A look shot across her face. Confusion. Wonder. Delight. With widening eyes, she reached up and grabbed on to his hair and forced his mouth back down to hers. He tried to lift it but Anna was having none of it. Her grip tightened and kept him in place as she started kissing him. Hungrily. Greedily. Over and over.

Then Anna broke the kiss. She searched his face, her breathing rapid, her body trembling.

"You're real," she croaked.

CHAPTER FIFTEEN

ANNA LOOKED AT Dez. He wasn't the Dez from her past. He was from now. She hadn't imagined him. She hadn't created him from the black hole of nothingness. It was really, truly Dez.

And he was here . . .

She wasn't mad after all. It had really happened. Dez had found her. He had rescued her from that vile asylum. He had taken her out and brought her to the place they loved.

She would never let him go.

"Yes, Anna. I am real. You are not at Gollingham anymore. Lord Shelton—your cousin, Tom—and I came and got you the minute we knew you were there."

Images flashed in her mind. Scattered and confusing. She remembered voices. A carriage. She thought of fragments this Dez—her Dez—had told her. She had heard some of it but pushed the rest aside, simply reveling in having him with her. But this was a flesh and blood man, not some imagined creature she had kept hidden in the recesses of her mind and resurrected when she most needed him.

This. Was. Dez.

Her Dez.

The love of her life.

He cradled her face tenderly. "You are free, Anna. You will stay free. I will see to that. I would give my life for you."

She knew he would. He had loved her. He had wanted to

wed her. And he had saved her.

"Dez . . ." She grunted the word since it was still difficult to speak.

It didn't matter, though. They were together.

And she wanted this man so badly.

She released the tight hold she held on his hair and stroked his cheeks. He wiped the tears that fell down hers. They stared at one another, drinking each other in. He was so beautiful.

Anna whispered, "Kiss me," and saw desire flicker in his eyes.

"Are you sure?" he asked.

She nodded, words beyond her at this point.

Dez's mouth returned to hers. The kiss began soft and sweet and tender but a storm raged within her. This man had been taken from her. Time had been stolen from them. She wanted it all back. Now.

She opened to him, letting him know she yielded. That she wanted to taste him. Crawl inside him. Anna clung to him as his tongue gently began exploring her. Though she wanted him to hurry, she understood he wanted to go slowly. To make sure she knew her own mind. She would follow his lead.

Because she never wanted to be parted from Dez ever again.

Anna allowed him to drink her in, hoping she still made his heart beat as fast as hers now did. It pounded so that she thought it might explode from her chest. Her blood seem to come alive and she could feel it flowing through her veins, calling his name, over and over. As Dez continued his exploration, she could wait no longer. Her tongue stroked his. He groaned, his hold tightening on her. Boldly, she now searched him, her tongue gliding along his teeth. Along the roof of his mouth. Rubbing against his tongue.

Then a passionate war erupted and they both fought for control. It was a game with no losers because each of them grew more excited and satisfied as they continued to kiss. She locked her hands around his neck, claiming possession. His fingers pushed into her hair, massaging her scalp as he had when he had tenderly washed her hair. Her emotions exploded and she whimpered.

Dez broke the kiss, his face worried. "Are you all right? I am sorry if I pushed too far but my God, Anna. I love you so, so much."

"I love you," she mouthed.

"Rest your voice, darling," he urged. "We will have much to talk about once you can." He paused. "You do know where you are? Who I am?"

She nodded and forced out, "I thought you were make believe before." Tears welled in her eyes. "Now, I know you are real."

He smiled with his entire face, his eyes lighting up. "I love you, Anna Browning." He threw back his head and shouted, "I love you!"

His gaze met hers and she nodded, the only way she could tell him she felt the same. Already, she seemed to wilt. The realization that she wasn't insane and had truly escaped from the Fiend had eliminated her energy. Her legs quaked and she almost collapsed but Dez swept her into his arms and took her back to the cottage.

"You are tired. I can tell," he said. "This experience has been overwhelming. You need to sleep, my love. Sleep will help restore your strength."

He carried her to the bed and placed her upon it.

"Stay," she whispered.

"I wouldn't go anywhere else in the world," he said.

She patted the mattress, her eyes beseeching him.

"You want me . . . to lie with you?" he asked, his voice breaking.

She nodded enthusiastically.

"It's not . . . oh, blast and bother," he exclaimed. "Who cares if it's not proper or what the *ton* might say? They aren't here. We are. And my dear, sweet Anna, I need you even more than you need me."

Dez climbed onto the bed beside Anna and gathered her into his arms. Her cheek nestled against his hard chest. His arms wrapped around her protectively. She sighed, utterly contented.

"Sleep," he urged. "I will be here when you awake."

Anna closed her eyes, finding peace for the first time since they had been parted.

❧

DEZ LAY BESIDE Anna, listening to her breathing as it became more agitated. She had been resting peacefully for an hour but now she began to grow restless, thrashing about, murmuring words that were incomprehensible.

Suddenly, she sat up, flailing, fighting with the bedclothes. He tried to calm her, placing his arms about her to keep her still, but she continued to fight, making guttural, animal noises.

"Anna!" he shouted, trying to get her attention. "Anna, you are fine. You are with me. It's Dez, Anna. Please, calm yourself."

Her eyes, wild with fright, looked at him and yet didn't seem to see—or recognize—him.

He lowered his voice, realizing his shouts had only upset her. He kept his arms banded about her but murmured soothingly to her.

"I am here, Anna. I am not leaving you. Ever. You are safe. You are here. With me. At the cottage. Nothing can hurt you. I won't let anyone ever hurt you again."

He must have gotten through to her because she shuddered and then quit struggling. He relaxed his hold on her but still kept her nestled in his arms.

"I thought . . . I was there again," she rasped.

"I know," he said, stroking her back. "It is only natural to have a nightmare regarding that place. You will never see it again, that I can promise you."

Anna blinked several times. "It was so real. And Matron . . ."

Her voice trailed off as she began trembling.

Dez continued to rub her back. Kiss her hair. Assure her she was safe.

Finally, he asked, "Would you care to talk about it?"

"I dreamed of Matron," she said dully.

He had only seen Dr. Cheshire and male attendants when he and Lord Shelton had entered Gollingham Asylum so it surprised him to hear a woman had been present in the madhouse. Still, she must have been a large presence in Anna's life for her to dream about her.

"Matron is not here, Anna. She never will be."

"She was so cruel," Anna whispered, as if this woman could hear Anna talk about her. "She delighted in making impossible rules and then punishing those who broke them."

After what he had witnessed during his brief time at the madhouse, Dez couldn't imagine what punishments this woman had dreamed up that could be worse than what he'd seen.

"You could tell she enjoyed hurting others. Lording her power over helpless women."

"Did she ever hurt you, Anna?" he asked softly.

She nodded. "Many times. She liked to have the attendants beat us with their fists while she counted the number of blows."

He kept silent, letting Anna take the lead.

"The worst was the heretic's fork. It was a metal rod with two prongs at either end, attached to a leather strap. Matron would tie the strap around my neck. One prong would rest on the fleshy part just under my chin. The other dug into my bone. Here."

She indicated her sternum. A sick feeling washed over him.

A faraway look filled her eyes as she continued in a monotone. "You had to keep your neck stretched and your head erect and absolutely still. If you moved, the prongs would penetrate your skin. Matron would have an attendant bind my hands over my head and attach them to a hook from the ceiling."

Bile rose in his throat at the thought of Anna being tortured in such a way.

"Matron said no vital organ would be pierced and blood loss would be minimal. She would leave me that way for hours." Tears cascaded down her cheeks. "I would try so hard not to move and keep my head still."

Dez kissed her brow. "She sounds as if she enjoyed seeing you suffer."

Anna blinked. "She did. I think she thrived on the misery of others, Dez. She enjoyed it when a patient broke her rules. She liked to torment us. See us in pain and agony."

Anna told him about being lashed with a horsewhip for not eating the food set before her. How when she spoke without permission her head was forced into something called a scold's bridle, which included a bit with tiny spikes being jammed into her mouth. The words poured from her in a torrent. He could only hold her close and try to keep from picturing the torture she endured.

Her voice faded and Dez looked down. Anna had worn herself out and had fallen asleep. He kept his arms about her, hoping it would comfort her and keep the nightmares away. Hours passed and morning turned into early afternoon. He remained with Anna, knowing it was important to be present when she opened her eyes.

He understood that his kiss had awakened her to reality. She had seemed in a fog until then, moving as if she glided through water, only taking in part of what he said.

Had she descended into madness during her time at Gollingham Asylum? Or had she retreated from its horrors and now emerged?

Even Anna might not have the answer to that. Dez only hoped that he could keep her here, in the present, and not have her slip away from him again.

He knew Coral would be coming soon. He had arranged for his valet to come early in the morning and again mid-afternoon. His presence had frightened Anna before and Dez hoped that wouldn't occur again. He needed to speak to the servant and tell him what to share with Lord Shelton.

Anna began stirring and he waited for her eyes to open. When they did, her gaze immediately rose to his face and she smiled. Her sky-blue eyes were clear. It was obvious she knew exactly where she was.

Dez kissed her brow and rested his cheek against it a moment before pulling away.

"Do you feel well rested?" he asked, not mentioning her previously awakening from a nightmare.

She nodded.

"My valet, Coral, will be here soon. He will bring us something to eat. Would you like to rise and refresh yourself? Brush your hair? Change your gown since it has wrinkled some while you slumbered?"

"No," she whispered, smoothing the skirt.

He could tell she liked being in the dress. He got out of bed and offered his hand, assisting her to her feet and leading her into the other room to the settee.

"Coral is supposed to go see your cousin this afternoon and bring him news of you. Tom very much wanted you to come back to Shelton Park but I persuaded him that you would be better off in my care."

She took his hand and kissed it, her gesture moving him.

"I know Jessa will also be eager to see you."

Anna smiled at the mention of her sister.

Dez heard the approaching sound of the horse's hooves clopping along and said, "Coral is here." He squeezed her hand. "Let me go greet him."

Going to the door, he opened it and went outside as the valet steered the horse and cart and brought them to a stop.

"Good afternoon, my lord," Coral called. "How does Miss Browning fare?"

"Remarkably well," he replied. "Let me help you carry things in."

They came inside. Anna sat alert, her eyes large.

To his credit, Coral set down the box on the table and went to her and bowed. "Good afternoon, my lady," he said, a blush rising on his cheeks like a schoolboy.

Dez went to stand by Anna, his hand on her back.

She nodded politely and gave him a smile.

"You are looking very well, my lady. I know Lord Torrington is happy because of that."

Again, she smiled.

"You can tell Lord Shelton that his cousin is feeling remarkably well. She is eating and sleeping and has been able to speak briefly. From my experience, she should regain use of her voice by tomorrow."

"I will let the viscount know, my lord. What if his lordship asks about visiting Miss Browning?"

He looked to Anna. "I think tomorrow might be a bit too soon. Why don't we say the day after?"

She nodded in agreement.

"Tell Lord Shelton that when you bring your report tomorrow that you will give him a time for him to call upon his cousin."

Anna tugged on his hand and sputtered, "Jessa?"

"Yes, of course." Dez looked to Coral. "Be sure to invite the other Miss Browning. For now, I would like you to help me haul more water from the lake."

"Certainly, my lord."

He took the two buckets from the cottage while Coral retrieved two from the ones he had brought in the cart. They made several trips and then Coral wished him well.

"Go straight to Shelton now," he urged. "I know the viscount is eager for news of his cousin."

After Coral left, they went through the same process as yesterday, applying the various solutions to Anna's hair and combing through it. He only found a few nits, which pleased him. He prepared bath water for her and helped unfasten the back of her gown. Before she could pull it off, he stopped her.

"You are much better today. I have left the cake of soap and a bath sheet for you. Can you wash your own hair?"

Disappointment crossed her face but she nodded.

"Then I will leave and give you privacy. I will be just outside if you need me."

Dez left and went to the chair sitting in the middle of the clearing, where he had Anna sit while he applied the treatments to her hair. He moved it back and placed it just outside the door to the cottage. He had left the door open so could he reach her quickly if needed. As he sat, he heard the water splashing, reminding him of when they would swim in the lake during summer. Anna, ever playful, would always splash with joy.

He listened carefully and heard when she stood and stepped from the tub. He decided when the sounds ceased that she had gone into the bedchamber to dress. He didn't know if she would put on another of Dalinda's gowns or if she would don a night rail. He knew how worn out she was and she might need to go to sleep again once he got some more food into her. Now that she was cognizant of her surroundings, he wanted to encourage her to eat small but frequent meals in order to help her regain her strength and put some weight back on her. Anna had always been thin but she certainly could stand to put on a stone or more.

She appeared on the porch, touching his shoulder. She wore a night rail. Her short hair was neatly combed.

"Are you tired, my love?" he asked, his fingers entwining with hers.

She bobbed her head.

"Very well. It's important for you to eat. Let's see what Coral brought for us and then we can put you back to bed."

They ate in companionable silence and then he insisted she sit as he cleared away the food and dishes and then emptied the tub where she had bathed. He escorted her to the bedroom. Her eyes pleaded with him to stay.

"I won't leave you," he said.

She got into bed and he brought the bedclothes over her.

"Talk to me," she said, her voice beginning to sound stronger.

"All right."

Dez told her stories of the army, making sure to make them lighthearted. He had her laughing, especially with tales of Rhys.

"Rhys has been a good friend to me. I hope that the two of you will meet one day."

"Dalinda?" she asked.

"Ah, Dalinda is doing quite well. She married. Not the man Father wanted to match her with but one of her own choice."

"How?"

He chuckled. "Father punished me by shipping me off to war without a university education. He thought Dalinda far too spirited and meddlesome, especially after she had helped you and me try to get to Gretna Green. He decided to marry her off to an old man who would exercise a firm hand on her. Naturally, Dalinda had other ideas. What she didn't expect was that a duke would come to her rescue."

Anna's eyes widened.

"Yes, you heard me correctly. Your best friend is now the Duchess of Gilford. She has two boys, Arthur and Harry. I met them and Gilford for the first time when I sold out and returned home to take on my title."

She frowned, her brows knitting together.

"I am Lord Torrington, Anna. My father, like yours, passed away. And my worthless brother, Ham, drowned. He was drunk and tipped over the rowboat he was in, killing himself and his countess."

Tears filled her eyes and he touched her cheek, wiping them away.

"I never met his wife since I was abroad. I do feel very sorry for her. The servants seemed to have liked her."

She yawned.

"I see you are getting sleeping. Close your eyes, sweetheart. We will have much to talk about tomorrow. And then the next day, Jessa and your cousin, Tom, will come and see you." He smiled. "You won't even recognize Jessa."

Anna bit her lip. "Why?" she asked.

"She's grown up now," he said matter-of-factly. "I saw her the other day when she and Tom and his new wife came to call. They showed me the letter from Dr. Cheshire, requiring the next yearly payment for your keep at Gollingham."

"How old?" she croaked, her eyes filling with panic. "How old is she?"

"Jessa is now eighteen," he said, taking her hand, wanting to calm her agitation.

"Eighteen," she said mournfully and then burst out in heaving sobs, slamming her hands against the mattress.

In that moment, Dez realized what a fool he had been. Anna hadn't had a clue how much time had passed. She hadn't known she had been locked away for a dozen years.

He reached for her and she flinched, rolling away and presenting her back to him. He could only listen helplessly as she cried for her lost youth and the years which had been stolen from her.

CHAPTER SIXTEEN

ANNA AWOKE ENVELOPED in warmth. She opened her eyes and saw the first rays of morning light beginning to stream into the room. She inhaled and realized why she was so warm.

Dez.

Her back was pressed against his chest. His arms enfolded her and one of his legs was atop hers. She swallowed as her throat thickened with tears.

She was old. Thirty. Over a decade had been taken from her. By her father. By Fiend and Matron. By all the cruel attendants. All for loving the man beside her and wanting to be with him.

Days had blended into weeks and months and finally years as she'd been imprisoned at Gollingham. She wondered how she could have lost track of time and then knew how easily it could occur. One day was much as the one before it and the one that followed. No dates were mentioned. No holidays celebrated. No visitors came to call with news of the outside world. Anna realized she had retreated so far within herself that time had been forgotten.

Just as she had.

A tear slid down her cheek again for the years which could never be replaced.

No wonder Dez looked so much older than she remembered. It wasn't that he was old. Thirty was a prime age for a man. His face and body had matured. He had been at war the entire time she had been at the asylum. If Dez was thirty, though, so was she. For a woman, looks faded faster. She already saw how thin she was and could feel how short her hair was. She wondered if her face had lines etched into it. She feared seeing herself in a mirror.

"Anna?"

"Yes," she answered, her voice sounding a little rusty from disuse.

His thumb stroked her forearm. "Do you think you can talk?"

"About how my father robbed me of the best years of my life?" she said, bitterness laced in her words.

He brought a hand to stroke her hair and said, "I would hope the best years are yet to come."

She turned so that she faced him. "My youth is gone. I missed my entire twenties, Dez. A time when I had thought to marry. Have children. Build a life—with you or a gentleman I would meet during my come-out. I will never be able to capture those years again."

He cupped her cheek. "No. The same is true for me. I spent the last dozen years at war. I know it was an honorable thing. To fight for king and country. But every shot I fired that felled a man. Every time my bayonet gutted an enemy soldier. Each battle I went into, I lost a piece of me." Tears welled in his eyes. "I was an excellent officer but I hated every minute of it, Anna. I hated killing strangers in the name of politics. I hated being away from England. Most of all, I hated that we had been separated. After I heard of your death, I longed for it myself on the battlefield."

"What?" she gasped.

He brushed back the hair from her brow. "Your father put out word that you had died. Dalinda wrote to me of the news. That you loaded your pockets with stones and walked into our lake and drown."

She laughed harshly. "That's exactly what I told him I would do when he told me I would be forced to wed Viscount Needham." She sniffed. "To think that he used that."

"Dalinda told me that because of the circumstances of your

death, you weren't buried in the village churchyard. When I returned to claim the earldom, that was a huge regret. Not being able to visit your grave. I didn't think your father would let me come to Shelton Park to do so." Dez sighed. "And then Tom came to see me, bringing his wife and Jessa with him."

He wiped his eyes. "Jessa and your mother were told of your death and were cautioned never to speak about you again. Jessa was young but she recalled the day you were taken away. She asked your butler about it when he was pensioned off."

"Beauchamp?"

"Yes. She was about eleven and he, too, warned her about ever mentioning you. Lord Shelton had said you were dead and you were to stay dead."

A chill caused Anna to shiver. Dez stroked her back.

"Your cousin and I went to visit Beauchamp. He confirmed you being taken away because you had been disobedient. He confirmed that you were placed in Gollingham and the general location of where it is located."

"I never liked Beauchamp. He was firmly my father's man."

"Still, his words—and the fact Dr. Cheshire had sent a request for the next year's payment—let us know you were alive. Though Cheshire never mentioned you by name, only initials."

"I had forgotten his name," she murmured.

"Didn't you see him every day?" Dez asked.

"Some days. Matron and the staff merely called him Doctor. I called him Fiend in my mind."

Dez cradled her cheek in his palm. "He can never hurt you again, Anna. Your cousin is now head of the Browning family. He feels terrible that he didn't know of your whereabouts. Jessa, too, must experience guilt."

"She was just a small girl."

He smiled. "She has turned into quite the beauty. She has your blue eyes but your mother's blond hair."

"Mama said one of her cousins had hair the shade of mine. Papa never liked it."

Running his fingers through her hair, Dez proclaimed, "I always loved it."

She reached up and tugged on it. "It is so short. I must be so ugly."

"Don't say that."

"I can't help it, Dez. I am bony and barely have any hair. I am sure my face is—"

His fingers pressed against her lips, silencing her. "Your face is the most beautiful sight I have ever seen. I love you, Anna. I have told you that several times and I will continue telling you until you believe it is true."

"Can you really love me the way I now am?" she asked sadly.

"You are more than your looks," his said fiercely. "You are kind and compassionate. You love people and flowers and music. You always think of others, be it humans or animals in need. You are intelligent and have a remarkable sense of humor. You are the sum of those things, Anna, and not merely your looks."

"I want to believe you," she said earnestly.

"You will. I guarantee it. You will grow stronger. You will add weight. Your hair will grow longer. But inside, your core, you always have been the same person I grew up with. The same girl I fell in love with. The one I still love."

He kissed her gently. The kiss held the promise of what might come between them.

If she would allow it.

"I won't ask you to marry me now," he told her. "I understand that after what you have gone through that you might never wish to wed. You may be more comfortable being the only one in charge of your life. But if the time comes when you decide you would like a partner to go through life with, then I will be here. Whether that is in a month. A year. Ten years. It doesn't matter." He smiled. "Until then, I am content to be your friend."

Anna wanted him desperately. As her friend. Her husband. Her lover. But she also thought Dez deserved much more than a broken human being. No, she wasn't broken. She had survived

Hell on earth and now stood proud and tall, knowing she had done so. It didn't mean, however, that she was the one for this wonderful man. He was now an earl. He needed a countess worthy of him. Not old, plain Miss Anna Browning.

She would let him help put her life back together because he so desperately wanted to—and she didn't think she could accomplish this alone. When the time was right, however, she would tell him that she would never take a husband.

To free him to take another as his wife.

Anna smiled. "I hope you will always be my friend, Dez. You have been my entire life."

He kissed her brow. "We should rise and get ready for the day. Coral will be here soon with breakfast for us. I also have an idea that I think you will like."

He left her to her ministrations and she heard Coral arrive. She came out from the bedchamber and the valet greeted her.

"A good morning to you, Coral," she said, a bit raspy.

"You have recovered your voice, Miss Browning," he declared. "I know you are happy to have it back."

"Miss Browning will need to keep gargling her salt water, however, and sipping on tea laced with honey," Dez added. "At least for the foreseeable future. Let me walk out with you, Coral."

She began setting out the dishes Coral had brought. Her stomach growled in hunger. At least she was getting good food and it tasted marvelous.

Dez returned and they ate and cleared the dishes. He told her to go and gargle while he began washing them. She did as he asked and then came in and began drying the plates.

"I thought we could walk again if you'd like," he suggested.

They strolled along the lakeshore. Dez pointed out a few things but had told Anna to rest her voice as much as possible in anticipation of tomorrow's visit with Jessa and Tom. They returned to the cottage and she went to lie down and rest while he sat at the desk and went over some paperwork which Coral had brought to him from Paul Lexington, whom Dez said was his estate manager.

She dozed for an hour and rose. Dez was still at work and she put on water to boil for tea. Coral had brought some raisin scones and Anna was determined to have one. She had always had a sweet tooth and would probably eat more than one scone.

When she had everything set out on the table, Dez joined her. He talked of a few incidents from their childhood and told her more about Dalinda's boys, who were nine and eleven. They seemed like a handful, which meant they took after their mischievous mother, in her opinion. Dalinda had always led Anna and Dez on a merry chase, devising all kinds of schemes in childhood. If they landed in trouble, Dez was quick to take the blame for his twin, claiming their actions had been due to his prodding. Anna had always thought it so gallant of him.

She heard noise outside and Dez said, "It's Coral returning. Come and see what he's brought."

When she stepped through the door, her heart began pounding. The valet had returned not only with the cart but two horses tied to it. She ran to them, excitement filling her.

Dez and Coral untied the horses, telling her which was his and which one she would ride. Anna stroked the horse, called Daisy, which was a deep brown in color and had a white blaze.

"Look in the cart bed, Miss Browning, and you'll find a few apples to give the horses a treat."

"Oh, thank you, Coral. That was very thoughtful of you."

"I aim to please, Miss," the valet said.

She took an apple and said to Daisy, "This is for you, my girl."

The horse made short order of the fruit and she offered one to Dez's horse, as well, not wanting his mount to feel left out.

"Shall I head to Lord Shelton's now, my lord?" Coral asked.

"Yes. Tell him Miss Browning is now speaking. That we had a lovely walk around the lake today and that we are now riding."

"What time should I say for him to call tomorrow?" Coral pressed.

Dez looked to her. "What do you think?"

She thought a moment. "I believe we should call on him," she said firmly.

"Are you certain? It would lead to many questions, you turning up with me after so many years away." He paused. "I am thinking of your reputation, Anna."

"I suppose you are right. I know in time I will need to return to Shelton Park, though." She thought a moment. "Shall we say ten o'clock?"

"Very good, Miss Browning," Coral said. "I am off to make my report." He looked to her. "Your cousin was very pleased at the news I brought him yesterday. He will be delighted at how much progress you have made in such a short time."

"Thank you, Coral. I am beginning to feel like my old self," she said.

The valet gave a jaunty wave and took up the reins, leaving the clearing.

"Are you ready to ride?" Dez asked.

Anna glanced at the gown she wore. "This would make it difficult to accomplish. Let me see if there is something else more appropriate."

She retreated into the cottage and went to the bedchamber, combing through the clothing. Though no riding habit was present, she did find a gown with a wide skirt that wouldn't restrict her movements much. She slipped from the simple gown she had worn today, not needing Dez's assistance, and changed into the new gown.

Coming back outside, she asked if he would help in securing the back and he did so. Feeling his fingers along her spine gave her a delicious feeling, making her want to kiss him again. She refrained from doing so, not wanting to be so forward—and not wanting to give him hope where their future relationship was concerned. Kissing him would only encourage his interest in her, as well as sadden her in the end. She would keep Dez as her friend and no more.

He helped her to mount Daisy and she stroked the horse,

telling her what a good girl she was and how much this ride meant to her.

They started off slowly, leaving the area since the forest was so dense, and working their way to more open land. Soon, they were cantering. Anna hadn't felt this free in so long. She and Daisy moved as one. She urged the horse on and Daisy took off. Glancing over her shoulder, she saw Dez nudge his horse and begin galloping after her. They raced across the open meadow and both pulled up when they reached the end.

"How is it?" he asked.

"Exhilarating!" she declared. "I think I missed riding almost as much as I missed you."

He laughed, the sound rich and deep, causing her insides to contract.

Anna loved Dez. He was the only man for her. She would have to free him, though. It would be foolish of him to tie himself to her. He needed a countess who glittered, one who could move easily through society. With his sister a duchess, Dez would move in high circles among Polite Society. She was a lowly viscount's daughter, one who had been locked away as mad, the *ton* made to believe she was dead by her own hand. Anna would not embarrass Dez in any way. He had done his time in the army and now he had a brilliant life ahead of him. He didn't need her as an anchor to weigh him down.

She spurred her horse on and Daisy took off. Dez gave chase and finally passed her as they reached the opposite end of the meadow. Slowing their horses, they walked them back to the cottage. Dez helped her dismount and they led the beasts to the lake, letting them drink their fill. Dez hurried back and retrieved a bucket and then poured water over the pair, cooling them off.

He handed her Daisy's reins and they led the horses back to the clearing, where Dez loosely tied them to a post on the cottage.

"Coral will return after he has visited with your cousin and take the horses back to Torville Manor. I hope you enjoyed riding."

"I did. Very much."

He seemed disappointed and Anna moved to him, the glow of the ride spilling from her. She hugged him tightly and said, "It has been a wonderful day, Dez. Riding was perfect."

She began to pull away but he held on to her. His gaze searched hers and her insides began to thrum. Anna swallowed, feeling suddenly awkward and nervous.

"I want to make every day a happy one for you," he said as he lowered his mouth to hers.

Kissing him would be wrong. She didn't want to lead him on. Yet when his lips touched hers, that wonderful jolt rippled through her and she knew she would not be able to resist his siren's call. Anna wrapped her arms around his neck and gave in to the kiss.

It was a sweet, leisurely one, with Dez nibbling and nipping on her lips and her answering him in return. Soon, it turned more heated, as they both began to take and then demand more of the other. Dez eased her mouth open and his tongue slipped inside, stroking hers. He tugged on her hair, tilting her head back, allowing him to deepen the kiss. Her insides began humming. The place between her legs started throbbing. Goosebumps sprang up on her arms.

Finally, he broke the kiss, both of them breathless, his forehead leaning against hers.

"I am sorry, Anna. I don't mean to push you too far. I know you are still recovering from your experience at Gollingham."

Anna realized they might never have this kind of time together. Alone. Isolated. She knew she couldn't have Dez for a lifetime—but she could have him for a little while. Enough to create a memory to sustain her once he had left and found happiness with another woman.

She cradled his face and brought it lower, kissing him with determination and the fever she felt.

Breaking the kiss, she said, "I want more than your kisses, Dez. I want all of you."

CHAPTER SEVENTEEN

ANNA ALMOST GIGGLED at the startled look on Dez's face.

"Do you understand what I am saying?" she asked. When he didn't reply, she said, "I want what was denied us by our fathers, Dez. What we would have had if we'd reached Gretna Green. I want that night with you. Now."

He cupped her cheeks. "Oh, Anna, do you think that is wise? You have been through a terrible ordeal. You need time to heal."

She glared at him. "I am not some fragile flower, Dez. I never have been. I am a strong woman, one so strong that she did *not* go mad when placed in a madhouse. I clung to my sanity in any way I could."

Moving away from him, she began pacing. "Do you know what it is like to sit on those hard benches all day? No conversing. No moving. Just sitting until every bone in your body aches. And those were the good days, sitting from the time they roused me and gave me a nasty gruel to eat and then escorted me to that seat. Sitting for hours upon hours upon hours."

She crossed her arms. "I won't even begin to tell you about the bad days."

Dez closed the gap between them and placed his hands on her shoulders, his face solemn.

"I saw some of what went on, Anna. What you were subjected to. I cannot imagine how you survived for so long."

Anna softened, seeing how affected he was by his trip to

Gollingham.

"Then you know what I am made of. I have come through it, out the other side, and while I know I must build up my physical strength, my character and heart and soul have never been stronger." She placed a palm against his cheek. "That is why I know my own mind, Dez. And I want to couple with you. You are my one true love. I owe it to myself to experience the act of love with you."

He enfolded her in his arms, kissing the top of her head. "If that is what you want, my love, then I refuse to disappoint you."

Sweeping her into his arms, he carried her inside the cottage, kicking the door closed with his foot. He crossed to the bedchamber and then eased her to her feet. Their gazes met and Anna was moved by the depths of love she saw in Dez's eyes.

He kissed her softly and then said, "I plan to worship you, Anna Browning, the way you were meant to be worshipped."

He undressed her slowly, kissing her in all different places. Where her neck met her shoulder. The inside of her elbow. Behind her right knee. Each kiss brought a delicious thrill and her heart sped up. Her breathing grew shallow and rapid. Her blood buzzed in her ears.

Dez guided her to the bed and helped her to lie down. Anna then watched as he removed his own layers of clothing, her mouth growing dry at the masculine beauty of his form. He had broad shoulders and narrow hips. Muscular thighs and beautiful calves. Flat belly and muscled chest. Her fingers itched to touch him.

He lay on the bed beside her, on his side, and his hands began roaming her body. She tried not to be embarrassed, knowing the yellow, faded bruises couldn't possibly be attractive, yet he seemed to ignore them. He kissed his way up and down her body, bringing chills of delight. She began touching him, too, gliding her hands along the planes of muscle, seeing them bunch beneath her fingertips.

Her breasts, though smaller now than before, seemed to hold

him spellbound as he caressed them with his hands and mouth. His tongue circled her nipples, bringing them to attention, and then he sucked hard on them, causing the place between her legs to throb almost painfully. She shifted, wondering if he could satisfy whatever urges she felt, desperate for him to touch her there and yet too afraid to ask.

Somehow, Dez knew what she needed. His hands slid along her legs, up her calves and thighs, back and forth. Each long stroke brought his fingers closer to her core. And then he touched it, a finger gliding along the seam of her sex, back and forth, almost sending her into a frenzy. Slowly, he parted the folds and slipped a finger inside her, shocking her and yet filling her need.

"You are wet for me," he said. "That means you want me."

Anna smiled. "I have always wanted you. Even when I didn't know I did," she said playfully.

A second finger joined the first and the caresses became longer. Deeper. They began to cause her to writhe. To whimper. All the while, Dez kissed her, long, drugging kisses that caused her body to grow fevered. Her fingers pushed into his thick hair and she held tight, never wanting him to leave her.

A pressure began building within her, something frenzied and exciting. New and bold and wonderful. His fingers continued working their magic, urging her on to some new, wonderful place. Then she seemed to explode within, erupting as a long dormant volcano might, something wild spilling from her. Anna heard cries and couldn't believe they came from her. She rode the crashing waves, Dez constantly kissing her. She clung to him, her moans becoming a shout and then she called his name a dozen times before falling limp.

He hovered above her, smiling. "Was it good?"

She managed a weak smile. "Very good, Lord Torrington. I would say remarkably good." She frowned. "But what of you?"

Glancing down, she saw his member at full attention and touched it, her fingers encircling it. He groaned and placed his hand over hers, stilling it.

"Not now, Anna."

"Why not? I must do for you what you did for me."

"That is for later. When we are wed. Only then will we consummate our love."

She hadn't known that wasn't what had just occurred but it made sense. She knew a couple somehow joined their bodies. That his cock needed to be inside her.

She squeezed it gently and he moaned. "I told you I want all of you, Desmond Bretton. That. Means. All."

He kissed her, hard and demanding, almost making her forget she held on to him.

Anna broke the kiss. "I will not be satisfied until we join together."

She began stroking him and he let her. His breathing grew harsh. His face almost pained.

"All right," he said roughly.

She released her hold on him, glad to claim victory.

"This will hurt," he warned. "It does the first time. Never after that."

"I don't care," she told him, knowing it would be the only time but happy to suffer whatever pain there was in order to make him happy.

His fingers teased her again, building her anticipation again, and then he pushed into her swiftly. The pain wasn't as bad as he had said. She had suffered far worse under Fiend and Matron. Anna wrapped her arms about him.

"Are you . . . did I hurt you much?" he asked.

"I am fine." To show him, she moved against him—and it felt divine.

"You are more than fine," he growled, kissing her. "You are perfect."

Dez began moving in and out. Instinctively, Anna rose to meet him. Their dance of love went from slow to frenzied. In the end, they both cried aloud, having reached a plain of heaven.

Afterward, she lay nestled in his arms, a drowsiness coming

over her. He stroked her arm.

"I am glad you felt safe enough with me to make love," he said.

"You have always made me feel safe, Dez. From the time we were children. When I climbed a tree, I knew you were below me and would catch me if I fell. When I swam to the center of the lake, I knew if I tired, you would never let me drown. You have always been my safe haven, Dez, even at the asylum. I would think of you and all the bad things would fall away."

He kissed her brow. "I love you so much, Anna. When I thought you were dead, a part of me died. Now that I have found you again, I feel whole and complete." He hesitated. "I know it seems soon, with everything you have undergone, but when you are ready I want to wed you."

Anna knew this moment had been coming. She steeled herself, determined to not give in to him, no matter how persuasive he tried to be.

"I don't ever plan to wed, Dez."

She sensed him tense. "Never? But . . . I thought you trusted me."

"I do. I always will."

"Is this because of the time you spent at Gollingham?" he demanded. "You are not to blame for that, Anna. You are a person of worth. I do not judge you for your time there."

"I can never marry," she insisted softly, knowing others would judge her—and him. She couldn't allow this wonderful man to be sucked into the vortex that would surround her, dragging him down with her. She loved him too much to see him hurt and ostracized by the *ton*.

Dez released her and sat up. "I never would have made love to you if I thought we wouldn't wed. I would never have compromised you."

She captured his hand and brought it to her lips, kissing it tenderly. "I appreciate all you have done for me. You saved me, Dez, but I cannot commit to you in that way."

Anna saw the hurt in his eyes. Hurt she had put there. She understood he would hurt for some time over her decision but, in the long run, he would thank her for allowing him to get on with his life. He could create a new one for himself, away from the war, now that he was the earl. He would wed. Have children. Find happiness. It was the thought of Dez being happy and fulfilled that made her push him away so hard now.

His gaze searched hers. "Are you certain, Anna? Certain this is what you truly want?"

"I am."

Without a word, he moved from the bed, collecting his clothes. He left the bedchamber, closing the door quietly behind him. She didn't move. If she did, she might rush after him. Hurl herself at him. Tell him she had made a mistake and that he should forget everything she had just said.

After some minutes, Anna rose and washed away all traces of Dez. She dressed. Combed her hair. Left the bedchamber.

Dez was already dressed himself, looking immaculate and handsome and stoic.

"Are you hungry?" he asked, his eyes not meeting hers.

"Yes," she responded, having no appetite but not wanting him to blame himself for that.

They prepared the dinner Coral had left for them, placing items on plates and sitting at the table in silence. She forced down as much as she could, her throat so tight with emotion that it hurt to swallow. Together, they cleared the remnants of the meal and washed and dried the few dishes.

Dez broke the silence. "I am going for a walk."

He left the cottage and Anna couldn't help herself. She followed him at a distance, worried about his state of mind. He went down to the lake and stood surveying it for a long time. Finally, he began shedding his clothes until he was naked. She couldn't help but admire the figure he cut. She loved his body. She had loved what he had done with it to her. She loved him. But she also knew she was doing what was best for him. Freeing him from the burden of her would be the greatest gift Anna could ever give him.

He swam, his strokes long, far across the water. She watched and waited until he finally headed back toward shore and began wading in. Knowing he was safe, she left the hiding place behind a large oak and hurried back to the cottage. She climbed into bed, her clothes still on, and pulled the bedclothes up, closing her eyes and pretending she was asleep.

Dez never entered the bedchamber, though. Her head—and heart—began to ache, knowing the hurt she had caused him. Silent tears streamed down her cheeks until she finally fell asleep.

CHAPTER EIGHTEEN

ANNA AWOKE, HER belly aching and her head pounding. She reached out and found no one beside her. She had forced a break between her and Dez yet she didn't know if she would be able to survive it. She reminded herself of what she had told him. That she was strong beyond measure. She would be resolute and endure whatever she must in order to free him. He didn't understand now the favor she did for him but he would in time. Perhaps one day, they might once more be friends.

And she would always have the memories of their time together.

She readied herself for the day, knowing she would be seeing Jessa and her cousin. The last time she had seen Tom they had both been children. Her father and his had some falling out and the two families had lost contact. She had wondered why but Mama had told her never to bring it up. As she matured, Anna believed it had to do with the fact Papa was disappointed and frustrated that Mama had not produced an heir for him and that his brother's son would become the next Lord Shelton.

Going into the other room, she saw Dez sitting at the table. He greeted her with the utmost politeness and offered her tea. She hated the stiffness between them but knew she couldn't encourage him. It would be wrong to give him hope only to dash those hopes again.

Coral arrived and it was obvious he sensed the gulf between

them. He opened the basket he brought, setting down poached eggs and a rasher of ham, along with sliced berries and cream.

"Are you doing well today, my lady?" the valet asked after Dez excused himself and left the cottage.

"Yes, Coral, I am very well. In fact, I will be returning to my home with my cousin when he calls upon me today."

The servant's eyes widened in surprise and she added, "You'd best take Daisy home with you when you leave."

He nodded, sadness shadowing his face.

"Will you look after Lord Torrington for me?" she asked. "He will need you."

"Of course, my lady," the valet agreed. "It is my responsibility to do so."

She met his gaze. "You know what I mean, Coral. He may be saddened by my departure. I only want the best for him."

"I see. Never fear, my lady. I will look after him to the best of my ability."

"Thank you, Coral."

The servant left and Anna found she couldn't eat anything. Dez had left his breakfast untouched and she didn't think he would return for it. So she cleaned up and then settled into a chair, waiting for her sister and cousin to arrive. She had chosen a pale yellow gown the color of sunshine and hoped it didn't hang on her too much.

She heard noise in the clearing and went to the door. Opening it, she saw Dez helping a woman dismount and then shaking the hand of the other rider. Her throat closed up with emotion as the woman turned.

Jessa . . .

Her sister had been only six years old when Anna had been removed from Shelton Park. Now, she was a young woman, fully matured. Her golden hair was piled high atop her head, little wisps of curls escaping to frame her face. She was tall, with a tiny waist. Love swelled within Anna.

"Jessa!" she cried at the same time her sister called Anna's name.

They rushed to one another, falling into each other's arms, tears of joy flowing. Anna clung to her sister for a moment and then pulled away to see her.

"You grew up!" she exclaimed. "You are so beautiful, Jessa. Or should I call you Jessica?"

The two women laughed. Her sister had been given the name Jessica but she had trouble saying it when she began to speak. It had come out Jessa and Anna and her mother had begun calling her that.

"I am still Jessa. Only Papa referred to me as Jessica and that was rare." She paused. "You know how it was. He had no use for a female. I think he often forgot I was around. My governess did her best to keep me out of his way."

Anna smoothed Jessa's hair. "I am sorry I missed seeing you grow up. Why, you must be eighteen now. Old enough to make your come-out."

"I will do so next Season. Papa died three months ago, else I would have done so this year."

She hugged her sister again. "We have much to catch up on." She released her sister and turned toward her cousin. "Tom. How very glad I am to see you after all these years."

The new Lord Shelton embraced her and then said, "I am happy to see you looking so bright-eyed and lively, Anna."

She took his hands. "I am sure I was a fright when you arrived at Gollingham." She squeezed them. "Thank you for bringing me from that place of horror, Tom."

Her cousin looked at Dez. "It was Torrington's forcefulness that helped remove you from the asylum, Cousin. Legally, I had the power to do so since I am now head of our family but this man should receive the credit for the way he stood up to Dr. Cheshire."

Anna thought if given the chance she could easily kill Fiend for all that he had put her and the other patients through. She refrained from saying so, aware she would always need to watch what she said in the future, knowing others would tread lightly around her. Even teasing might be misconstrued and she wanted to be above reproach. She didn't want the situation to color Jessa's chances of making a match.

The sunshine suddenly seemed too bright. Anna felt herself tiring and needed to sit. Or perhaps it as the penetrating look that Dez gave her which she avoided.

"I have also expressed my appreciation to Dez," she told Tom, her voice a little unsteady. "Would you and Jessa like to come in?"

Her sister linked her arm through Anna's and they strolled toward the cottage and entered it. Anna felt relieved to be out of the warm day and went to sit on the settee. Dez and Tom followed them inside.

"It's a bit rustic but we can offer you some tea," she told their visitors.

"No, we don't need anything," Jessa said. "I am just thrilled to be sitting next to you. Oh, Anna, you don't know how awful it was to think you were dead all these years. And to now find you alive." She paused. "What was the asylum like?"

Anna stiffened. Though she heard the concern in Jessa's voice and knew she meant no harm by her question, it left her speechless.

"Jessa, Gollingham is something Anna must put behind her," Dez said gently, speaking up for Anna. "Although you are Anna's sister and love her, you must understand that she may never be able to talk about the horrible time she spent there. She needs to put it firmly in her past—and look to her present."

She nodded, her eyes conveying her gratitude to him. "Dez is right." Echoing his words to her, she said to Jessa, "I am a person of worth. I can't blame myself for Papa's actions."

Jessa threw her arms around Anna. "Oh, I am so sorry. It was thoughtless of me to force you to talk about it." She pulled away. "Tom was so worried when he arrived at Shelton Park but other than you looking pale and thin, you seem like the old Anna. My

Anna."

Anna knew she would never be that young woman again. She could never erase what Fiend and Matron had done to her. What she could do is not let them rule any of her life. She was responsible for herself now. She was alive and outside the asylum and free. That was what was important.

"Tell me of home. Of our tenants. Of what you did growing up," she encouraged. "You and Tom."

Jessa and Tom took turns talking of the years Anna had missed, with Tom finishing up by telling them of his recent marriage after last Season.

"I wanted to bring my wife today to meet you but I did not want to overwhelm you. She is eager to meet you, though." He smiled. "I think the two of you will get along splendidly."

Dez cleared his throat. "I know I was the one to cease talk of Gollingham but I do have a question for you, Anna."

She braced herself, not wanting to be dragged back into that quagmire. "What?" she asked tersely.

"Did you know a Lady Jergens while you were there?"

"I know who she is. We would surreptitiously share our names upon arrival but I know little about her or any of the other patients. Why they were brought there." She paused. "You recall the circumstances."

She saw he remembered how the patients sat in silence for hours, physically close to one another yet so very far apart.

"I believe I can help free Lady Jergens," he said quietly.

"How?" she asked. "You have no legal authority over her."

"She spoke to Shelton and me briefly before she was led away."

Fear quickened in her belly, knowing what the consequences would have been for the woman by having spoken to an outsider.

"I mean to help her," Dez said. "She was placed at the asylum by her husband but she revealed they had not consummated the marriage. That legal technicality would be grounds for an annulment, I believe. Her father would be the one responsible for her. Not Lord Jergens."

He pushed a hand through his hair. "Even if it's just the one, I will move heaven and earth to get her out from under Cheshire's grasp."

Anna felt her heart burst with new love for him. "You are a knight in shining armor, Dez. I hope you can save as many as you can."

She watched him as he considered her words.

"Perhaps you are right, Anna. There may be more that I can do."

Silence blanketed the room and then Jessa said brightly, "I heard you rode yesterday. That man, Coral, told us you did. You used to be so fond of riding, Anna. How was it?"

The talk turned to horses and how much she had enjoyed riding Daisy.

"I plan to ride every day now that I can," she declared.

"I told you I would make my come-out next year," Jessa said. "Will you be home by then Anna? Would you come to London and help me?"

It had been so long since she had made her own come-out. Just a few, brief weeks before she and Dez had made for Scotland.

"The *ton* thinks I am dead," she said flatly. "If I show up, half of Polite Society would be struck with apoplexy. No, Jessa, I plan to remain in the country." She looked to her cousin. "In fact, if you will allow it, Tom, I would like to go home with you today."

Dez shot to his feet. Anna watched as he started to protest and then said, "You must do what you feel is best, Anna."

She knew her words had wounded him to his core but that he was gentleman enough to let her go.

"I do think returning to my family and Shelton Park is the right thing to do," she said.

"We would be delighted to have you back at home, Anna," Tom said.

Anna focused on Dez, who now sat. "Would you mind if I took Dalinda's clothes with me? Looking at Jessa, she is far taller than I am. If I borrowed any gowns from her, they would drag the floor."

"They are yours," Dez said. "Dalinda hasn't worn them in over a decade. She would be glad that you are getting some use out of them."

Jessa took Anna's hand. "Oh, you will get new gowns, Anna, once we fatten you up. It will be fun choosing fabrics, won't it? Why, we can even start thinking about what gowns I will need for my own come-out."

As Jessa prattled on, Anna could feel Dez slowly withdrawing. She met his eyes and his look told her that he understood.

"Shall we leave then?" she asked. "Give me a few minutes in which to pack."

"I can help you," Jessa volunteered and the two sisters went into the bedchamber.

Anna showed her the valises and they made quick work of placing the borrowed gowns inside them.

Returning to the other room, Dez offered to collect the luggage and disappeared.

Tom said, "The carriage is nearby. We couldn't bring it all the way to the cottage."

Dez entered with the suitcases in hand. Tom took one and they set out for the carriage, reaching it after a few minutes' walk. A footman handed her inside the vehicle and Jessa and Tom joined her.

"Goodbye, Dez," she said, doing her best to keep her face void of emotion.

"Goodbye, Anna," he replied. He looked as if he wished to say more but glanced away.

As the carriage started up, Anna couldn't look back though she longed for a last glance at him. She thought if she did, she might turn to a pillar of salt as Lot's wife did.

Anna hoped he would have the strength and courage to move forward. As far as she was concerned, Dez Bretton would always have her heart.

CHAPTER NINETEEN

London

DEZ HADN'T BEEN in his family's London townhouse since he'd been sent packing, escorted to his new regiment by two ruffians who never let him out of their sight until he had been delivered to his commanding officer. The place had never felt like home to him because he and Dalinda had spent so little time here. They had been left in the country a majority of the time, only coming to London on rare occasions. Dalinda had spent a few weeks in the townhouse, thanks to her making her come-out, but she had not been back since her marriage to Gilford.

It had been difficult to write to his twin but he had done so, letting her know that Anna had been found alive at Gollingham Asylum. Dez had tried to write dispassionately about the circumstances but he remained haunted. By how he had found Anna. And by how she had left him. His heart told him that she loved him, as he did her, but she had some foolish notion that they couldn't be together because of her time at the asylum. He had picked up on that when she referenced the *ton* being shocked by her return from the dead.

She was right. Once Polite Society discovered she was alive, it would only be a matter of time before someone found out where she had been and spread ugly rumors. That was the likely reason she wouldn't accompany Jessa to town for her come-out. Anna would want her sister to secure a husband before her presence was made known, else it would jeopardize Jessa's chances of ever making a worthwhile match.

Dez believed Anna thought to protect him, as well, from the gossipmongers of society. He didn't care what they said of him. He was determined to wed Anna. They belonged together. Still, he knew despite what she said that she had to be emotionally fragile after enduring so many years locked away from the world. He told himself he would give her time to adjust being back. Only then would he pursue her in earnest. Dez had always had a stubborn streak. When it came to Anna, he would do whatever it took to convince her they belonged together.

In the meantime, he wanted to do what he could to rescue Lady Jergens. He had already put steps into motion over the last week, having met with the head of the Bow Street Runners, who assigned a man named Haggard to the case. Dez had explained to the runner in detail everything he knew about Gollingham Asylum and Lady Jergens and why he believed there was a strong possibility of liberating the woman from being a patient.

Haggard agreed and Dez pressed further, asking that the runner go to Gollingham and see if he could obtain a list of all the patients at the facility. He explained that if there were even one woman that he might be able to help, he wanted to do so and had given the man one hundred pounds to use as bribes, as well as traveling expenses. Haggard had left immediately for Hampshire and was gone four days. When he returned, the agent had a handwritten list of twenty-three women. Beside each name was listed the man who had committed her to the institute. Dez didn't ask how Haggard had gotten the information and the runner hadn't volunteered how he came to possess it.

What he did ask was that the agent find out what he could about the men and women on the list. If they could find another circumstance similar to Lady Jergens', then he would take action. For now, he concentrated on her case.

He made his way to the drawing room because he was expecting guests. Dez had written to Lord Morton, whom Haggard discovered was Lady Jergens' father, and asked the earl to call upon Dez, bringing along his solicitor and physician. He stressed that it was a private, urgent matter, one which he couldn't explain except in person, and begged the earl to adhere to his request for a meeting in person. Morton had responded in the affirmative, probably curious as to why a former officer and new peer would seek him out.

Entering the drawing room, he found Haggard already present and greeted him. The agent was of average height and weight, with brown hair and brown eyes, not memorable in any way. It was probably what made him such a good investigator, along with his keen intelligence.

"Thank you for coming today," Dez told the runner.

"I am happy to be here. I hope Lord Morton will come and be as eager as we are to get Lady Jergens out of that awful place."

Haggard had shared that he had been inside the asylum once, late at night, and even someone hardened by all that he had seen had been shaken by his observations. He had told Dez that he would stay on the case as long as needed and hoped they could get as many women out of the asylum as possible.

His butler entered. "Lord Morton. Dr. Caymon. And Mr. Black."

"Thank you, Johnson," Dez said, stepping toward his guests. "Lord Morton, thank you for coming."

Skepticism filled the earl's face. "This is Dr. Caymon, my personal physician, and Mr. Black, my solicitor." He frowned. "I have no idea what you are up to, Torrington. The only reason I came is because you aren't your brother. He was a rake of the worst sort and a drunken ass." He sniffed. "Of course, I have no idea who or what you are. No one in London does, other than you were in the military."

"Yes, Lord Morton. I served a dozen years in His Majesty's Army, attaining the rank of major."

"Hmm. I am a former naval officer myself. Very well. Let's get this done."

Dez indicated seats and the five men took each took one.

"I would like to introduce you to Mr. Haggard, of the Bow Street Runners."

Distaste crossed the earl's face. "Get to the point, man."

He took a calming breath. "The point, my lord, is your daughter. Lady Jergens."

Morton drew in a quick breath. "You have news of her?" he asked anxiously. "Jergens is even worse than your brother. I learned too late that he is a dissolute gambler and skirt chaser. He has cut off all contact between Alice and me. I see her at no social events. My letters to her are returned unopened."

"That is because Jergens committed his wife to a madhouse."

Horror crossed the earl's face. "No!" he gasped as both the physician and solicitor shifted uncomfortably.

Then Morton shook his head, tears brimming in his eyes. "Then my Alice is lost to me. I know the law. A husband exercises full rights over his wife."

"*If* he is a true husband," Dez said.

Immediately, he explained how he had met Lady Jergens in the asylum while helping his neighbor retrieve his own relative and what she had been able to reveal to him before she had been taken away.

"If this is the case," Mr. Black said, "Lady Alice is still legally married and the marriage could not be annulled. Non-consummation is not grounds for an annulment."

"Then what is?" Dez demanded. "I am appalled that Jergens wed her for her dowry and never touched her."

The solicitor said, "The grounds for annulment include three instances. One is impotence—and a couple must have been wed three years before this charge can be brought." He cleared his throat. "Insanity is another instance. Very few families are willing to seek an annulment claiming this since it taints the entire family. From what you say, Lord Torrington, Lady Jergens could actually *be* sane but has been legally declared to be mad. This does occur when a man wants to discard his wife, I am afraid."

Dez began to lose hope but asked, "What is the third circumstance? You mentioned three."

"Fraud," Mr. Black said. "This would involve promises in the marriage that were not kept."

"What kind of promises?" demanded Lord Morton.

Black thought a moment. "Breach of contract might include a non-consenting bride at the ceremony, which wasn't the case with Lady Jergens. Or a promise of housing that has already been sold. A vanished dowry."

He jumped on that. "Wouldn't Jergens' use of the dowry apply in the case?"

Black thought a moment. "I did draw up the marriage settlements, along with Lord Morton." He turned to the earl. "Do you remember the clause in regard to where your daughter would live if Lord Jergens predeceased her and no heir had been born, allowing his lordship's younger brother to assume the title?"

"I do," the earl said. "Alice was to be given an unentailed estate in Sussex. Why do you ask?"

"We should investigate that at once," Black recommended. "If Jergens' debts are so large and the estate unentailed, he might have sold it—which would breach the marriage contracts established."

Morton's eyes narrowed. "I wouldn't put it past the bastard. He is young and arrogant. He would think he would outlive Alice—and me. If I weren't around to hold him to the marriage settlement, and poor Alice was already locked away, he would believe he could get away with it."

"If that is the case," Black continued, "then we could have the marriage annulled due to fraud. Jergens would have to return the entire dowry, which I am sure would be impossible, considering his gambling debts."

"I don't care about the damned dowry!" shouted Lord Morton. "I just want my Alice back." He looked to Dez. "I have heard rumors of these places. Is it as horrifying as they say?"

"You will want to remove Lady Alice as soon as possible," he said gently. He turned to the solicitor. "As a peer, I wasn't aware of non-consummation not being grounds for an annulment. I doubt the physician running the asylum or any attendant would be, either."

Understanding dawned in the earl's eyes. "You are saying we should go and claim that anyway in order to have Alice removed and placed into my custody."

"I do," Dez said. "Even if Mr. Black cannot prove fraud and annul the marriage, she would be free of that place. I know legally Lord Jergens could simply send her back—but he would have to find her first. You could have her go abroad. Even to America. Anywhere would be better than Gollingham."

"I agree," Lord Morton said firmly.

"My carriage is waiting and we can leave for Hampshire immediately. We could be there by late afternoon." Dez hesitated. "That is, if you would allow me to accompany you."

Morton sprang to his feet. "I am ready and would appreciate your company, Torrington." He looked to the two men who had accompanied him. "Will you go with me?" he pleaded.

Dez added, "Mr. Black will be able to explain the so-called legalities to the physician in charge. I thought it would be wise to ask Dr. Caymon to come, as well, so that he might examine Lady Alice and verify that her hymen is intact. Even though we now know that is not grounds for annulment, I believe we can get away with it and spirit her away." He gestured to Haggard. "Mr. Haggard helped me track you down, Lord Morton, and verified the connection between you and Lady Jergens."

The earl went to Haggard and offered his hand. "I regret I was so dismissive of you before, Mr. Haggard. I offer you my thanks from the bottom of my heart."

The runner shook Morton's hand. "I only hope you can remove your daughter from Gollingham, my lord. Others, too."

The earl frowned. "Others?"

"Yes. I have a list of the other patients who have been committed to the madhouse. Lord Torrington is having me look into each one to see if there is a possibility of freeing any of these women, such as Lady Alice."

"Then I wish you the best of luck, young man." Morton looked to Dez. "And I will pay for Mr. Haggard's services, reimbursing you for anything you have spent, as well as any other costs incurred with regard to these other women."

"That isn't necessary, my lord," Dez assured the earl.

"It may not be to you but I want to help in whatever way I can. Shall we split the bill?"

He grinned and stuck out his hand. "You have a bargain."

The men shook and he suggested the earl also take his carriage.

"Why?"

"Having just removed a patient from the same facility, I can tell you that Lady Alice will be quite fragile, both mentally and physically. I am not saying she is mad. She seemed far from it but she has suffered inhumane treatment and been without hope. She may not wish to be in the presence of others as we return to London. I would be happy for your physician and solicitor to return with me. As it is, you will need to stay overnight. It will be too late to begin the journey to London. Grantham is the nearest village to Gollingham. Alton is a bit larger and might be a better place to stay the night."

"I will take your advice, Torrington," Morton said. "Would you ride with us for a bit? At least to whatever inn we stay at. My daughter might recognize you and be comforted by your presence."

"I would be happy to do so."

"Then we should leave at once," the earl declared.

"I can have messages sent to your homes and offices," Dez offered to Black and Caymon.

Both men took him up on the offer and they quickly dashed off notes. Black said his would ask for his associate to look into

Lord Jergens' financial affairs and determine whether or not he had sold the estate, which was to have gone to his wife, according to the marriage settlements. Dez gave the notes to his footman to deliver. With that accomplished, the five men ventured outside, where Dez's carriage waited next to Morton's.

"I won't be going along, Lord Morton," Haggard said. "You have the men you need with you to bring your girl home. I will remain in London, running down leads on the list I brought back."

"Thank you again, Mr. Haggard," the earl said. "I will ask to see you once I return to London with Alice."

"Very good, my lord," Haggard said and took his leave.

The earl asked Dez to ride with them and he instructed his coachman to follow. The driver already knew the final destination and nodded.

✌

THEY REACHED GOLLINGHAM at close to four o'clock that afternoon. As they disembarked, Dez told his coachman that they would return to Alton and spend the night in order to allow the horses to rest.

"Do you have need of me, my lord?" the driver asked, glancing up at the structure before them.

"If I need an extra pair of fists, I will know where to come," he replied. "Hopefully, it won't come to that."

He rejoined the others and they made their way to the door. Lord Morton pounded on the door and shouted, "Open up!"

After a few moments, the same servant who had answered before when Dez had come calling with Shelton opened the door. His eyes darted among the four men standing in front of him and paused when they landed on Dez.

"No. Not again," he proclaimed and slammed the door in their faces.

Before the attendant could throw the lock, Dez turned the knob and pushed it forward forcefully. It slammed into the man and he went crashing to the floor.

Quickly, he scrambled to his feet and began shouting, "Matron! Matron!" as he scurried up the staircase.

"Follow me," he told the others and he hurriedly ascended the stairs in pursuit of the man.

They reached the landing and turned to go up the next flight when a commanding voice from above said, "Stop right there."

For a moment, he obeyed and saw a large woman with hair as gray as iron and a sour look upon her face. Behind her was the attendant, who said, "He's the one in front. The one who took her. He's back again."

Matron stared down at them. Dez ignored her glare and continued up the stairs, willing the others to follow him as he had done on the battlefield so many times. They reached the top and the woman had to step back to accommodate them.

"We are here for Lady Jergens," he said calmly. "Fetch Dr. Cheshire."

"He ain't here," she said belligerently.

"It doesn't matter." Dez indicated the man to his left. "This is Lord Morton, her father."

Matron sneered. "A father won't do much good in this circumstance," she said haughtily. "Only the lady's husband can extract her. From what I know, that will never happen. That woman will die in here, decades from now."

Lord Morton choked. Whether in sorrow or rage, Dez didn't know but he did know a bully when he saw one and stepped toward her, forcing her further back until she bumped against the wall.

Drawing near to her face, he hissed, "You *will* send someone for Cheshire. In the meantime, you will find Lady Jergens. The law is on our side, Madam. She is not Lady Jergens at all but rather Lady Alice."

As he stepped back, he saw both anger—and fear—in the

woman's eyes.

Mr. Black crisply said, "The marriage is to be annulled because no marriage existed. Marital relations did not occur, thus rendering things invalid."

Understanding lit Matron's eyes. She remained defiant, however, as she said, "That will be up to Dr. Cheshire to decide." Glancing to her right, she told the hovering attendant, "Fetch the doctor. Be quick about it."

He hurried away, throwing a glance over his shoulder.

"Produce Lady Alice," Dez said, his voice ringing out.

"I am here," a voice called.

Looking past Matron, he saw the usual line of silent women hunched on the hard benches they inhabited for all of their waking hours. One woman had risen, however, and unsteadily made her way toward them.

"Papa?" she asked as she drew closer. "Papa?"

"Alice. Alice." Morton rushed to her and wrapped her in his arms.

She began weeping profusely, clinging to him. Dez had to look away because the emotions flooding him were so powerful. He glanced to his companions and saw they, too, had a hard time watching the reunion between father and daughter.

"Stay here," Matron said and she moved down the staircase.

Dez walked down the corridor, looking at the various patients. Not a one met his eyes or said anything. No one moved other than the attendants, who began hurrying off, making themselves scarce. He withdrew the list Haggard had composed from his pocket.

"Miss Stone?" he called.

When no one replied, he repeated the name. Finally, a voice said, "I am here."

He started toward her and came to a halt. "I want to talk to as many of you as I can before Dr. Cheshire arrives. I need to ask why you were placed here."

In the next few minutes, Dez tried to speak to every woman

on Haggard's list. Seven of them knew their names and little else so he moved on, eager to gain as much information as he could in the short amount of time he had. Three patients looked at him in such fear when he addressed them that he believed they regretted even giving their names to him. All three became mute afterward, despite his pleas that he was here to help them. Regretting having to abandon them, Dez again shouted out a few names from his list, despair filling him. Two of the women came forward when he did so but they hurried back to their seats when he tried to question them regarding why they were placed at Gollingham.

He tried again, his desperation growing. Another two women began weeping hysterically, waving him away as he approached, fear evident on their faces. Having remembered the punishments Anna told him about, he understood their reluctance to speak out and suffer such dire consequences.

Finally, the dam broke. Nine of the patients sprang from their seats and surrounded him, revealing why they had been put away. Only two from this group, a Miss Stone and Lady Eastman, were lucid enough to answer his questions rapidly and succinctly and seemed to have a chance of being helped.

"I cannot promise you anything," he told the two women, "but I will speak to your families and see if I can have you removed."

Lady Eastman burst out into tears, returning to her bench and placing her head in her hands.

Miss Stone said, "Thank you, my lord. For giving me hope." She kissed his hand. "Thank you."

She, too, returned to the bench she had occupied and, minutes later, Matron returned with Dr. Cheshire in tow. Dez hid his dismay, knowing he would not be able to help the vast majority of the women locked away in this madhouse. He steeled himself, though, ready to confront the warden of this asylum once again.

The physician glared at him. "You're back again, stirring up trouble, I see. What is it now, Lord Torrington?"

"Find a room where Lady Jergens can be examined," Dez said and nodded to Mr. Black.

Quickly, the solicitor outlined the case and then Dr. Caymon stepped forward.

"I will examine the patient to see if her hymen has been breached. If it hasn't, then she is not the wife of Lord Jergens but Lady Alice. Mr. Black can serve as a witness and testify to the court, if necessary."

"And she will be leaving with me—her father," Lord Morton roared, his arm about his daughter, who huddled against him.

Dez approached her. "My lady, do you remember me?"

"I do, my lord. You came back."

"Have you heard what has been said and understand?"

"Yes. I will swear in court if I must that Jergens never touched me beyond a few kisses during our courtship. That he only wanted me for my dowry."

"Do you understand why Dr. Caymon must examine you?" he pressed. "And that Dr. Cheshire must be in the room to confirm the diagnosis?"

"Yes," she said, her tears beginning to fall. "Will you go with me?" she begged.

"Wouldn't you rather have your father with you?" he asked gently.

She looked to her father. "Papa, I don't want you to see me like that. Surely, you understand."

The earl's eyes filled with tears. "I do, my precious. Go with them now. Lord Torrington will protect you."

She eased away from her father and gripped Dez's arm.

"I am ready."

He turned and saw the fury on both Cheshire's and Matron's faces but they both wheeled and moved down the hallway. Dez led Lady Alice while Black and Caymon followed. They entered a room similar to the one Anna had slept in.

"Lie on the cot," barked Cheshire. He now held a lantern in

his hand. "Raise your skirt and spread your legs."

Lady Alice turned to Dez. "Will you stay by my side? Hold my hand?"

"It would be an honor, my lady."

She went and laid on the cot. Dez moved to where he was close to her head and knelt beside her. He took her hand and she gripped his as she pulled up the rag she wore.

Dr. Caymon moved closer and instructed her to put her feet flat on the cot, bending her knees and spreading her legs. She did as asked, squeezing her eyes shut. Dez watched her face as the doctor called for Cheshire to hold the lamp close as he examined her.

Moments later, he rose and said, "She is intact." The physician stared at Cheshire. "See for yourself. And if you break her hymen and she bleeds, I will know what you did."

Cheshire knelt before Lady Alice. Dez kept concentrating on her face. She flinched when Cheshire touched her but she didn't cry out.

"You are correct. Lord Jergens did not see to his duty. Get her out of here." Cheshire stalked to the door and then turned. To Dez, he said, "I hope never to see you here again."

"And I hope you rot in the bowels of Hell," he snapped.

Cheshire left the room. Dr. Caymon lowered Lady Alice's skirt and Dez helped her sit up. When she stood, her knees buckled and he swept her up, carrying her past all the silent patients and out of the asylum. Lord Morton's footman set the steps down and Dez climbed into the carriage with her. Lord Morton followed and closed the door.

"The others will follow us," he said tersely. "I only wish I could kill that doctor and Jergens. Black says to leave everything to him."

As they drove away, Dez vowed to return and do everything in his power to free Lady Eastman and Miss Stone.

Finally, Lady Alice spoke. She scooted from Dez's lap and sat next to him.

"How can I ever repay you, my lord?" she asked softly. "I will never be able to show my gratitude."

"By living a good life," he replied. "The life you were meant to live. It will take time to recover but you are now free."

"What of the woman you came for—Miss Browning? How does she fare?"

He smiled. "Thank you for asking. She is doing quite well. She has returned to her family and was overjoyed to be reunited with her sister, who was only six when they were separated."

A smile lit her face upon hearing that news. "Miss Browning was the strongest of us all, my lord. She would slip small bits of bread to those who looked as if they needed it most. She would catch your hand and squeeze it reassuringly when the attendants were distracted. When Matron became perturbed at a patient, Miss Browning would step forward and ask to take their punishment. She was so strong and unwavering. I admired her a great deal."

Pride filled Dez at hearing of Anna's incredible bravery. "Miss Browning is very resilient," he said, his voice breaking with emotion.

Lady Alice studied him. "You love her, don't you?"

"I do," he confirmed. "I don't know if she will ever be able to return my love, though. Her experience in the asylum was difficult."

She nodded. "Miss Browning was quite rebellious. She dared to do what none of us did. She fought back." She gazed into his eyes. "Give her time, Lord Torrington."

Dez only hoped that Lady Alice was right.

CHAPTER TWENTY

Shelton Park

ANNA WALKED WITH Jessa to the stables for their daily ride. In the month since she had come home, riding had been what made her happiest. Dez had sent Daisy over, knowing she had been comfortable on the horse. She hadn't wanted to accept such an expensive gift but she knew his gesture was heartfelt and she couldn't bear to hurt him more by turning it down.

He had obviously written to Dalinda about Anna's resurrection from the dead because shortly after her arrival at Shelton Park a thick letter had arrived from her friend. In it, Dalinda expressed how happy she was that Anna was back home and shared what had happened in her life since that fateful day long ago. Dalinda explained why she couldn't come for a visit to reunite with Anna. Gilford had taken a turn for the worse and she refused to leave her husband, not knowing how long he had and wanting to spend every minute with him that she could. She did issue an open invitation for Anna to come to Gillingham whenever she liked so that she could meet the duke and Arthur and Harry.

Her friend had closed the letter asking that Anna keep an open mind and give Dez every chance. Anna knew Dalinda referred to Dez wishing for them to wed. She didn't know if Dez had mentioned it to his sister or his lack of referring to it clued

Dalinda in that something was amiss.

She missed Dez every day even though her days were filled. She walked and read. Played the pianoforte. Did some gardening. Rode. She had gotten to know Tom and his wife quite well and thought her cousin was doing an excellent job as the new Lord Shelton. Anna's life was peaceful. No ups or downs, just a smooth glide. Despite that, she couldn't help but think she would be complete if Dez were by her side.

She hadn't seen him since they'd parted. Besides sending Daisy to her, he had thoughtfully sent a note telling her he was going to London for business and would be gone several weeks. He would let her know when he returned and perhaps call upon her if she were agreeable. Hoping that time and distance from him would lessen her heartache, Anna had discovered it only enhanced it. She would allow him to call once he returned but she would have to make it absolutely clear that it was merely a call between neighbors and old friends.

Not the beginning of him pressing his suit.

They reached the stables and Jessa stopped in her tracks.

"Oh, bother. It is Thursday. I am supposed to attend an altar guild meeting at church."

As of yet, Anna hadn't left the property. She had not gone into the village, even though Jessa had encouraged her to see the seamstress. Her excuse had been she wanted to wait until she put on some weight and settled into the size she would be. For now, Dalinda's clothes would suit her. She hadn't attended church services either. Though word must be out by now of her reappearance at Shelton Park, thanks to their servants, she wasn't ready to step out and venture beyond Shelton Park.

"Do you mind?" Jessa asked.

"Go," Anna urged. "I have never been one for sewing."

Her sister hesitated. "If you are certain you don't mind."

"Not a bit."

They had the grooms saddle their horses and Jessa asked that one of them accompany her into the village. Anna gave a jaunty wave as the two set off. She turned in the opposite direction.

It had been nice to explore Shelton Park again, both on horseback and foot. The estate was a beautiful one. She had avoided talking with any tenants so far, only waving or nodding as she passed. She knew she was the object of gossip and wasn't yet ready to confront it. The day would come when she knew she would be ready. It just wasn't time yet. When she did, it would be imperative not to show any emotion when the inevitable questions came. Where she had been all these years. What the asylum was like. Whether she had truly been insane. Whether she still was. Anna knew there would always be those who judged her, be it Polite Society or the locals. Being ready to stand up for herself was important.

She rode the perimeter of Shelton Park and then turned inward, drawn to the lake. Knowing Dez was gone, she had ridden to it several times. She did so now, knowing the water brought her solace. Without meaning to, she crossed from Shelton Park onto Torrington lands and soon found herself at the cottage. Dismounting, she tied Daisy's reins to a post and tried the door. It was unlocked and so she stepped inside.

This was the place she had truly regained her sanity. Anna had never been mad but she knew for long periods she had retreated within herself. It was here that Dez brought her back to reality. In her short time staying at the cottage, he had helped her regain confidence in herself. There would always be instances when doubts occurred. That was only natural. But after her time with him, she had learned to trust herself.

She walked to the doorway of the bedchamber, standing there as memories of making love with Dez flooded her. She was still glad she had coupled with him. The only regret she had was that it had been selfish on her part, tying Dez to her when she was trying to free him. Still, it would be the only time she would ever be with a man and she was glad she had done so. Everything about the experience had been perfect. It was a well from which she would draw over the years.

"Anna," a voice softly said and she winced.

Dez had returned.

She turned slowly. He stood several feet from her, dressed in fawn breeches and a bottle green coat and waistcoat. His hair, always slightly wavy, was mussed from the breeze. There would never be a more handsome man as far as she was concerned.

"You returned from London," she said, stating the obvious. "How did your business go?"

Anna hated that her tone and greeting sounded stiff to her ears but she couldn't help it. She had to create distance between them in order to keep herself from rushing to him and throwing her arms about him.

"It went well." He swallowed. "It involved you to a degree. Could we sit a moment? I'd like to explain because it will affect you."

"Of course."

She bravely went to the settee and was surprised when he didn't sit next to her but took the chair next to it.

"I hired a Bow Street Runner," he began. "I wanted to track down Lady Jergens' father and inform him of her situation."

"Were you successful?"

He nodded. "The runner found Lord Morton and I accompanied him to Gollingham."

Dez explained how they had also brought along the earl's solicitor and personal physician and how they were able to liberate Lady Jergens from the asylum, albeit it not quite legally.

"She is now Lady Alice again," he concluded.

"I am sure she is very grateful to you for all you did on her behalf."

"She is," he agreed. "News of her release and petition for annulment, due to fraud, will eventually make the London newspapers. My agent ascertained Lord Jergens' gambling debts are already growing again."

"They will never see her dowry again."

"That didn't matter to Lord Morton, only that he had his

daughter returned to him." Dez hesitated. "Anna, once the newspapers get hold of the story, there will be talk of investigating Gollingham. You see, Mr. Haggard, the agent I engaged, was able to obtain a list of all of the women there. When we went to retrieve Lady Alice, I was able to speak to each of them briefly. As a result, I have contacted two other families who have relatives who are patients there. I believe that at least Lady Eastman and Miss Stone will soon be released."

A wave of emotion flooded Anna. "I remember the two of them. That is certainly good news."

Dez cleared his throat. "With Lady Alice now safely away and petitioning for an annulment—as well as the two other women I mentioned—I cannot keep your name out of any newspaper articles. I never gave anyone your name and Mr. Haggard wouldn't either but if an investigation is launched by a journalist? One of the attendants is certain to speak for a price. It will come out why you were committed to a madhouse and that you had recently been released."

She sat numbly, taking in what he said, wanting to retreat into herself again, into a world where she was safe. Anna shook her head vigorously. No, she wouldn't do that. She was safe at Shelton Park. She need never return to London again. Let the gossips have their heyday at her expense. She would never hear what they said.

"I sent a note to you when I returned this afternoon and would have told you all of this when I called upon you," Dez explained. "You may disregard it now. I just wanted you to know. I am sorry that—"

"Don't apologize," she interrupted. "Lady Alice gained her freedom. Two other women might, as well, thanks to your actions. I don't care if the newspapers mention me."

"But your reputation, Anna."

"I don't care about that either, Dez. What I do care about is yours. I know you still have feelings for me. You must put them aside. I insist."

He shook his head sadly. "Love is not a spigot to turn on and off at will. I have loved you for years—even when I thought you were dead. I will go on loving you until I am in my grave. You may not love me, Anna, but you cannot change the fact that I love you."

Tears filled her eyes. She tried to speak but nothing came out.

"You still love me," he said. "I know you do. You are trying to be noble and cut ties between us, thinking that I will wed and start a new life with that wife."

Dez took her hand. "No, Anna. I could never wed. Unless it was you. I have an heir in Dalinda's older boy. He can become the next Earl of Torrington." He squeezed her hand. "Oh, why can't you see that the obstacles you have placed between us are of your own making? I can't stop thinking about that night, Anna. The night we spent together, joined as one.

"I want you in my life. You aren't the only one who is damaged. The war did the same to me." He took her chin in his hand and forced her to meet his gaze. "Can two damaged souls come together and find salvation? If any can, it is you and me."

The dam she had built to contain her emotions collapsed. Anna blindly reached for Dez, tears obscuring him. He brought her to her feet and embraced her, a solid wall of comfort, bringing warmth to her cold, shattered soul.

"I love you," she repeated over and over.

"I love you, my darling. For now and always. Always," he said fiercely.

Dez kissed her, a kiss so tender, so loving, so romantic, that it magically mended the broken pieces within her.

She loved this man. He loved her. Who cared what the world said?

They belonged together. For eternity.

Anna broke the kiss. "Love me," she urged.

"I do."

"No. *Love me,*" she repeated.

Understanding flickered in his eyes and he said, "I will—on

the condition that you agree for the banns to be read three days from now. This Sunday and the following two. That you will sit with me and hear them proclaimed, letting the world know of our love. That you will marry me and be my countess. My wife. My best friend. The love of my life."

"Yes," she whispered and then more loudly, she proclaimed, "Yes. I will sit beside you and hear the banns and marry you and wear your ring. I will share everything with you. My joy. My sadness. My anger. My happiness. And children. Oh, sweet heavens, I want your children, Dez. Your sons and daughters."

He kissed her swiftly, over and over. Her lips. Her eyelids. Her cheeks. He returned to her mouth and the long, drugging kisses heated her from the inside out. She matched him, kiss for kiss, joy spreading through her.

Suddenly, he swept her up and carried her to the bed, spending the next hour kissing every inch of her. Even her core. She hadn't known she could be kissed there and thought it wicked—and wonderful. His lips and tongue brought her to the heights of passion and it spilled out from her.

She loved this man. With her body and soul. They were meant to be together.

As she lay in the aftermath of their lovemaking, smoothing the hair on his broad chest, Anna said, "I was foolish to try and keep us apart. Fortunately, you are stubborn and persisted."

Dez kissed her. "Who knew being headstrong and unyielding could end with such delicious results?"

And he made love to her again.

CHAPTER TWENTY-ONE

ANNA DRESSED WITH care, knowing she would be the object of fascination for every parishioner present this morning. She placed one of Jessa's bonnets on her head and tied the ribbon under her chin, glad that it would cover her short hair. She still missed her long tresses but already it was beginning to grow back quickly. Dez assured her that no matter what its length, he would always enjoying running his fingers through it.

She made her way downstairs, nerves humming within her, and joined her family for the short carriage ride to Draymott, only three miles away. It was mandatory for her to be present when the banns were read for the next three Sundays but after she and Dez had talked it over, Anna wanted to be there. She was done hiding. The villagers and tenants from both their estates would gossip no matter what. She would turn a deaf ear to it because, in the end, she would be wed to the man she adored.

They reached the village church and she saw the worshippers heading toward the doors as the bell began to peal. Only Dez waited and he handed her down from the carriage.

"Are you ready to run the gauntlet?" he asked.

"With you by my side, I doubt it will be daunting," she said lightly, trembling slightly.

He placed her hand on his sleeve and escorted her inside. A hush fell over the church as he led her to the front pew. They were joined by her sister, cousin and his wife. Jessa sat next to

Anna and took her hand, squeezing her fingers. Jessa had been a rock to her ever since her return from Gollingham and it comforted Anna to know that they would be close. At least until Jessa made her come-out and a marriage of her own.

A clergyman appeared, one she was unfamiliar with. He couldn't be more than thirty and had dark, curly hair and an impish look about him, as if he were more devil than angel. He led the congregation through the service. She tried to listen to his sermon but she still found it difficult at times to sit still and concentrate. She was used to withdrawing into herself anytime she was made to be still after so many years of doing so. That's why she preferred being outdoors, digging in the dirt or walking or riding.

The service drew to a close and she prepared herself for the recitation she had heard many times over the years. The good reverend asked that all parishioners be seated and then began to speak.

"I publish the Banns of Marriage between Desmond Bretton, Earl of Torrington, of Draymott Parish and Miss Anna Browning, also of Draymott Parish. If any of you know cause or just impediment why these two persons should not be joined together in Holy matrimony, you are to declare it. This is the first time of asking."

Anna knew the objections which had been part of the recitation were the point of the Calling of the Banns. Those banns were not to inform the worshippers of the coming marriage or give them an invitation to the wedding. Rather, they were to inquire of those present if they knew of any obstacles to the marriage. A person objecting would proceed to speak with the clergyman directly in order to present evidence why one of the parties wasn't free to wed.

She sat ramrod straight and very still, listening to see if anyone would come forward. She worried that someone would cite her years in the madhouse as reason enough for Dez not to consider marriage to her. Thankfully, no one spoke out. The banns would be called twice more and if no one named any hindrance, then she and Dez would have ninety days in which to marry. They hadn't talked about a date but Anna hoped it would be soon after the third and final calling.

The clergyman then looked out over the church and said, "I am new to this parish but I am aware that this couple has known each other from childhood. I look forward to performing their ceremony."

He then looked at her and smiled, bringing tears to her eyes.

Everyone rose and a final hymn concluded the ceremony. People started to file out but Dez took her arm.

"Reverend Hummert wishes to speak to us a moment," he told her.

Tom nodded and escorted his wife and Jessa from the church.

Once everyone was gone, the clergyman came to them and said, "I am Reverend Hummert, Miss Browning. I wanted to personally welcome you back to Draymott."

"Thank you, Reverend. And thank you for what you said after calling the banns."

"I have only been here two years and have just gotten to know Lord Torrington." The clergyman's eyes twinkled. "He is an improvement upon the previous holder of the title, as is your cousin. I must say that Lord Torrington has convinced me not only how much he admires and respects you but that you are a love match."

Anna glanced to Dez, who slipped his hand around hers.

"I am sorry you were parted so many years ago," Hummert continued. "I look forward to getting to know you both better and hope you will be active participants in the parish."

"Thank you for your support, Reverend," Dez said.

"Do you have an idea when you wish to wed?" the clergyman asked.

"The day after the third calling," Dez replied quickly, causing Hummert to chuckle heartily.

"I will place the event upon the church calendar. Any time in mind?

"I will leave that up to my bride-to-be."

"How about ten o'clock?" she suggested.

"I suppose I can wait that long," Dez said, squeezing her fingers.

"Thank you, Reverend Hummert," she said. "I will see you next Sunday. Or perhaps at the altar guild meeting this week?"

Hummert shuddered. "I stay away from that. Too many bossy women. However, they are good parishioners. My vestments and the altar linens are always in impeccable shape. The guild members also prepare the church for services and straighten up afterward. They will be the ones who decorate the church for your wedding."

She smiled. "Then I think it is high time I begin attending meetings with my sister."

"If you'll excuse me, I should go and speak to any members of the congregation who still linger. I always have one or two who compliment me on my sermon." He grinned. "A few others who tell me I spoke too long or not long enough."

They laughed and followed Hummert up the aisle, stepping out into the warm sunshine of the June day. Anna came to a halt as she looked out and saw the entire congregation still present, formed in two lines. The moment they saw her, hearty applause broke out, along with smiles on the faces of so many. Tears came to her eyes and she gripped Dez's arm for support.

She recognized Mr. Harmon, a longtime tenant at Shelton Park, who stepped forward.

"Miss Browning, you always had a smile and a kind word for all of your father's tenants. You visited the sick and brought baskets of goods to every family—and not just at Christmastime. You have been sorely missed during your time away and we, the people who are at Shelton Park, are grateful for your return. We are happy to share you with those who live and work on Torrington lands and tell them that they are getting a wonderful mistress."

"Thank you, Mr. Harmon," she managed to say loudly and clearly before emotion closed her throat.

Everyone applauded again and Dez led her down one of the lines and back up the other, allowing her to greet tenants and villagers alike. She saw so many familiar faces and felt their love and support as gratitude filled her. Polite Society might not welcome her back but she would always be at home in the country with these good people.

When they finished, Reverend Hummert stepped up and said, "I see you are much beloved, Miss Browning. I am grateful to number you among my flock."

Anna thanked him and turned to Dez. "May I make an announcement?"

"Of course."

She looked out at those gathered. "I am sincerely touched by your charity and generosity. Usually, a wedding breakfast is attended only by family and close friends. I would like my marriage to Lord Torrington to be more of a celebration, however. Think of it like a country ball. I hope all of you will attend our wedding ceremony three weeks from tomorrow at this very church and then return with us to Shelton Park for a breakfast and dancing."

Cheers erupted from the crowd. Dez slipped an arm about her waist and kissed her cheek.

"You will make for a wonderful countess, Anna Browning."

"I feel accepted by them," she explained. "They may be the only society who accepts me. I want them to help us celebrate our union."

"I think it a perfect way to begin our life together," he said.

THREE WEEKS AND one day later, Anna took Tom's hand as he helped her into the carriage that would take them to the church.

The others had already gone ahead to see that all the flowers and decorations were perfect, leaving her with her cousin. Though they hadn't seen each other since they were young children, Anna had grown close to Tom ever since her return to Shelton Park.

"You are marrying a good man, Anna," he said as the carriage started up. "Torrington loves you a great deal."

"I know. I am most fortunate. We have loved each other since childhood and had reconciled the fact that our fathers had other plans for us. University and the military for Dez and my come-out and marriage to a peer for me. When Papa wished to wed me to a man older than he was, Dez stepped in and tried to change things. Unfortunately, that did not work out for us."

"Everything will work out today. I promise you that," Tom swore. "I cannot tell you how glad I am to have a man of Torrington's caliber as my neighbor and your champion."

"It's thanks to you and Dez that I am here today, Tom."

"And Jessa," he added. "Don't forget her role. She insisted you were alive and that the two of us must seek you out."

Anna sighed. "It's so hard to see her all grown up. When I was spirited away, she was only a child, six years of age. Now, she is a grown woman, lovely and sweet and kind. I regret missing all those years of her maturing."

"Don't look to the past, Anna. Keep your focus on the future."

Her belly began to roil and her hand flew to her mouth. Tom looked at her in concern and called for the coachman to stop the vehicle. The moment he did, her cousin threw the door open and she leaned over, vomiting. She sat upright and gave him a weak smile as he handed over a handkerchief and she wiped her mouth.

"Are you ill, Cousin? Or are your nerves frayed with excitement?" he asked, his concern obvious.

"Neither," she said. Rubbing her belly, she said, "You mentioned the future. The future is here."

His eyes widened. "I see. Does Torrington know?"

She shook her head. "I have only known for a couple of days

myself."

He leaned over and swung the door closed and the carriage started up again.

"A baby is just the thing to help you heal from the experience you have endured. It will bring the two of you even closer together."

"Dez will be pleased," she agreed. "Please don't say anything just yet. I want to tell him first and then let us bask in the knowledge that soon there will be three of us."

Tom took her hand. "Your secret is safe with me."

"Thank you."

They arrived at the church and Tom handed her down. Excitement filled her, knowing in but a short time, she and Dez would be husband and wife.

Tom led her to the doors of the church and kissed her cheek. "Are you ready?"

Anna grinned. "I have been waiting for this moment all my life."

He opened the door and ushered her in. She glanced about and saw the church filled to the brim, faces smiling her way. Jessa waited at the front to the left, ready to stand up with her sister. In the middle stood Reverend Hummert. He nodded to the side and Dez joined him at the altar.

Her heart practically leaped from her chest when she saw her handsome groom. As Tom led her down the aisle, they only had eyes for one another. Getting to this day had taken a lifetime but it had been worth all the pain and sorrow to belong to this man.

Tom placed her hand on Dez's sleeve and then moved to the right, where he would act as their other witness.

"You are so very beautiful," the groom said so softly that only she could hear. "I cannot believe you are mine."

"I won't be until we speak our vows," she replied playfully.

"Then we better commence," he said and they faced Reverend Hummert.

The clergyman bestowed a smile upon them and began. As

he spoke about love and marriage, Anna said her own prayer of thanksgiving for leading her to Dez.

"And as it is written in the Song of Solomon, *I am my beloved's and my beloved is mine. I found the one my heart loves.* This is true of the couple that stands before me and I will now ask them to speak their vows before God and man."

Hummert had them face one another and said, "Desmond Bretton, wilt thou have this woman to thy wedded wife, to live together according to God's law in the holy estate of matrimony? Wilt thou love her, comfort her, honor and keep her, in sickness and in health; and, forsaking all others, keep thee only unto her, so long as ye both shall live?"

Dez's voice rang with conviction. "I will."

"Anna Browning, wilt thou have this man to thy wedded husband, to live together after God's ordinance in the holy estate of matrimony? Wilt thou obey him, and serve him, love, honor, and keep him, in sickness and in health; and, forsaking all others, keep thee only unto him, so long as ye both shall live?"

Anna gazed into her groom's eyes. "I will."

The ceremony continued, with both of them making promises to the other, plighting their troth. Dez placed her wedding ring on the Bible the clergyman held and he took it and raised it high for all to see. The gold band, studded with diamonds, had even more significance to her since her groom had told her it belonged to his mother—and had been the ring he had wanted to give her at Gretna Green so many years ago.

"Bless, O Lord, this ring, and grant that he who gives it and she who shall wear it may remain faithful to each other, and abide in thy peace and favor, and live together in love until their lives' end. Through Jesus Christ our Lord. Amen."

Hummert returned the ring to Dez and he placed it on her hand, his fingers remaining on it as he said, "With this ring I thee wed; with my body I thee honor; and all my worldly goods with thee I share; in the name of the Father, and of the Son, and of the Holy Ghost. Amen."

Reverend Hummert had them kneel and prayed, "O eternal God, Creator and Preserver of all mankind, giver of all spiritual grace, the author of everlasting life: send thy blessing upon these the servants, this man and this woman, whom we bless in thy name; that, living faithfully together, they may surely perform and keep the vow and covenant betwixt them made, whereof this ring given and received is a token and pledge; and may ever remain in perfect love and peace together, and live according to thy laws; through Jesus Christ our Lord."

A peace settled over Anna, knowing her welfare and life were in Dez's hands and his in hers, as well. Hummert added a few words, pronouncing them man and wife and then offered a final blessing.

"God the Father, God the Son, God the Holy Ghost, bless, preserve, and keep you; the Lord mercifully with His favor look upon you; and so fill you with all spiritual benediction and grace, that ye may so live together in this life, that in the world to come ye may have life everlasting."

The ceremony continued with a reading of the Psalms and communion and then the clergyman gave a final prayer. He then allowed them a kiss to seal their vows and it was the most tender, beautiful one she had experienced, full of light and goodness, sealing the vows they had made toward one another in front of their guests.

Reverend Hummert told those present that they should head to Shelton Park and he led them, Jessa, and Tom back to sign the church's registry.

"It is official," the clergyman said, a wide smile on his face. "You are husband and wife."

Dez kissed her again with enthusiasm and then led her from the church, where everyone still awaited them, tossing rice in the air. As it showered upon them, someone called out, "May you be blessed with many children."

Her new husband led her to his awaiting carriage and they began the short journey to Shelton Park.

"I have something to tell you," Anna began.

"Yes, Lady Torrington?"

She was taken aback for a moment and then realized he referred to her.

"My, that is certainly a mouthful," she proclaimed.

He captured her hand and brought it to his lips, nibbling upon her fingers. "I rather like the sound of it. I have my countess. I am an old, married man."

"We are the same age, my lord," she said, laughing. "I don't want to consider myself old. Especially when it comes to having our child."

He laughed along with her and then suddenly stopped, his eyes searching her face. "Do you . . . is that . . . are you saying . . ."

Anna cradled his face in her hands. "I am with child, Dez. I believe I conceived our first time together."

His hands touched her belly. "Oh, Anna. I hope you are happy with this news."

"Happy—and a bit nauseous," she teased. "I have had a hard time holding down my breakfast these last two days so don't be surprised if I don't choose to eat much this morning."

He kissed her deeply, love from him pouring into her. In that moment, Anna felt the last restraints of the past melt away. This man was her present. Her future. Her now and always.

They arrived at Shelton Park an hour after the ceremony and went into where the wedding breakfast would be held. Guests poured in, from residents of the village to those who worked the fields and served at both estates. Anna ate more than she had thought she could, her earlier queasiness gone. Toasts were made and then the orchestra broke out and the dancing began in earnest.

She danced with Mr. Meadows, the Torrington butler, after her first dance with her new husband, followed by one with Coral. She made her away around the room after that, talking with their guests. Dez convinced her to dance again and once the music came to a close, he led her from the room and up the stairs.

Giggling, Anna asked, "Do you think anyone will miss us?"

"I doubt it. They are all having a good time. Besides, I want you all to myself."

Even now, with all that had passed between them, she felt the heat rise in her cheeks.

"You are a beautiful, blushing bride," he told her. "And I happen to be the luckiest groom in the world."

They went to her bedchamber and made sure to lock the door. Dez made slow, sweet love to her, making Anna feel cherished and ever so lucky to have this man in her life.

Rejoining their guests an hour later, Jessa caught Anna's eyes and winked.

"My sister knows what we've been up to," she told her new husband.

He slipped an arm about her waist. "I hope Jessa will be lucky enough to find love herself."

"She's to make her come-out next year. She had asked me to help her."

"And you are reluctant to do so?"

"How will the *ton* think of me, Dez? I don't want them to judge Jessa based upon me and my experience."

She knew, too, that they would soon be heading to London to visit with Lord Morton and his daughter, as well as meeting with Mr. Haggard, the Bow Street Runner Dez had hired. If Lady Jergens gained her annulment, the newspapers would be full of it and Anna felt somehow her name would be a part of their reporting.

"Let next Season take care of itself. We don't have to worry about it now," he said. "Things might have changed by the time April comes."

"You're right," she agreed. "I won't borrow trouble."

After more dancing, they made their farewells, encouraging their guests to continue the celebration while they made their way back to Torville Manor.

Or so she thought.

Instead, Dez brought her to their cottage and said, "I couldn't think of a better place for us to spend our wedding night."

Inside, candles burned brightly. Food and wine were laid out. Flowers adorned the entire room.

Anna smiled. "You are the best husband in the world—and this is the perfect place to spend our first night together as man and wife."

Not much sleep occurred—but when morning came, Anna felt very, very married.

CHAPTER TWENTY-TWO

D EZ GAZED DOWN at his sleeping wife as the carriage turned onto the lane leading up to Gillingham. They hadn't gotten much sleep last night and he had encouraged her to nap during their journey to Kent. They had stopped twice to change the horses and Anna had curled up, her head in his lap, after the last time. He smoothed her hair and decided he should awaken her since they would be arriving soon.

His thumb stroked her cheek and she smiled in her sleep, a small sigh escaping her rosebud lips. They had to be the most kissable lips in the world. He would never tire of kissing her. Making love to her. Simply being with her.

After their night at Torville Manor, they now headed to see Dalinda. They would spend a week or so at Gillingham and then make their way to London.

"Lady Torrington?" Dez asked softly, his thumb now rubbing against Anna's full, bottom lip.

Her eyelids fluttered and then she gazed up at him, love for him shining in her eyes.

"Are we there?"

"Almost."

He helped her sit up and she smoothed the skirts of her traveling outfit before gazing out the window.

"Oh, I think I see it," she proclaimed. "What a lovely house."

The carriage arrived several minutes later and the minute the door opened, Dez saw his twin standing nearby.

"Dez!" she cried, a wide smile on her face. "Anna!"

He leaped from the carriage and snatched his sister up, spinning in a circle as the footman placed the stairs before the opening. Quickly, Dez turned and handed Anna down and she fell into Dalinda's arms. The two women clung to each other, sobbing, and he stepped away to give them a private moment together, giving instructions to his coachman and greeting the Gilford butler who had also been on hand to meet them.

"Hello, Bellows."

"Good afternoon, Lord Torrington. Did you and Lady Torrington have a safe journey?"

"It was very good and we are happy to be here," he replied.

"Mrs. Paul has prepared a heavy tea. Would you care to freshen up before it is served?"

He looked to his wife and sister, who still had their arms about one another, babbling at the same time.

"I think tea sounds splendid," he proclaimed. "I will be sure the ladies get there and you can inform Mrs. Paul to send it up to the drawing room."

"Very good, my lord."

Bellows left and Dez went to the two people he was closest to in all the world.

"Shall we go inside? I hear a marvelous tea is coming."

"Of course," Dalinda said, her arm going around Anna, leading her inside.

He followed, happy to see these two reunited after so many years apart.

They arrived in the drawing room and sat as the teacart was rolled in.

"I am famished," he declared, looking at Anna. She had lost her breakfast almost immediately after she'd eaten it this morning, which had worried him, but she said it was perfectly normal to do so at this stage of quickening.

"I am, too," she said, her look reminding him that she did

better keeping food down later in the day.

As Dalinda poured out and handed them their cups and saucers, they all filled their plates.

"Tea is the last large meal we usually serve," his twin said. "The boys have a light supper. I am usually with Gilford then, trying to persuade him to eat something."

"Is he so very ill?" Anna asked, her eyes sympathetic.

"Yes. He was doing slightly better when Dez was here a few months ago but I can see him going downhill every day. The doctor said he has seen these cases before and has told me more than likely, we only have a year together. Perhaps less."

Dalinda took a sip of tea. "I hope you understood that is why I had to miss your wedding."

"You were by your husband's side, where you belong," Anna assured her friend.

"He is eager to meet you," Dalinda shared. "I have talked about you so much over the years. Especially at the beginning, when I missed you so much." Tears glistened in her eyes. "To receive Dez's note and learn you weren't dead was a joyful moment." She smiled. "And now to have you as my best friend and sister-in-law is simply amazing."

The two women clasped their hands together, a look passing between them.

"Were you surprised when we wrote to tell you of our betrothal?" Dez asked.

Dalinda shook her head. "Not at all. Your marriage corrected the mistakes of the past. Mistakes our fathers were responsible for making. Now that they both are gone, we are all living the lives we chose."

"You are happy with Gilford?" Anna asked.

"I have been," Dalinda said. "He lost his wife many years before we met and hadn't planned on wedding again. Somehow, my story touched his heart and he offered for me." She chuckled. "My stepson, Reid, is only a year younger than I am. He is Gilford's heir and the only child from his first marriage."

"What did he think of having a stepmamma his age?" Anna asked.

"We didn't talk about it much. Reid left soon after we wed to attend university and then he went directly into the army afterward. So quite frankly, I don't know him very well. I have written to him, asking him to come home because of his father's health but Reid is quite the patriot and determined to keep serving in His Majesty's Army."

Anna frowned. "Isn't that quite unusual? A marquess and duke's heir a military officer?"

"It is but Reid always wanted to serve his country. His closest friends, Gray and Burke, also joined him in this endeavor."

They chatted for an hour, Dez carefully watching Anna as she ate slowly but definitely well. She seemed more partial to sweets now that she was with child and ate her fair share of a sponge cake and a few tarts. Dalinda looked to him, a question in her eyes, and he nodded. They had always been able to communicate without words. His twin's eyes twinkled and he knew she was happy for the news.

Suddenly, the door swung open and Arthur and Harry bounded in.

"Uncle Dez!" they both cried, running to him.

He hugged them. "It's so good to see you boys. I have someone I want you to meet."

They both turned and eyed Anna with interest, stepping to her and bowing.

"I am Arthur Baker. You are the Countess of Torrington. Mama told us you were coming."

Harry squeezed past his brother. "I am Harry Baker. Mama said you are her best friend ever and Uncle Dez is lucky to have you."

Anna laughed, charmed by the pair. "I would say I am the fortunate one. I grew up on the estate next to your mama and your uncle. We were neighbors and did everything together."

"Like what?" Harry asked eagerly.

"We liked to walk both estates. Ride. Swim. We fished together but neither your mama nor me would place the worm on the hook."

"That's boy's work," Arthur proclaimed. "I can do that if you want to go fishing with us, my lady."

"Will you be here long enough to fish?" Harry asked. He looked to Dez.

"About a week or so. Plenty of time to fish and do other things. Your new aunt is terrific at skimming stones across the water. Perhaps she can teach you how."

"I'm bloody awful at that," Arthur said.

"Arthur! Language," Dalinda admonished.

"Sorry, Mama." He glanced to Anna. "Sorry, my lady."

"I would be pleased to be called Aunt Anna," she told him.

Arthur's eyes lit up, as did Harry's and Arthur asked, "May we, Mama? Call her Aunt?"

Dalinda nodded her approval and then said, "Would you like some tea?"

"Yes!" the boys cried.

"And tarts," Harry added. He looked to Anna and confided, "They are my favorite."

"Mine, too," she said. "I have always loved sweets but even more so now."

"Why?" Arthur asked before taking a huge bite of his sandwich.

She glanced to Dez and he nodded.

"You are going to have a cousin," she revealed. "When a woman carries a baby inside her belly, sometimes she gets cravings."

"What are those?" Harry asked.

"A longing for something. It can be quite intense."

"When will our cousin come?" Arthur piped up.

"Next year," Dez said, not wanting to mention the month. He didn't know if Gilford—or Dalinda—had told the boys anything about how babies were made or how long they took to come.

"Finish eating, boys," Dalinda said. "Your governess will be coming for you soon."

"I need to finish my cravings, Mama," Harry said, using his new word, if incorrectly. "Auntie Anna and I like our sweets."

The boys concentrated on eating as the adults talked a bit about those who had attended the wedding. Once Harry and Arthur had been collected by their governess and vacated the drawing room, Dalinda hugged Anna.

"I am thrilled you are going to have a child."

Anna smiled ruefully. "We started a bit early so the baby will naturally come a little early."

"Do you hope for a boy or girl?" she asked.

"Either," Dez answered for them both. "We hope for a healthy babe and many more to follow."

"What if you have twins?" his sister asked. "They run in our family."

"Oh." Anna looked blank for a moment. "I hadn't even considered that possibility."

"I had wondered if Gilford and I might have twins. Our boys are spaced just over two years apart. Arthur turned eleven in April and Harry became nine last week."

"Our baby should come in February," Anna revealed.

"How are you feeling?" Dalinda asked.

"Miserable in the mornings. That started less than a week ago."

"It will run a few months and then you will feel fit as a fiddle," Dalinda reassured her. "Would you like to meet Gilford now? I usually go up after tea and spend time with him."

"I would like that," Anna said.

They accompanied Dalinda to the duke's rooms and Dez saw the difference in Gilford the moment they entered. While he had been weak during Dez's visit, the duke was obviously quite ill. His color was poor and he seemed frail as he gestured from his bed.

"Back for a rematch?" Gilford asked, a twinkle still in his eyes.

"I would like that, Your Grace. May I present to you my new wife, the Countess of Torrington."

Anna moved close to the bed and curtseyed. "It is an honor to meet you, Your Grace." She took his hand. "Thank you for saving my friend all those years ago. You have made her quite happy and your boys are lovely."

Gilford smiled up at Anna. "It is Dalinda who saved me," he said and he glanced to his wife. "She gave me a new outlook on life and the chance to be a father again, twice over."

They stayed a few minutes and then Anna caught Dez's eyes and he said, "We have traveled a good distance today and need to retire. Perhaps we can visit again tomorrow, Your Grace."

"I would like that," he said weakly.

"Bellows can show you to your room," Dalinda said, pulling the cord to summon the butler.

When the servant arrived, they bid the duke and duchess goodnight and retreated to their guest bedchamber.

Once alone, Anna said, "Gilford seems quite nice but he's not long for this world. Poor Dalinda."

"My sister will be fine. She has her boys, wild though they may be."

"It surprised me they were here and not finishing their term at school."

"I understand they were asked to leave their last school," he revealed. "I fear Dalinda has spent too much time with her ailing husband and her boys are rebelling somewhat."

He slipped his arms around her and brought her close. "Our children will be perfect, I'm sure. They will never be tossed from their schools. Never tattle on one another. Never put toads in their governess' bed."

Anna laughed. "I hope they are just as we were as children. We had some wonderful times together—you, Dalinda, and I."

Dez laughed and kissed her hard. "How about I show you a wonderful time tonight?"

And he did. More than once.

CHAPTER TWENTY-THREE

DEZ AND ANNA arrived at Lord Morton's London townhouse, along with Haggard, the Bow Street Runner. They were to meet with Lord Morton and his daughter first and then others helping in the case against Lord Jergens would join them.

The butler showed them to the drawing room and before Dez could introduce Anna to the earl, she and Lady Jergens fell into each other's arms. Tears and a hurried conversation occurred and then Lady Jergens presented Anna to her father.

"I am so pleased to meet you, Lord Morton," Anna said, wiping away her tears.

"It is an honor to meet you, Lady Torrington," the earl replied. "Your husband was instrumental in removing my daughter from Gollingham Asylum."

"How are you feeling, my lady?" Dez inquired.

"Quite well, Lord Torrington, thanks to you."

"Has your husband contacted Lord Morton or tried to have you removed from his care?" he asked.

"No. We have heard not one word from Jergens," she revealed. "I would have thought he would be enraged and stormed my father's townhouse."

"We wouldn't have allowed that, my lady," Haggard interjected. "Both your father and Lord Torrington have seen to having men placed at the front and back entrances to your residence."

"Still, it seems odd we wouldn't have heard from Jergens," Lord Morton pointed out.

"Unless Dr. Cheshire neglected to notify Jergens of his wife's removal from Gollingham," Dez said. "If Jergens had already paid the annual fee for Lady Jergens' care as a patient, Cheshire might be biding his time."

"He is sly," Anna said. "I would not put it past him to keep the news from Lord Jergens for as long as he can." She turned to Lady Jergens. "Do you remember when your husband placed you at the asylum?"

"It was last September." A shadow crossed her face. "We had been married less than a month."

"It is July now so Cheshire has a little time to try and think of a way to notify Jergens that you have left the facility and are in your father's care," Dez said.

"He will know everything in a few minutes," Lord Morton said. "I have asked him to come see me—along with his solicitor. I told him I would warrant no excuses and if he knew what was good for him, he would be prompt."

Morton called out and the door opened. The butler ushered in Mr. Black and Dr. Caymon and they joined the group. Dez introduced Anna to them and they all sat.

"Share with them what you have learned, Mr. Black," the earl urged.

Black explained how Lord Jergens had been thoroughly investigated and that they would press for an annulment based upon their findings. Dr. Caymon told of how he and two other physicians had examined Lady Jergens and found her to be of sound mind. Mr. Haggard added that Lady Jergens had seen no other physician before being placed at Gollingham, being committed solely on Lord Jergens' word.

"That harkens back to the Hawley case from 1763," the solicitor said. "Various madhouses acts were the result, though these govern facilities in and surrounding London—not ones as far away as Gollingham."

"Then how will you fight for Lady Jergens' freedom?" Anna asked, shuddering.

Dez threaded his fingers through hers, trying to calm and comfort her.

"Oh, Lord Jergens has definitely committed fraud," Black assured them. "We will confront him on that issue today."

The butler entered and announced, "Lord Jergens and Mr. Withersby."

Two men entered. The one obviously dressed well stormed ahead of the other, ready to confront his father-in-law. He strode across the room.

"Why do you think you can threaten and demand . . ." Lord Jergens' voice trailed off. Surprise registered upon his face. "You!" he said, spying his wife and then wheeling to face Lord Morton. "What the dickens is this bloody bedlamite doing here?"

The earl rose to his feet, towering over Jergens, and said, "Don't you dare throw your curses at my daughter. *You* are the bloody bastard who should be beaten to death for what you have done to my Alice."

Haggard stepped to the earl and took his forearm. "Have a seat, my lord," the runner said calmly. "This will be over in a few minutes."

Morton's face, red with anger, looked as if he might explode but he took Haggard's advice.

The runner said to Jergens, "You and your man take a seat. You won't be here long."

When an exasperated sigh came from Jergens, Dez said, "Do as you're told, man."

"Who are you?" Jergens demanded.

"The Earl of Torrington. Sit."

Jergens finally did so, motioning his solicitor, who looked terrified, to do the same.

Mr. Black took the lead and said, "Lady Jergens will sue for an annulment, with her father's support."

Jergens shot to his feet again. "My wife will go back to where

I placed her. Legally, she is mine to do with as I wish."

"As long as you are wed," Black continued. "Part of that is honoring the marriage settlements. The contracts you signed along with Lord Morton."

Dez watched as a crack in Jergens' confidence appeared and he took his seat again. Anna squeezed his fingers and he nodded to her.

"A stipulation in the settlements was for Dunhaven, one of your unentailed estates in Sussex, be made available to Lady Jergens and serve as her home in case you predeceased her in death and no issue from the marriage had occurred to become the heir apparent."

"What of it?" Jergens asked warily.

Black cleared his throat dramatically. "When the contracts were signed, you no longer possessed Dunhaven. It had been sold to help pay off some of your immense debts."

"So?" the viscount asked testily. "I would have merely given her another place to go. As it was, I received a wife who was damaged goods. A lunatic."

Dr. Caymon spoke up. "A woman with whom you never bothered to consummate your marriage. Yes, I have examined Lady Jergens, as did Dr. Cheshire at Gollingham Asylum, and we both ascertained she remains a virgin."

The words badly shook Jergens, who grew pale.

"You also did not have a physician examine her for her mental capacity," Dr. Caymon continued. "She was committed to Gollingham strictly on your word, which violates several laws." He looked to Black. "I believe you mentioned the Hawley case."

Jergens' eyes cut to his own solicitor, who began shaking his head in surrender.

"You wed my daughter strictly for her dowry," Lord Morton accused. "Though that very act happens time and again in Polite Society, you never even bothered to make her a true wife and committed her to an asylum. You signed the marriage contracts, knowing full well what you offered to her as property was no longer available, thinking I would never outlive you and Alice would be locked away and in no need of a place to live upon your death."

Lord Morton stood and closed the distance between him and his son-in-law. He spit into Jergens' face. "You disgust me."

The viscount wiped the spittle away with his sleeve and looked to his solicitor. "Withersby?" he pleaded.

Withersby shook his head. "I am sorry, my lord. You are in violation of the contracts. Lord Morton and Lady Jergens will bring about the charge of fraud. It is grounds for an annulment. The case will be tried in an ecclesiastical court by the Bishop of the See in your local parish. In this case, that would be Sussex."

Jergens gasped. "That would make me a social pariah." His eyes cut to his wife. "You, too, Alice." He smiled, trying to appeal to her, rising from his seat and going to kneel before her. "You don't want that, do you? No man would think to wed you after an annulment. Why don't the two of us settle this between us, darling? There's no sense you going back to Gollingham. I see now that wasn't the solution for us. We can live separate lives as many in the *ton* do. We can even—"

Lady Jergens slapped her husband, knocking him over. She rose to her feet.

"I am not—and never will be—your darling, Jergens. You are a fool. A gambler. A licentious bastard. I would rather die a free spinster than be bound to you in marriage for a moment longer."

With that, the viscount broke down sobbing. He began blubbering, asking for forgiveness, clawing at his wife's skirts.

"I will leave it to you gentlemen now," Lady Jergens said and she quit the room.

The viscount's head fell into his hands. "What do we do now?" he asked.

Mr. Black responded. "I will see that a hearing in the ecclesiastical court is placed upon the calendar as quickly as possible. Mr. Withersby and I will meet with the bishop beforehand to see what evidence is required and what testimony will take place. In the meantime, Lord Jergens, I suggest that you refrain from discussing the matter with anyone but your solicitor and that you do not try to write or see your wife or father-in-law. Can we agree to those terms?"

"They are acceptable," Withersby responded. "Let me know when we are to travel to Sussex, Mr. Black." To the viscount, Withersby said, "Come, my lord. We have no further business here."

The solicitor grabbed the viscount's elbow and hoisted him to his feet. He led his employer from the room and an audible, collective sigh came from those still present.

"I have already written to the bishop and received a reply," Black revealed. "A note was delivered to Withersby's office during our meeting, informing him that we leave tomorrow morning to meet with the bishop regarding the affair."

The solicitor and doctor excused themselves and Dez turned to Haggard.

"What else have you found?" he asked the runner, knowing Lord Morton and Anna needed to be apprised of the investigator's findings.

"I have looked into the cases of the two women you spoke with at Gollingham, Lord Torrington. In the case of Lady Eastman, she lost her husband three months before giving birth to their only child, a son, who was then named the new Lord Eastman. Her brother-in-law, a Mr. Sillwell, had come to live at the estate, waiting to see if he would become the new viscount or if she produced a male child. From what I learned, Lady Eastman had been severely depressed upon the death of her husband but had roused herself upon the birth of her first child."

"But this brother-in-law wished to be the new viscount," Dez stated.

"Yes," the runner agreed. "Mr. Sillwell felt it best for the child to commit the mother. He claimed she had tried to harm the boy, telling him that he needed to die and be with his beloved papa."

"All a lie, I am sure," Anna said bitterly. "What has happened to the baby?"

"Mr. Sillwell was named as guardian for young Lord Eastman," Haggard said.

"I worry for the child's welfare," Anna said. "This Sillwell wants to be a viscount. The only thing standing between him and the title is a baby."

"I fear you are correct," Haggard said.

The runner explained a few ways for them to proceed and both Dez and Lord Morton granted him the power to do so.

"And Miss Stone?" Dez asked, thinking of the other woman who was as lucid and sane as he was, even as she sat rotting away in Gollingham Asylum.

"Miss Stone taught at a school run by her father. Upon his death, Mr. Stone left the school to his daughter—and not one penny to his profligate son. Though unmarried women can own and maintain property in England, Mr. Stone had his sister committed and has taken over the running of the school. Into the ground, I am afraid."

Once more, they debated ways to help Miss Stone and authorized the Bow Street Runner to pursue them.

As they readied themselves to leave, Lord Morton said, "Mr. Black said that you might be called upon as a witness to my daughter's case, Lord Torrington."

"I will be happy to testify to what I know," Dez said.

"If I am needed to do so, I would also speak my piece," Anna added.

"Thank you both," the earl said. "I am grateful to have Alice back. Even if her reputation is ruined by this whole sordid affair, at least she is free of that cursed place." He smiled at them. "The fact the two of you have wed and appear quite happy brings me joy."

They thanked him and left. In the carriage, Dez placed an arm about his wife, drawing her close.

"Do you think Lady Eastman or Miss Stone have a chance of being released?" Anna asked hopefully.

"I will do everything in my power to help restore them to society," Dez said fervently.

CHAPTER TWENTY-FOUR

ANNA DIDN'T MIND that she and Dez remained in London. The Season was winding down and, already, many of the *ton* were leaving town with the increase in the heat, retreating to their country estates and house parties. It wasn't as if they would have been invited to any events.

She didn't know what their status would be come next Season. By then, they would be parents. She placed a hand protectively against her belly. Her giving birth in February probably meant that they wouldn't even bother to come to London. She hoped her cousin and his wife would chaperone Jessa for her come-out. Tom's reputation was impeccable and would help Jessa far more than Anna's might even though she was now a countess.

They had been to visit Lord Morton and his daughter twice in the last two weeks. Anna and Alice were now on a first-name basis and had left the men on their own to talk while they retreated to a parlor Alice had claimed as her own. Her new friend confided that she still had nightmares about Gollingham but expressed her gratitude for being free of the asylum.

The petition for annulling the marriage of Lord and Lady Jergens' marriage had been heard recently by the bishop. Neither Dez nor Anna had been called to testify. Mr. Black had sent word that their presence would not be required. Dez had thought that would be the case. They waited now for word regarding the decision.

As she gazed out the window, she asked her husband, "Would you like me to ring for a pot of tea?"

"No. Just sit here with me."

"Gladly."

Anna joined Dez and they sat together, their hands finding one another. Having known only brutish physical contact for so many years, she found she craved his touch, in and out of bed. He seemed to understand her need for it and always tried to sit next to her, his fingers laced through hers. Last night, he had curled up with her, his head in her lap. She constantly ran her fingers through the thick waves, reassured by his presence.

"Would you like me to read to you?" he asked.

"No. I am afraid it would be a waste of your voice for I don't think I could concentrate on the words. Not until we hear from Lord Morton."

Johnson, their butler, slipped into the room. "Mr. Haggard is here, my lord, and asking to see you at once."

"Send him in," ordered Dez.

Moments later, the Bow Street Runner entered the drawing room. He withdrew a folded page from his pocket and handed it to Dez. Eagerly, Anna looked as her husband opened the note and they both read it. Relief filled her when she learned the bishop had granted the petition for annulment.

"Were you with Lord Morton and Lady Jergens when they received word?" she asked Haggard.

"I was, my lady," Haggard said, a smile lighting his usually stern countenance. "Both father and daughter were quite happy at the outcome. Lady Alice's dowry is supposed to be returned but I doubt Lord Morton will receive any of it. From what I ascertained, most of it has already been spent. Lord Morton could press for it in court but it would add to the already brewing scandal."

"You think the scandal will break now?" she asked anxiously.

"It is inevitable, my love," Dez said. "Lord Jergens won't be able to pay his debts again and when his former wife appears in society as Lady Alice once again, the tongues of the *ton* will wag. He will never be able to find a bride and I am afraid she will not be able to find a husband."

"Even though she is not at fault?" Anna demanded.

"Polite Society is cruel to women," he said. "I know that she will always have a friend in you, however." Looking to Haggard, he asked, "Any progress on the other matters?"

She knew he referred to Lady Eastman and Miss Stone, who still remained at Gollingham.

"I cannot find the doctors who examined them and judged them to be insane," the runner shared.

"If that's the case, then do you think there is hope of them being able to leave Gollingham?" she asked hopefully.

"It is early yet, my lady," Haggard said. "Both your husband and Lord Morton have told me to keep on it."

"Thank you for bringing us the good news, Haggard," Dez said.

The agent took his leave and she threw her arms about her husband, soundly kissing him.

"This calls for a celebration," she said.

"Is that a wicked glint in your eyes, Lady Torrington?" he asked playfully.

"I don't know, Lord Torrington. Is it?" she responded coyly.

He pulled her to him for a searing kiss. Anna had thought she would never get her fill of him but ever since she learned she was with child, she seemed to be even more frisky when it came to bedding her husband.

"Would you like to retire for an afternoon nap, my lady?"

She yawned. "I do feel rather tired. Perhaps a nap would be just the thing."

Dez pulled her to her feet and gave her a lingering kiss. "Then nap you shall. And I will supervise you in this endeavor."

They crossed the room and before they could exit it, Johnson opened the door.

"What is it, Johnson?" Dez asked.

The servant frowned. "There is a Mr. Jefferson here to see you, my lord."

"Jefferson? I don't recall knowing any Jefferson."

Johnson handed over the card he carried, distaste on his face. "He said you would say that."

Anna glanced down and saw the name Jefferson. Underneath it was the name of the largest newspaper circulating in London.

"A reporter? Whatever could he want?" she asked, her heart speeding up, especially as she saw the worry reflected in Dez's eyes.

"I will see him," he informed Johnson, whose brows arched for a moment. "Bring him up."

When the butler left, Dez said, "Go to our bedchamber. I will—"

"I will not!" she protested. "If this is about me—and Gollingham—then I have a right to hear and be a part of the discussion."

He sighed. "You are right. I only wished to protect you."

"And you have," she reassured him. "But remember, Dez, we are in this together. Our vows spoke to that."

He kissed her softly. "You are so wise, my dear countess."

Johnson announced their visitor and Mr. Jefferson came toward them. He was tall and thin and had inquisitive brown eyes.

"Good afternoon, Lord Torrington. Lady Torrington. I am Mr. Jefferson, a journalist investigating Gollingham Asylum." He looked to Anna. "You are looking well, my lady, for having been a recent patient of the facility."

Dez took a step toward the man, partially shielding her. "You go too far, Jefferson."

"I don't go far enough, my lord," the reporter countered. "You and Lord Shelton were successful in removing Lady Torrington from the place. I am trying to do the same for other women."

"We should hear him out," she said. "Won't you have a seat, Mr. Jefferson?"

Anna indicated a chair and the journalist took it while she and Dez seated themselves by one another. She knew members of Polite Society never chose to meet with reporters but she was curious about what this man was up to.

"What is the scope and nature of your investigation, Mr. Jefferson?" she asked.

He looked at her frankly. "Thank you for even seeing me, my lady. My lord. I doubted you would but since you didn't refuse, I believe you to be more openminded than most members of Polite Society." He took a deep breath and exhaled it slowly. "I am not one who writes of *ton* gossip but rather a serious journalist who writes stories on political and economic issues."

"How does a madhouse qualify as either?" Dez asked sharply.

"The story has become more personal for me," Jefferson revealed. "My fiancée, Miss Blair, teaches at Stone Academy, and is close friends with Miss Stone. Miss Stone's father passed away several months ago, leaving her the school—and nothing to her worthless brother. When Miss Blair arrived one day, Miss Stone was nowhere to be found. Her brother was there and said that she had left him in charge and he would be the new headmaster."

Jefferson shook his head. "I know Miss Stone through my fiancée and she would never have walked away from Stone Academy, much less left a fool in charge of running things. I discovered Stone had his sister sent to Gollingham Asylum and began researching the facility and its staff, trying to find out how and why Miss Stone was placed there."

"I knew Miss Stone," Anna said. "Patients were not allowed to speak to one another but we did so on rare occasions. She was a lovely woman but stayed in trouble with the staff, much as I did, because she rebelled against the treatments."

Jefferson grimaced. "I have learned of some of those treatments." He paused. "Would you be willing to speak to me about them? And the conditions at Gollingham?" He looked at Dez. "I have already learned from my investigations that you and Lord Morton have been able to remove his daughter from the place and that she was granted an annulment from Lord Jergens."

"You are remarkably well informed," Dez said.

Jefferson shrugged. "I have a way with people, drawing them out. And when that doesn't work, I have learned a sufficiently greased palm will loosen all manner of tongues."

She turned to her husband. "We should help him."

"I agree," Dez said quietly. "We will share what we know with you, Mr. Jefferson. I have had a Bow Street Runner working on our behalf. I will have him summoned."

He rang for Johnson and told the butler to send a message to Haggard to return at once.

"While we wait for Mr. Haggard's arrival, I will answer your questions," Anna said.

"Thank you, Lady Torrington. I am writing a series of articles exposing the treatment of patients in madhouses, as well as how they came to be there. A goodly portion of patients institutionalized are women, placed their by husbands or fathers who did so to silence their voices or opinions. Females in our society are naturally rendered more vulnerable based upon our laws. If not submissive?" Jefferson shrugged. "They are controlled in these asylums, whether sane or not."

"They are terrible places. At least Gollingham was," she began. "Our nights were spent in cramped, cell-like rooms with poor ventilation. They would tie us to the beds with ropes, saying that prevented anti-social behaviors and kept us from harming ourselves or one another."

"With a straitjacket?" Jefferson asked.

"Sometimes. Those would bind our arms to our bodies and prevent movement but we were still often bound to the beds in addition to being restrained by the straitjackets. Left to soil ourselves."

"How did the staff treat you?" he asked gently.

"Brutality and neglect were common. We were constantly told we were demented and that there was no cure for what was wrong with us. We were merely to be confined, away from our families and society. We were abused both physically and mentally. The food mostly consisted of a gruel broth, with the occasional spoiled beef provided. Dirty, undrinkable water accompanied each meal."

"How did you spend your days?"

She swallowed. "In silence. Sitting upon hard benches for twelve hours or longer. Waste was everywhere. Rats scurried about freely."

"Were you punished for speaking to others?"

"Always," she said vehemently, her insides tightening.

Dez took her hand, stroking it with his thumb, calming her.

She continued to answer Jefferson's questions until Mr. Haggard arrived. Dez gave the runner permission to share all he had learned and the two men spoke back and forth quickly, sharing information.

"I don't need your permission," Jefferson said, "but I would ask your blessing. I am ready to go to print with this."

Anna turned to her husband. "If we can help even one woman . . ." Her voice trailed off.

He nodded and looked to the journalist. "Go ahead."

"I will protect you as best as I can, Lady Torrington," Jefferson said. "I will not name you as a source regarding what I will write but your name will be mentioned as having been a patient at Gollingham."

"Go ahead," she said boldly. "I have my life back, thanks to my husband and cousin."

Jefferson said, "I hope my investigative work will be able to free Miss Stone and possibly others. Comparing notes with Mr. Haggard, neither of us can find any physician who diagnosed Miss Stone as mad. I believe she was placed there merely on her brother's word, in order for him to gain access to the school and monies left to her by her father.

"You are a very brave woman, Lady Torrington," he continued. "To share with me the horrific conditions you endured."

"I hope something good will come from your articles, Mr.

Jefferson," she said. She rose. "Thank you for coming."

Knowing they were dismissed, both Jefferson and Haggard left the drawing room. Dez pulled her into his arms.

"You have more courage than any man I ever saw on the battlefield, my love. I want us to raise our children with conviction. To teach them to always do the right thing. I want our girls to know they are as valued and loved as our boys." His palm flattened against her belly. "This little one, son or daughter, will have two parents who will give it our love. Our time. I want our children to grow up free to express their opinions to us, while at the same time learning to always be kind to others.

She touched his cheek. "You are a remarkable man, Desmond Bretton. I doubt a handful of men in Polite Society would feel as you do. It's just one of the reasons I love you so very much."

He kissed her and then said with a smile, "I would enjoy showing you how much I love you, Lady Torrington. I believe you were to take a nap before we were interrupted by our unexpected guest."

Anna laughed. "Let us keep the world at bay for a few hours then."

Dez swept her into his arms, carrying her to their bedchamber, and did just that.

CHAPTER TWENTY-FIVE

DEZ AWOKE TO a bloodcurdling shriek. Anna thrashed on the bed, in the grips of a terrible nightmare. Coral rushed in and ran to the bed, halting when he saw Anna's arms striking out violently at empty space.

The valet blanched but quickly said, "What can I do, my lord?"

"Nothing, Coral. Go," he commanded and the servant sadly turned away, quietly closing the door as he exited the bedchamber.

Dez captured his wife's wrists and lowered them to her sides, securing them there.

"Wake up, Anna, my darling. Wake up. You are with me. Dez. Your husband. Wake up, sweetheart."

Her eyes flew open, darting about as she quickly assessed her surroundings. Slowly, the tension eased from her body. He released her wrists and lay beside her, pulling her close. Even now, her heart beat rapidly, like a wild animal caught in a trap, thumping against his bare chest. Dez didn't speak. He merely held her to him, hoping to warm her chilled body. After some minutes, he no longer could feel the pounding of her heart against him and he sensed her relaxing.

"Another nightmare?" he asked.

Anna continued to have bad dreams about her time in the madhouse. They had seemed to lessen in frequency, however.

The intensity of this one bothered him.

"Yes," she finally replied. "I thought I was getting better. I am afraid talking with Mr. Jefferson yesterday brought up things I had locked away."

"You don't have to see or speak to Jefferson again, my love," Dez said, hoping to soothe her.

"No. It's all right. If I can help him to gain the release of even one woman existing in that living Hell, then I want to continue to see him and assist in whatever way I can." She smiled up at him. "Besides, I have the most handsome, loving husband in the world to offer me comfort and chase away the lingering feelings of my nightmares."

He hated that the reporter's visit had caused another setback in Anna's recovery but Dez knew his wife must follow her heart and do what she could to liberate any patient she had known.

"I dreamed of Matron again," Anna said. "Above all the others, she haunts me most."

"Perhaps because of her extreme cruelty," he suggested. "Your most terrible experiences were at her hands."

"I suppose so. I wonder why she took such joy in tormenting those under her care."

He kissed her temple. "She wasn't caring for you or any of the others, sweetheart. She made no attempts to help heal anyone. Matron was merely a jailor, keeping innocent women prisoners."

She remained quiet in his arms for several minutes and then softly said, "Make love to me. It helps me to remember I am free and alive."

Their lovemaking began slow and tender but became more frantic. Dez could understand why. After a battle, men wanted to prove they were still alive and had cheated death. Many soldiers sought out camp doxies for that very reason. Lovemaking was the ultimate physical experience. Anna had come through an entire war during her stay at Gollingham. Wanting to assert herself through making love was a natural extension of proving to herself that she was free from the dark shadows of the madhouse.

She slipped from her bed and shrugged into her dressing gown. "I have certainly worked up an appetite," she joked. "I will meet you downstairs for breakfast."

She cut through this dressing room to return to her own bedchamber. Dez rang for Coral.

"Is Lady Torrington all right?" the valet asked, his concern obvious.

"She will be. It simply will take time to get over what she went through."

"Lady Torrington has you in her corner, my lord," the servant said. "I can think of no greater champion to spur her on."

Dez went to Anna's rooms and found her about to leave.

"Good," he said, slipping her arm through his. "I am in time to escort my beautiful wife to breakfast."

As they came into the breakfast room, Johnson hovered nearby.

"What is it?" Dez asked the butler.

"The morning newspapers, my lord. They are on the table." He lowered his voice and leaned close. "You and Lady Torrington are mentioned in them. Thanks to that reporter," he added with disdain.

He stared down the servant until Johnson flinched.

"Do you have a problem working in this household, Johnson?"

Panic filled the butler's face. "No, my lord. Never. I live to serve you and the countess."

Anna said smoothly, "Thank you for letting us know, Johnson. It was very thoughtful of you."

She moved to take her seat and the butler pulled out her chair and pushed it up once she had sat upon it.

"I believe I will take two poached eggs this morning with my toast," she said airily. "And tea now."

Johnson looked to a footman, who brought the teapot over and poured the brew into her cup.

"Coffee for me," Dez said abruptly and the second footman responded quickly. "A rasher of bacon and three eggs for me, Johnson."

"At once, my lord."

The butler hurried off and he and Anna doctored their drinks the way they liked them. He noticed how she added an additional sugar cube, something she had never done before the baby.

"Do you really think you can eat two poached eggs?" he asked, clasping her fingers.

"Not at all," she said. "I doubt I can force one down but I wanted to give him something to do. He's quite upset. If the butler or housekeeper are upset, then all the servants are." Anna smiled. "Johnson is merely looking out for us. He disapproves of us speaking to Mr. Jefferson yesterday."

"Remember, we agreed not to care what Polite Society thought. We should do the same for our servants," he said quietly. He picked up the newspaper Jefferson wrote for. "Shall we?"

"You read it first," she told him. "I will look at the gossip column and see what poor soul is being lambasted today."

Dez opened the paper and saw the bold headline.

Horrific Conditions at Gollingham Asylum.

With a deep breath, he began reading.

By the time he finished, the breakfast Johnson had brought had grown cold. He motioned for a footman to take it away and asked for more coffee and then dismissed the servants, giving him and his wife privacy for their discussion.

"Well?" she asked.

"The piece is very thorough. Jefferson is concise and yet leaves no stone unturned."

"Let me read it then."

He watched her face as she did, reaching for the toast she'd left untouched and finishing it and her eggs off, along with his coffee.

She finished and set the newspaper aside.

"It was bold of him to list the names of all the patients. I wonder if he got that from Haggard," she mused. "And he does detail Lord Jergens' role in having his bride committed and the annulment issued by the bishop. Jefferson has excellent sources."

"Jergens will be ruined. He already was on shaky ground, owing creditors all over town. No parents will ever allow him to court—much less wed—their daughters. Lady Alice came off as very sympathetic, I thought."

"Yes, but we both know how gossip eviscerates people, Dez. Women, in particular, even if they are blameless."

He thought she spoke of herself. "His details are comprehensive and precise regarding Miss Stone and the happenings at Stone Academy. I am sure parents will be clamoring to have their children removed."

"I like how he asks at the end just how many patients who are kept at Gollingham are actually mad. He pointed out several instances where women were committed solely on the word of a male relative. I wonder how this will affect Fiend and Gollingham?"

"Who?"

Anna flushed. "Dr. Cheshire is Fiend. It was my name for him. I did not even dignify him with his title of doctor."

"He treated you very badly, didn't he?" Dez asked softly, his fingers entwining with hers.

"He did." Though tears glistened in her eyes, he saw defiance there, as well. "I only hope some of the women mentioned in Mr. Jefferson's article will be given a second chance by their families."

"The authorities may very well become involved," he said. "Though the Madhouse Act only pertained to asylums in London and its outskirts, Jefferson may have stirred up the proverbial hornet's nest with his investigation. It wouldn't surprise me if the local magistrate in Alton decides to take a look for himself."

The door opened and an apologetic Johnson said, "Lord Morton and Lady Alice are here, my lord. Do you wish to see them?"

"Yes, of course," he said. "Show them to the library. We will be there soon."

"Very good, my lord."

Anna looked at him worriedly. "Do you think they will be upset about Mr. Jefferson's article? Perhaps we should have warned them it would be published soon."

"He was going to print it regardless. He may have gone to them as he did us and allow them input. We will see."

Dez escorted Anna to the library, where Lord Morton was seated with Lady Alice. Both rose and they greeted one another before taking a seat again.

"I assume you have read the morning newspapers," Lord Morton began.

"We have just finished," he said. Looking to Lady Alice, he asked, "Are you terribly upset, my lady?"

"Not one whit," she declared, her smile genuine. "Papa and I are happy this Mr. Jefferson made known what a scoundrel Jergens is. Yes, my annulment is referenced but I believe by next Season, it will be old news and some newer scandal will have taken its place. I plan to partake in the Season again. I'll be frank, my lord. I want children more than anything in the world. Papa says he will provide me with a generous dowry. I am hopeful there is a good man out there willing to overlook my previous mistake. If not, at least I am free of both Jergens and Gollingham."

Anna reached and took Lady Alice's hand. "You have fortitude and courage, my friend. I do believe you will find the gentleman meant for you."

"Are you upset about being mentioned?" Lady Alice asked in return.

"No," Anna said firmly. "I hope my plight—and yours—will bring attention to the women wrongfully imprisoned at Gollingham."

"I hope that as well," Lord Morton said. "For now, Alice and I are retreating to the country. London is hot and smells dreadful this time of year. We wanted to come by and tell you both goodbye."

"We are leaving soon, as well," Dez shared. "We both prefer the country over town."

"Will you return next Season?" the older man asked.

"It will depend," he said, not wanting to reveal their news just yet. "I am sure Anna will write to you and tell you of our plans."

The two women embraced as the men shook hands. Lord Morton mentioned keeping Haggard on the case for now and Dez agreed. They walked the pair downstairs and to their waiting carriage, waving farewell.

As they returned inside, Anna asked, "Are you ready to return to Torville Manor because I certainly am."

He brought her hand to his lips and kissed it. "I have never been more ready to return to the country."

ANNA WAS SEATED on a blanket on the front lawn, her legs stretched out in front of her, her back leaning against Dez's chest. His arms were gently wrapped around her. A slight bump protruded, marking the presence of the baby growing inside her. They had been back at Torville Manor for almost a month now and her initial sickness every morning had begun to calm. She only occasionally awoke feeling nauseous and had regained her spotty appetite. They had settled into a routine, with Dez learning more about the business of running his country estate from Mr. Lexington, their steward. Anna had worked with Mrs. Abbott, the housekeeper, and Mr. Meadows, the butler, learning the names of servants and the customary practices. She had changed a few things with her husband's encouragement and had also begun refreshing a few of the rooms that they spent the most time in, including the drawing room, the library, and their bedchamber. She shared one with her husband and enjoyed waking up each morning snuggled close to him.

"More lemonade?" he asked, bring the cup toward her.

She sipped the cool, tart liquid, which tasted refreshing in the early afternoon heat. Her eyes began to droop and she gave over to the sleepiness.

In her ear, Dez said, "Wake up, Anna. It looks as though we have guests coming."

She stretched lazily and yawned, allowing her husband to bring her to her feet. An unfamiliar carriage headed up the lane. Their only visitors since they had returned to Surrey had been their neighbors. Anna was growing close to Tom's wife and getting to know the mature Jessa more, delighting in how her younger sister had turned out.

"Who might be calling?" she wondered aloud.

They strolled to the drive and waited for the carriage to arrive. When it did, she recognized the crest upon it.

"Lord Morton and Alice? But they did not write of their visit," she said. "I will need for Mrs. Abbott to prepare rooms for them."

She signaled Meadows, who had arrived and stood to the side. He hurried over.

"We'll need two guests rooms prepared at once and others for Lord Morton's servants who accompany them. Wait a moment so we can see who alights from the carriages."

"I only see the one," Dez pointed out. "Perhaps they left their valet and lady's maid at home?"

Anna chuckled. "Would Coral allow you to go anywhere without him? I think not. Any valet worth his salt would demand to accompany his lord."

The vehicle rolled to a halt and the door opened. Surprise filled her when Mr. Haggard bounded out, followed by Mr. Jefferson. Anna held her breath as two women were helped to the ground. One she did not recognize but the other could only be one person.

"Miss Stone!" she called and rushed to meet the woman.

Miss Stone gave her a shy smile. "Miss Browning," she said fondly. "Or I believe I should say Lady Torrington."

"Yes, I have wed since I left Gollingham." She indicated Dez. "I believe you have met my husband before."

Dez bowed. "It is good to see you again, Miss Stone. Especially away from the confines of Gollington Asylum."

"You were instrumental in helping me obtain my release." She turned to the other woman. "My lord and lady, I wish to present to you my dearest friend, Miss Blair."

"How do you do?" asked the pretty young woman with lively blue eyes hiding behind a pair of spectacles.

"You are Mr. Jefferson's fiancée, I believe," Dez said. "Welcome to Torville Manor, ladies and gentlemen."

"I know we were unexpected," Mr. Jefferson said. "But Mr. Haggard told me he was coming down to give you a report in person. Miss Stone wished to thank you herself. Miss Blair and I tagged along."

"You are all very welcome," Anna enthused. "Meadows, our butler, will see that your things are taken to your rooms. Would you care to join us in the drawing room for tea?"

"Tea would be lovely," Miss Stone said. "I hope we aren't putting you out."

"We have a large house and can think of no better visitors to invite to stay with us," Dez said. "Shall we?"

They entered the manor and went to the drawing room, Anna dispatching a footman along the way to give Mrs. Abbott the news of their guests and rooms to be prepared.

Tea arrived and the travelers spoke briefly about their journey from London before Miss Stone said, "We bring news from London. Mr. Haggard, would you be so kind as to share with the earl and countess what they have missed since they returned to the country?"

"Of course, Miss Stone," said the Bow Street Runner.

Dez found her hand and laced their fingers together. Somehow, Anna knew what the agent would share would be very important.

"As you can see, Miss Stone has been released from Gollingham. There was quite an outcry from the parents of students at Stone Academy after several of Mr. Jefferson's articles were published. Miss Blair here helped increase the awareness."

"Mr. Haggard is being kind," Miss Blair said. "I quite stirred the pot over the matter. I couldn't believe Mr. Stone had his sister locked away and tried to take over the running of the academy. The parents couldn't have been lovelier."

"They increased pressure on the authorities," Mr. Haggard continued. "With help from Miss Stone's uncle on her mother's side, they fought for her release."

"Where is your brother now?" Anna asked.

"Gone," Miss Stone said. "I assume back hiding under whatever rock he climbed out from. He's not an honest sort, my lady. Never took an interest in his education or the school and had been estranged from my father and me for years. You could have knocked me over with a feather when he showed up. The next thing I knew, I was being physically restrained and taken away."

She paused, wiping a tear from her eye. "I know I am one of the lucky ones. You pressing Lady Torrington's case. Hiring Mr. Haggard. Lord Morton, too. It's thanks to all of you and my uncle and the parents who rallied around me." She took her friend's hand. "And for my wonderful Miss Blair. If she hadn't gone and convinced Mr. Jefferson to write about Gollingham, I wouldn't be sitting here today."

"Have any other women been released?" Dez asked.

"Lady Eastman," Haggard noted. "Mr. Jefferson's investigation called into question her brother-in-law's placement of Lady Eastman at Gollingham with only his say and no physician examining her state of mind. It seems her son, the new Lord Eastman, had been experiencing ill health ever since his mother was removed. The Lord Chancellor himself took over the matter, placing the infant under his own household. Remarkably, the child began to thrive again."

The agent shook his head in disgust. "After strong pressure, the wet nurse hired confessed that she was withholding milk from the babe, slowly starving it. The heir presumptive had paid her to do so and promised to take care of her once he became the viscount."

Anna gasped. "That is horrible! He slowly kills a babe for position and a title."

"What did the Lord Chancellor do?" Dez asked.

"He went himself to Gollingham," Haggard continued. "And removed Lady Eastman to his care. The brother-in-law has been imprisoned and will go to trial. The wet nurse pled guilty and will serve a reduced sentence for her cooperation in the matter." Haggard sighed. "Lady Eastman will be returning home—with her son—in the next week or so."

Anna felt her heart racing at hearing this news. "Any other women who found their way out of the asylum?"

Haggard detailed four more families who had claimed their female relatives under the mounting pressure and said the Lord Chancellor demanded that impartial physicians be brought into Gollingham to examine every patient left.

"That is happening as we speak, my lady," the agent said. "There is hope more will be released. And if found mad, the other patients will be taken to different facilities. Gollingham is to be shut down."

Anna burst into tears. Dez wrapped his arms about her, murmuring soft words of comfort.

"Forgive me," she said to their guests after her tears subsided and she dried her cheeks with her husband's offered handkerchief. "I am so emotional regarding this topic."

"It doesn't mean that all asylums will close," Mr. Haggard said. "As long as there are very rich men who hold the power over their women, these places will exist. But, my lord, you and your wife have helped more than a few women."

"I am a testament to your doggedness," Miss Stone said.

"Mr. Jefferson played a key role," Dez said. "It was crucial to get the public involved, as well as the crown. You are to be congratulated, sir."

Jefferson said, "Newspapers have been a way to communicate for a good many decades now. Though in London, they are most popular for the gossip columns, which the *ton* eagerly reads each morning, I am pleased that my investigation has brought about change, even though it is small. I plan to continue my work. Looking into the downtrodden and weak. The helpless and powerless. I wish to make their stories known. Hopefully, some good will come of my efforts."

He smiled at his fiancée. "I tried to convince Miss Blair to join me in my efforts, helping me with the research, but she is loyal to Miss Stone and the Stone Academy."

Miss Blair said, "Miss Stone will retire from her teaching duties and serve strictly as headmaster and administrator for the academy." She gave her friend a fond smile. "I have been named lead teacher. It is a role of great responsibility and one I take seriously. We will have to work hard to undo the harm Mr. Stone caused during his time at the helm."

"How are you situated for money?" Dez asked.

"We have lost several students," Miss Stone admitted. "Hopefully, some of them will return now that I will be in charge once more."

"I would like to make a donation to Stone Academy," Dez said.

He named a figure and even Anna gasped.

"Are you serious, Lord Torrington?" asked Miss Stone. "Why, I could keep the school running for several years on that amount. It would allow me to hire additional staff members. New books and supplies."

"Consider it done. Let me know who your banker is and I will make the arrangements."

Anna cradled Dez's face in her hands. "This is why I married this incredible man," she told the others. "He is generous to a fault and his heart is filled with kindness. I love you, Dez."

Despite the presence of others, Anna chose to kiss her husband thoroughly.

CHAPTER TWENTY-SIX

ANNA CHECKED WITH Mrs. Abbott regarding the week's menus and then said she was off to the kitchens.

"Claiming more carrots for Daisy?" the housekeeper asked, not bothering to hide her smile.

The doctor had told Anna to curtail further riding until after the baby had been born so she satisfied herself by visiting her horse each day.

"I have already been to see Daisy earlier today," she said. "I am going to visit Mrs. Milken. She had her baby three days ago and I promised to come back and see her. I've had Cook roast a chicken for the Milkens."

"You are very thoughtful, my lady. Tell Mrs. Milken I wish her the best."

She went to the kitchens, where Cook spied her.

"I've got everything ready for you, my lady. In the burlap sack over there as you requested. Even the scones you asked for."

"Thank you, Cook. I know the Milkens will be appreciative of your efforts."

Anna slipped the strap of the bag over her head, which allowed her hands to remain free. It was the only way Dez would allow her to carry things these days. She had reached the five-month mark and had experienced a new burst of energy during this period. The doctor had agreed that walking was good for her and so she had continued to do so every day, enjoying the cooler weather as autumn took hold of Surrey. Being outside still felt liberating to her and she would continue to dig in the dirt and walk as long as possible.

She cut across the estate and headed straight for the Milkens' cottage. Reaching it, she rapped on the door and then opened it, calling out, "Mrs. Milken? It is Lady Torrington come to call."

"Here, my lady," a voice sounded and Anna removed the sack and placed it down on the table before crossing the main room and heading into the bedchamber.

The new mother was in bed, sitting up, pillows behind her. In her arms her infant was fussing.

"I am not sure what is wrong with her."

"May I?" she asked and held her hands out.

Mrs. Milken handed the baby over and Anna cradled the girl in her arms.

"She has been crying ever since I finished nursing her."

"Did you burp her?" she asked, remembering how the young mother hadn't even known to do that after she'd given birth days earlier.

"I did as you said, my lady." As the baby wailed, Mrs. Milken added, "Whatever is wrong with her?"

Anna brought the child to her shoulder and began swaying back and forth, gently patting the girl's back.

"Sometimes, they need to burp more than once. I used to help care for my sister, Jessa, when she was born. I was twelve years old and like a little mother to her. Jessa often became fussy because she had taken in more air than she should have."

She continued moving slowly back and forth as she patted the infant. Suddenly, a loud burp sounded and the wailing ceased.

"There, my little one," Anna said, rubbing the baby's back and kissing the top of her head before returning her to her mother's arms.

"She belched as loud as Mr. Milken does after he's had more ale than he should have," the young mother marveled. "For a sound like that to come out of a wee babe is almost frightening."

"Just remember to keep at it for a few minutes each time after you feed her," Anna gently reminded. "You will learn as much about her as she does about you over the coming weeks and months."

"I worry that I will never learn everything," Mrs. Milken said, sighing heavily.

"It will get harder before it gets easier," she warned as she rubbed her own belly. "But this tiny one is so worth it."

"When will your babe come, my lady?"

"In February. The second or third week."

"You look ever so pretty. You have a glow about you."

Anna knew Mrs. Milken wasn't using mere flattery. As she had put on a little weight after leaving the asylum and then more as the baby grew within her, she had noticed her features softening, although she tended to think being in love also had something to do with her appearance.

They chatted for a few more minutes and then she mentioned that she had brought a roasted chicken for them to eat from for the next few days.

"I also had Cook bake you some scones," she added. "I have found I have a fondness for them while I have been with child."

The younger mother giggled. "I have always had a fondness for scones, child or not. Thank you for your thoughtfulness, my lady."

"I am happy to do it for you."

"All the tenants talk of how lucky we are that his lordship wed you. That you both care for this estate and its people, more so than the previous earl ever did."

Having known Dez's brother and his wayward tendencies, it didn't surprise her. She merely smiled graciously and told the woman that she would be back in a week to visit and see how things were coming along.

She removed the food from her sack and slipped it back over her head. As she started out, the October afternoon's breeze had picked up and the sting of cool was in the air. She gathered her shawl about her as she left the Milkens' abode and headed back to Torville Manor. On her way, she decided to cut through the woods and go by the lake, still one of her favorite places to walk. As she passed by what she fondly thought of as her and Dez's cottage, she thought the door stood ajar.

Leaving the path by the lake, she cut toward the cottage and as she approached it, she saw the door was definitely open. She wondered if they had failed to secure it properly after their last visit here a week ago and today's wind had blown it open. She reached the door and started to close it when she noticed dirty dishes on the table. Frowning, Anna stepped inside, wondering if someone had come across the cottage and thought it unoccupied.

She ventured further in and crossed to the bedchamber, finding the bed unmade, the bedclothes hopelessly tangled. Some unauthorized person had definitely been staying here. She would alert Dez the minute she reached home. He could have a footman or groom stationed at the cottage and warn the trespasser off. It would also be wise to have a maid come down to the cottage and clean it. Anna didn't like a stranger having been where she and Dez came for brief respites. Perhaps they should start locking the place up when they left each time, even if it did stand on Torrington lands.

As she turned and came back into the main room, a figure stood in the doorway. The way the sun streamed in, the person's face was in shadow.

Before she could ask who stood there, the person took a few steps forward.

Matron.

A chill rushed through Anna. Then she saw the light reflect from something in Matron's hand and saw the woman held a knife. Fear now seized Anna and she dug her nails into the palms of her hands to keep from screaming.

"What are you doing here?" she asked, her voice calm despite the nerves rippling through her. "Have you been staying at this cottage? If so, I must ask you to leave. You are trespassing. I won't tell my husband but you need to go. Now."

Matron took a step forward, her wrist turning the knife she held menacingly.

"Oh, I'm not going anywhere, Miss Browning. You always were a troublemaker, from the moment you came to Gollingham."

"I am Lady Torrington and this is not Gollingham. Leave, Matron," Anna said firmly.

"You can act all high and mighty—but you're not going to chase me away. I came for what's due me."

Anna bit her bottom lip to still its trembling.

"First you. Then Lady Jergens, Lady Eastman and Miss Stone. Then a few others. Men came. All the patients were removed. And it was all your fault. You and that husband of yours."

The blood pounded loudly in her ears. She didn't think she could get around Matron and make it out the door. She locked her knees, trying to keep from swaying.

"It was my place. *My* place!" Matron shouted. "I handled the patients and staff. Dr. Cheshire merely came in from time to time, pretending to know what went on." An evil smile lit her face. "I would be the one who whispered in his ear what to do. I decided who would undergo which treatment. I was like a queen, controlling my own little kingdom. I issued orders and they were followed to the letter."

Matron continued to ramble on. The more she spoke, the more Anna believed that the woman herself had dipped into madness.

"He killed himself, you know. When they shut down Gollingham. Cheshire was a fool."

Though she couldn't feel regret for the death of the man she'd called Fiend, she said, "I am sorry for your loss."

Matron sneered. "I never cared for him. He was weak. Not as I am. I am strong." She began twisting her wrist again, the blade of the steel knife catching the light.

"You need to leave, Matron," Anna said again, hoping to get

through to her.

"And go where, you bitch?" the woman shouted. "I am out of a job with Gollingham closed. Cheshire died without writing me a reference. Even if I did have one, what good would it do? I have already tried to find another position. No one wants to hire someone from the infamous Gollingham Asylum. Not that all the other madhouses are any different. They're all the same."

Matron raised the knife in her hand and, instinctively, Anna brought her hands to her belly, shielding it.

"I will give you coin to help tide you over until you find another position," she said.

"Money? You offer me money?" Matron shrieked. Then an evil smile settled about her lips. "I want much more than money, dearie. I want your life. Yours—and your child's."

DEZ CLOSED THE ledger and rubbed his eyes. He had enough of numbers today.

What he needed was Anna time.

His love for his lovely wife had only grown stronger since their wedding ceremony. He had loved Anna with boyish devotion throughout their childhood and mourned her loss as an adult. When he had discovered she was alive, it was as if the still-burning ember inside him ignited, fanning the flames of love and desire until they engulfed him. Now that she carried their child, he felt his love multiplying daily and couldn't wait for its birth, when they would become a family of three.

He rose from his desk and decided to look for Anna. He would probably find her digging in her garden or at the stables with Daisy. She loved the freedom of being outside. Dez grinned. He would suggest that she was dirty and chilled from being outdoors and that a hot bath would be the best cure. Naturally, he would join her in it and then they could spend the afternoon in their bedchamber as he made sweet love to her.

Leaving his study, he passed a maid and asked, "Have you seen Lady Torrington?"

"Not for an hour or so, my lord. She was with Mrs. Abbott."

"Thank you."

He made his way through the house and located the house-keeper, inquiring where his countess might be.

"She went to visit Mrs. Milken, my lord. Took her a basket of food."

Dez remembered the woman had given birth a few days ago.

"Thank you, Mrs. Abbott."

He headed to the kitchens and had Cook prepare a basket with bread, cheese, and wine. If Anna was out walking, she would have worked up an appetite. He would meet her and they could stop at their cottage for a few hours of love play.

Once out the door, he noticed the wind had picked up. The previous few days had seen warm afternoons, while the nights were cool. It seemed today was the day the tide changed and autumn had arrived in full force. He worried, hoping his wife had taken a shawl with her. Dez decided to detour to the cottage and leave the basket there. He would bring in some firewood and place it upon the hearth so it would be ready to light when they arrived. Stopping would be a nice surprise for Anna and offer her a respite before they continued on to Torville Manor.

As he arrived in the clearing, he noticed the door to the cottage stood wide open. He chided himself for not having secured the door after their last sojourn there and hoped no animal had gotten inside and torn up the place. Reaching the cottage, he stepped inside and was startled to find two figures before him. One, a large woman, had her back to him. Beyond her stood Anna, her face white with fear.

"I want your life. Yours—and your child's."

Dez recognized the voice of Matron, the woman in charge of the patients at Gollingham. He dropped the basket and sprang forward as the woman lunged at Anna.

His wife was prepared, though, and as she leaped to the side, she yanked something over her head and swung a strap over the hand that held a knife. Anna jerked hard and the force caused Matron to drop the blade.

Dez grabbed the attacker from behind, pinning her arms back as the large woman struggled against him.

"Get the knife, Anna,!" he shouted hoarsely.

She swept it from the floor, gripping the hilt, her breathing rapid.

"Get a bedsheet," he instructed calmly.

Anna hurried from the room, returning quickly with a bedsheet. He had her tear it into strips and as he held Matron, he had Anna secure the first one around the woman's ankles.

"Tie it firmly. Use strong knots."

Matron cursed loudly, language Dez hadn't even heard used in the army by the coarsest of soldiers.

"Bring another strip," he told his wife as he slid his hands from grasping Matron's elbows down to her wrists, holding them together as Anna bound them as she had Matron's ankles.

"Another strip for good measure," he suggested and Anna complied.

Their prisoner was now thoroughly restrained, though she shrieked as if he had stabbed her several times with the knife she had brought. He shuddered, thinking of what might have happened to Anna and shoved all thought of it from his mind, else he might murder Matron.

Taking another piece of the bedsheet, he used it to gag the woman, muffling her shouts and the torrent of curses.

"We must go for the magistrate," he said. "She meant to kill you."

"Secure her to a chair," Anna suggested. "I fear if someone comes along, they might free her. Better yet, I will stay with her."

The thought horrified him. "I won't leave you with her, Anna."

She placed a hand on his forearm. "I will make sure she goes nowhere." Glancing to Matron, she added, "I will show her the mercy she never showed me."

He gripped her shoulders. "Are you certain, my love?"

"I will be fine. Fasten her to a chair and then be quick."

Dez did as she asked, dragging Matron to a chair and using additional bits of the torn bedsheet to fasten her to it. The woman growled beneath her gag, her eyes bulging and furious.

He took Anna's hand and led her outside, where he enfolded her in his arms. She clung to him, tears now coming. He kissed them away and then searched her face.

"I could have lost you. And our babe."

"But you didn't," she said. "Go, Dez. I am fine. I will even sit out on the porch so I don't have to look at her."

"I'll be quick as I can." He kissed her hard. "Oh, Anna, I do love you so."

Her sky-blue eyes gazed upon him with so much love, he felt it fill him and spill over.

"I love you, my precious husband. I always will." She kissed him. "Go and bring the magistrate back so that we can close this ugly chapter forever."

Dez cradled her cheek. "I will be back before you know it."

EPILOGUE

Four months later . . .

DEZ TRIED TO focus on his correspondence and gave up, pushing it away. He hadn't seen Anna or the baby in close to two hours and needed to remedy that.

Their lives had changed radically in the week since their son's arrival. It amazed him how full of love his heart was in an instant, the moment he saw the perfect little person they had made together. He was endlessly fascinated by his son's tiny fingers and toes and though he knew it was impossible, he knew Charlie smiled anytime he or Anna talked to him.

A knock sounded on his study door and he replied, "Come."

Johnson entered bearing a silver tray.

"A messenger has arrived from Gillingham," the butler said.

Dez lifted the parchment from the tray. "See that he has something to eat and tell him to wait."

The clocked chimed three and he added, "No, tell him he will be staying overnight and can leave first thing in the morning. It is already too late for him to start out and, this way, I can take my time and compose a reply to my sister by then."

"Very good, my lord."

He stood and stretched, deciding to take the letter upstairs so he and Anna could read it together. He found her in the small parlor she had been drawn to, sitting before a cheery fire.

"And how are my two favorite people faring?" he asked.

"The same as we were when you asked two hours ago," she said, smiling sweetly and lifting her face for his kiss.

He sat beside her. "May I?"

She handed the baby over and love once again blossomed deep within him. He kissed Charlie's head and sighed.

"Were two parents ever as besotted with their child as we are?" he asked.

"I doubt it," she replied playfully. "What's that?"

He passed the letter to her. "It just came from Dalinda. Why don't you read it aloud?"

Anna broke the seal and began to read:

My dearest Dez and Anna –

I received your note that your baby has come and I know your joy knows no end that he is here and healthy. I can still remember when Arthur first arrived and how I thought my heart would burst from pride and love every time I gazed down upon him. I will admit that I worried once I discovered I was with child again because I just didn't think it possible to love another baby as much as I did Arthur.

Then Harry showed up, his own little person, so very different from his brother—and I learned a lesson all parents do— that the love in your heart isn't limited. It merely magnifies and grows larger and larger each time a new child appears. You will be the same and I do hope you will have many, many children.

I must share a bit of sad news. My heart is heavy because Gilford is no more. It was a long time coming and I thought I had prepared myself, but I still am quite sad at his loss. We held his funeral the day I received your joyous note. I did not send word of his death to you earlier because I did not want Dez torn between coming to comfort me and missing the birth of his first child. He needed to be with you, Anna, as you become a family.

Reid has arrived at Gillingham and taken up the title. The boys are a little wary of him, coming in and taking charge the way he has. Being a military man and officer, I know it is natural for him to do so. Quite frankly, I am relieved that he is here to make decisions that are rightfully his. It looks as if he will be a good influence on my boys, though, and is thinking of placing Arthur and Harry at a local school.

I do love and miss you both. Once the boys are settled at Dunwood Academy, I would like to come and meet my new nephew and spend time together. I will let you know more of my plans once I know Harry and Arthur are established.

All my love,
Dalinda

Anna folded the letter and set it on a table. "Poor Dalinda."

"I know," Dez said. "She did have some good years with Gilford. At least she has Arthur and Harry. Her stepson taking over will be a huge relief."

"She is young," his wife pointed out. "I wonder if she would ever consider marrying again."

"Perhaps. I do hope she will come to see us soon. I know she sounds strong in her letter but I believe she needs us even more than she herself knows."

Charlie began to fuss and Dez told his son, "I do believe it is time for your nap."

Anna kissed the infant's head. "I'll see to tea while you get him settled."

He took his boy upstairs to the nursery and handed him over to Nanny. She began rocking him, rubbing his back, making soothing noises. Dez waited until Charlie quieted and then went to the drawing room, where the teacart sat.

"This came for you," his wife said, handing him a letter. "Read it while I make you a plate."

Recognizing the handwriting, he said, "It's from Rhys." He broke the seal, quickly reading the few lines written on the page.

"I cannot wait to meet Colonel Armistead someday," Anna said. "You have had such good things to say about him. I hope this war will end soon."

Dez glanced up. "You will meet him shortly. Rhys has returned to England. His cousin has always been sickly. He writes to tell me he is the new Earl of Sheffington—and he wants to pay us a visit."

"Why, that is marvelous," she exclaimed. "I suppose I will get my wish to meet him sooner than I expected."

Anna handed him his plate and they spent the next hour talking of Rhys and what his return to England would mean.

"I know Rhys hadn't heard from Lord Sheffington since he joined the army at eighteen so it must have been quite a surprise for him to learn he is now the earl."

She touched his sleeve. "You never thought you would be the Earl of Torrington yet look what a marvelous job you are doing. You will have to help your friend, Dez. Just as Dalinda needs us, so will Rhys."

Setting her saucer down, she said, "Shall we go and see Charlie now?"

Dez took Anna's hand in his, drawing warmth and strength from the simple contact, and led her upstairs to the nursery. They slipped inside and Nanny rose from her rocker.

"Lord Charles is still fast asleep," she reported. "I'll give you a few minutes alone with him but then he'll need to wake and feed."

They went to the crib and gazed down at their son.

"He's our little miracle," Anna said. "A physical manifestation of our love for one another."

Dez slipped his arm about his wife's waist. "Our story started in innocence and turned to heartbreak yet we found our way back to one another. My love for you grows stronger each day, Anna. Charlie only adds to our blessings."

He bent and kissed his son's head and then he gazed at Anna, his heart bursting with love.

"Have I told you today how much I love you, my dearest?"

She smiled. "Once or twice, I believe. But I have always believed actions speak louder than words."

With a hearty laugh, Dez's lips touched hers.

THE END

About the Author

Award-winning and internationally bestselling author Alexa Aston's historical romances use history as a backdrop to place her characters in extraordinary circumstances, where their intense desire for one another grows into the treasured gift of love.

She is the author of Regency and Medieval romance, including: Dukes of Distinction; Soldiers & Soulmates; The St. Clairs; The King's Cousins; and The Knights of Honor.

A native Texan, Alexa lives with her husband in a Dallas suburb, where she eats her fair share of dark chocolate and plots out stories while she walks every morning. She enjoys a good Netflix binge; travel; seafood; and can't get enough of *Survivor* or *The Crown*.

www.ingramcontent.com/pod-product-compliance
Lightning Source LLC
Chambersburg PA
CBHW070338200726
48294CB00003B/706